BONES OF A GIANT

BRIAN THOMAS ISAAC

BONES OF A GIANT

A NOVEL

RANDOM HOUSE CANADA

PUBLISHED BY RANDOM HOUSE CANADA

Copyright © 2025 Brian Thomas Isaac

All rights reserved under International and Pan-American Copyright Conventions. No part of this book may be reproduced in any form or by any electronic or mechanical means, including information storage and retrieval systems, without permission in writing from the publisher, except by a reviewer, who may quote brief passages in a review. No part of this book may be used or reproduced in any manner for the purpose of training artificial intelligence technologies or systems. Published in 2025 by Random House Canada, a division of Penguin Random House Canada Limited, Toronto.

Random House Canada, an imprint of Penguin Random House Canada Limited
320 Front Street West, Suite 1400
Toronto, Ontario, M5V 3B6, Canada
penguinrandomhouse.ca

Random House Canada and colophon are registered trademarks of Penguin Random House LLC.

The authorized representative in the EU for product safety and compliance is Penguin Random House Ireland, Morrison Chambers, 32 Nassau Street, Dublin D02 YH68, Ireland. https://eu-contact.penguin.ie

Library and Archives Canada Cataloguing in Publication

Title: Bones of a giant / Brian Thomas Isaac.
Names: Isaac, Brian Thomas, author
Identifiers: Canadiana (print) 20240419634 | Canadiana (ebook) 20240419758 | ISBN 9781039011779 (hardcover) | ISBN 9781039011786 (EPUB)
Subjects: LCGFT: Novels.
Classification: LCC PS8617.S215 B66 2025 | DDC C813/.6—dc23

Cover design: Andrew Roberts
Text design: Andrew Roberts
Typesetting: Terra Page
Map: Andrew Roberts
Interior art: Adobe Stock
Cover art: E.J. Hughes
   Above Okanagan Lake, 1994
   watercolour on paper
   50.8 x 61 cm
   Collection of the Kamloops Art Gallery, gift of the Artist
   Photo: Cory Hope
   Copyright: E.J. Hughes Estate

Printed in Canada

10 9 8 7 6 5 4 3 2 1

This book is dedicated to my best friend, my confidante and my lover, whose belief in me carried me through, right up to the last page.

My wife, Marlene.

"For a moment he feels the possibility of all things new, then it vanishes."

–Claire Keegan, *Walk the Blue Fields*

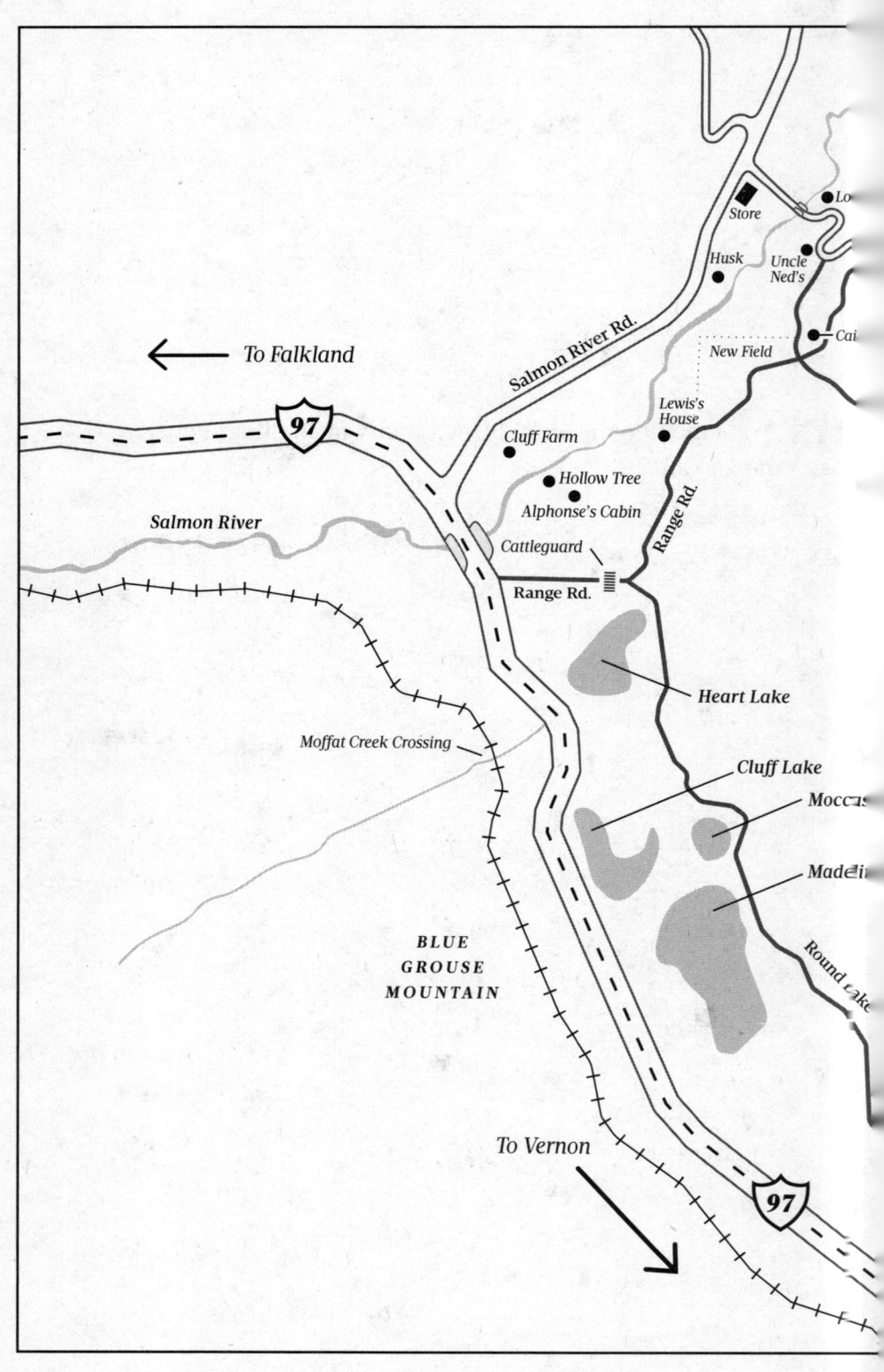

Heywood Armstrong Rd.

To Armstrong →

ROSE SWANSON
MOUNTAIN

Upper Range

Old Smith Cabin

SALMON VALLEY AND RANGE

Range

Round Lake

500m

N

CHAPTER 1

THE SIGNAL LIGHT TICKED as the driver braked to make the turn. Lewis Toma pointed to the shoulder of the highway. "Just drop me off here, Roland."

"I don't mind taking you home," Roland said, as he swung onto the gravel road. Loose stones peppered the floorboards and the car juddered across the cattle guard onto the Okanagan Indian Reserve.

"Pull over. I want to walk from here," Lewis said.

Roland leaned forward to see past his friend Clay, who sat in the middle, his full attention on the car radio as he hunted for a station. "What's the matter? Don't you want us to see where you live?"

The mocking tone in his voice caused heat to rise up Lewis's neck and spread across his face. When he realized Roland had no intention of stopping, he reached over Clay, knocking him against the seat back, and grabbed the steering wheel, cranking it hard toward the fence. Roland jammed on the brakes and the car slid to a stop.

Opening the door, Lewis said, "If I wanted you to come to my place I would have asked you." He slammed the door shut, giving a hard stare at his white classmates, and went down the dirt road.

"You don't have to bite my head off," Roland called after him. "You're the one missed the bus on the last day of school. I was doing you a favour."

Lewis shouted back over his shoulder, "Thanks."

Roland backed up the car and spun around, then pulled out onto the highway, tires squealing. A southbound tanker truck sounded its air horn and didn't let up until the car went around the corner, the truck right on its tail. Lewis heard its whistling exhaust pipes as it sped up the highway to Vernon. He picked up a stone and threw it hard at a fence post, where it caromed off the barbed wire.

When he passed the trees that blocked the view of his house from the highway, he stopped and studied the place where he and his family lived. The house had never looked or felt the same since his big brother, Eddie, came home from the hospital after being in a terrible accident with his not-so-secret love, Eva Cluff. When he found out she had been killed instantly, he disappeared.

No one knew where Eddie was, not his mother, Grace, or her best friend, Isabel, who came for a visit and never left, or his Uncle Alphonse, whose cabin perched above the river was only a stone's throw away from them. When they realized Eddie was missing, Uncle Alphonse began a search of the area. He had picked up Eddie's tracks but they petered out by the shore of the river. Though he never spoke of it to his sister Grace, Alphonse told Lewis that Eddie had either fallen in and been carried away by the current, or jumped in because he couldn't bear the thought of losing Eva. His mother hadn't spoken of Eddie for the two years since, which left Lewis feeling alone and abandoned.

Their house was a small and basic shelter by town-people standards. His uncle had built the porch using whatever lumber he could lay his hands on, and it was obvious he hadn't mastered the skill of carpentry. Boards of all lengths, widths, and a mix of cedar, pine and fir, were nailed down on unpeeled rails in an ugly patchwork. Blocks of firewood from the woodshed supported the deck. The cheap grey asphalt siding and the blood-red shingles, a roof colour he had never seen anywhere else except on his place and his uncle's cabin, declared this to be an "Indian" house.

The clothesline ran from the corner of the house across the yard to a large fir tree. At one time it had leaned in the opposite direction, but the weight of wet clothes had caused the tree to bend toward the house. The clotheslines he saw in town had painted poles at either end and a spacer with wheels that held the line up so the clothes wouldn't hang down to the ground. His uncle's broken-down cars were parked all over the property and caused many an argument between him and Lewis's mother. She wanted them hauled out of there, but in his uncle's thinking, the wrecks were a symbol of accumulated wealth. "All I need is a couple parts and I can get that thing purring like a kitten," he'd say.

One day when everyone was away, Alphonse had parked a new wreck right beside the house, axles resting on the ground, hood lying on the roof. The paint, burnt by the sun into patches of red rust, only added to its nasty appearance. The car was the first thing a visitor saw. When his mother complained, Alphonse had said, "I don't know why you're so mad. The *summas* in town got a pink flamingo in front of their house. You got a pinto one."

She didn't think it was funny.

Lewis resumed walking, his hands shoved deep in his pockets. As he was about to turn down his driveway, he noticed a blue pickup truck he didn't recognize pull up to the gate that opened into their new field. Then he heard a gunshot and ducked as a ricocheted bullet whined overhead. The strangers had shot off the padlock that his mother had asked him to put on the gate to keep out trespassers.

From where he crouched, he watched a tall man carrying a rifle unhook the barbed-wire gate so the other could drive the truck through. The driver, a red bandana wrapped around his head, stepped out and they both walked over to the bulldozer that Alphonse and his buddy Abel had used to clear the trees in the field. After looking it over for a few minutes, the two men began walking toward the river.

Lewis took off for his house at a run. Isabel's car was gone, which meant she and his mother would be off somewhere because one seldom went without the other. He kept going until he came to his uncle's small house. He opened the door, calling his uncle's name, but Alphonse wasn't there. He pulled the door shut and ran to the old trail along the river, low branches brushing his head. When he came to the big tree that had fallen halfway across the river, he jumped on, slid over to the other side and dove into the cold water, his skin tightening against his ribs. Swimming downstream, he came to where a finger of land jutted away from the bank and stepped on shore.

Lewis entered the forest as quietly as he could, but only a few feet in, a grouse was flushed out of the bush. Its sudden drumming wings startled him and he shouted and stopped. With a hand over his mouth, he waited to see if he had been discovered. Seeing no one, he carried on. He went in the direction he thought the men were going, slipping through a tall patch of skunk cabbage and dense fern and into the trees along the swamp, carpeted with green algae. Hearing voices, he ducked behind a trunk as the two men appeared, fifty feet from where he hid.

"Watch that gun, Moose," the driver said. "If you trip over them big feet of yours, I'll get shot in the back, sure as hell. I told you we didn't need it."

"Stop calling me Moose."

The shorter man laughed. "I can't help it if you remind me of the guy in the Archie comics."

"I don't like it when you make fun of me."

"All right, I'll stop—just watch where you're pointing that damn thing."

The big man said, "If a bear comes along, you'll hide behind me like a little girl."

A light wind shook the tall grass near the swamp. Birds fluttered overhead and two trees rubbing together clicked and squeaked. "What's that?" the big man asked.

"It's the sound of the bush. What, you've never been out to the bush before?"

"I don't like it here. It feels like something is watching."

"You scaredy-cat. Just let me step this out to see if the shop will fit, and then we'll be outta here before you piss your pants."

As the man in the bandana began to walk toward his tree, Lewis went down on his stomach and crawled into the thick undergrowth. He kept still as his heart thumped in his ears. The man stopped so close to him, Lewis was afraid he would get stepped on. He shouted back to his friend, "All we gotta do is fill in that little swamp and we'll have nice flat ground for the yard. Everything we need is right here. There's water and firewood—hell, we can even go fishing if we want. It's just the way he said it would be. And he's pretty sure he can get power down here."

Chilled in his wet clothes, Lewis began to shiver. Easing his knees up to his chest to warm himself, he rustled the vegetation.

"What the hell was that? Jesus, Moose, get over here. I think you're right. Somebody is watching us."

"I ain't moving." Moose said.

A rock hit the tree beside the man.

"Look out—it's right behind you," Moose shouted. "It's a alligator."

"I'll bounce a rock off your bald head," the man said.

Lewis waited until he heard the two walking away, still arguing. When he thought they were gone, he stuck his head out of the bracken just as the driver looked back. Lewis ducked, thinking for sure he had been spotted. Minutes went by before he checked again. They were gone.

It was just before supper when the car pulled up in front of his house. Isabel, Alphonse and his mother climbed out.

"Where were you guys, anyway?"

Grace laughed. "In town, where else?"

Isabel opened the trunk and grabbed a paper bag of groceries. "We got some good stuff to eat for the schoolboy on his last day. Are you hungry?"

"I'm starving," he said.

As his mother and Isabel went inside, Alphonse began walking toward his house. Lewis caught up to him and told him about the two strangers. "What do you think? Should I tell Mom?"

Alphonse scratched his chin. "Let me go have a good look around first. Don't know what to make of this yet."

CHAPTER 2

LEWIS FILLED THE WOODBOX by the stove, then took the swede saw and cut off the boards sticking out on the porch deck. Then, with the axe, he cut away the bark from the supporting blocks. After he tossed all the bits and pieces into the woodshed, he stood back to have a good look at his work. Finishing Alphonse's job hadn't been that hard and he wondered how long it would take him to rip the boards from the deck and replace them all. But buying new wood was out of the question, so he walked back to the shed and hung the saw on its nail. The great carpenter, done for the day.

He went into the house, grabbed the empty buckets and made for the river. Along the way boisterous birdsong sounded through the woodland. It was already hot, but he didn't care because school was out and he had the whole summer ahead of him. Sleeping in was something he had been looking forward to more than anything else. Just lying in bed knowing he didn't have to get dressed and run for the school bus had made him laugh out loud.

At the river's edge, he dipped the buckets into the water. It felt as if he had been doing this chore ever since he could walk. Even though the Indian department had built a pumphouse months ago and installed pipes in a ditch thirty feet away from their house, the waterspout and shut-off tee poked out of the ground like useless sculptures.

"The water should be hooked up any day now," his mother kept saying. But it still hadn't been done, so every day he struggled back with the heavy pails bumping against his legs, sloshing water onto the ground. Today, dripping with sweat, he climbed the steps, kicked off his water-soaked runners and walked into the kitchen, his wet footprints dissolving into nothing behind him as if he were being followed by a ghost. The grey cat lay in a pool of warm sun and watched the footprints disappear.

The house always felt warm in the mornings because Isabel and Grace wanted to have all the cooking done for the day so they could let the fire go out. The old kitchen stove cracked and bumped as he opened the reservoir, curls of steam drifting to the ceiling. After filling the reservoir, he set the pails on the water stand, where they fit into the black rings on the linoleum top. After washing his hands in the basin, he sat down to a breakfast of mush, a slice of bread with jam and a glass of cold grape Kool-Aid.

After he finished eating, he stepped out onto the porch. The sun beating down on his sneakers had already dried them and he banged them together, specks of dust churning in the air like midges.

He sat on the step to put his shoes back on, then looked toward the trees that shielded the river. Birds flew up, scattering in all directions as if they couldn't make up their minds where to settle. Crows on treetops presided over the world below. The river was quiet now, unlike in the spring, when it had risen so high it had spilled onto the shore, the current so strong he could feel a gentle shivering in the bed‑springs at night.

Lewis jumped off the porch steps and wandered past the outhouse to the network of forest trails he and Eddie had made long ago to throw off anyone trying to find them. Now they were overgrown with thick brush and weeds. He threaded his way along a barely visible path he thought was the shortcut through the woods. But he was quickly surrounded by rose bushes and hawthorns. Ducking under a branch, he tripped over an exposed root and fell, scratching his face, and knew he was on the wrong trail. Backtracking, he came to the pointy stump where he and his brother had taken turns to hack away at a tree with an axe. When he spotted the large fir riddled with holes that looked like they were made by a shotgun blast instead of diligent woodpeckers, he knew he was getting close to the water. Entering a small clearing, he saw the burl shaped like a woman's breast on the trunk of another tree that he and Eddie rubbed for good luck each time they walked by. Minutes later he stepped out onto the riverbank, surprising a blue heron. It gave a honking squawk that echoed like a trumpet as it scrambled off the river. Water fell in glassy ribbons from trailing feet as powerful wings lifted it skyward. Tipping to its side, it glided around the bend like a great prehistoric bird.

Lewis's eyes were drawn to a heap of broken trees on the far side of the river. His heart began to race. Was that someone's legs caught up in the tangle? Afraid of what he might find, he waded across and picked up a stick to prod at the legs. When he realized it was just an old pair of jeans, he pulled them out and tossed them into the brush.

Downriver was the large cedar he had crawled over the day before. When he was little, he would straddle the trunk like he was riding a horse, toss in his fishing line and watch the baited hook float downstream on top of the water. It was a place where a person could fish and never leave empty-handed.

Lewis stumbled over slippery stones until he reached a wide spot on the bank and sat down. Sweat burned his eyes, so he cupped a handful of the water and splashed his face. A light wind shook the leaves of the trees around him and small birds lifted into the air from the branches. For a moment he sat watching them, then he stood, brushing off his rear end. He jumped onto the cedar log and slid down the other side, his feet sinking in the mud close to shore. He waded through the shallows until the cool river water came up to his chest, and he was thankful for the instant relief.

The sun beat down hot on his head, so he dove in. Water burned his nose and pressure pushed at his ears until he surfaced. He waded onto a rock-strewn bar of land and tipped his head back to shake the water from his hair. Just ahead was the bottomless hole he and his brother had discovered a long time ago, where part of the river disappeared underground. His uncle said he was sure this was the place where Eddie had ended his life. When Lewis asked his mother if it was true, she walked out of the house and over to Alphonse's place and yelled at his uncle to stop saying such things. Lewis thought about Eddie every day.

Lewis went down on his stomach and cupped his hands around his eyes to look past the reflections and down into the hole. Unable to see much, he stood and picked up a piece of soaked driftwood and tossed it into the centre of the hole. He watched the stick fight back for a moment, twisting and reaching up like a desperate arm, before the river sucked it down into the gloom. A pebble bounced off the rocks, striking his leg. He turned to see his Uncle Alphonse standing near his fishing log, rubbing his sore back with one hand while waving for him to come back with the other. Ever since he injured his back in a sawmill accident a few years ago, his once-muscular physique, toned by years of working on the green chain pulling heavy lumber off the line, now caused him such bother that he walked with a stoop, like he was falling forward on his legs.

Lewis went over to him.

His uncle asked, "Whatcha doing?"

"Just looking around."

"I seen you staring into that hole. It's darker down there than three feet up a cow's ass, ain't it? I don't know what you're hunting for, but I found something you should take a look at."

As Alphonse led the way through the thick brush along the bank of the river, Lewis kept his eyes down to watch for booby traps left by nature. Once, when he'd tried to walk across a deadfall of branches, he had fallen in and his legs were badly scratched. Brushing up against devil's club was the worst. Its needles shot out such hot, searing pain that, now, walking through the stinging nettles that grew hand-high didn't hurt much at all.

His uncle stopped so suddenly Lewis bumped into him.

"Listen," Alphonse whispered.

Lewis heard a low hum but couldn't see what was making the sound until his uncle pointed to wasps circling above a small hole in the ground. Both stepped quietly away. They passed the place where Lewis filled his water pails and continued until they came to a clearing at the edge of the river a hundred yards from the Salmon River Bridge. Alphonse pointed to where a huge cottonwood had broken off six feet above the ground. The rest lay on the forest floor, its large broken branches reaching out. Bark hung down like ragged clothes on bleached arms. Eddie had told Lewis the tree looked like the bones of a giant.

"I seen this before but didn't notice there's a trail that goes right up to the stump. Maybe a bear used it," Alphonse said. "Listen to all the birds whistling and singing. It's like a different world down here."

No one but Lewis knew that this was Eddie's hidden place. And Lewis had only come upon it because he followed Eddie to the spot and saw him crawl inside the tree stump. Eddie never would have caught his little brother spying if Lewis hadn't sneezed. When he tried to run away, Eddie grabbed him by his T-shirt and made him promise not to tell anybody his secret or he would get the beating of his life.

When he sat here by himself, Lewis could almost feel Eddie's presence.

Alphonse walked over to the riverbank, sat and pulled off his shoes. He peeled off his socks, rolled up his pants and eased his burning feet into the water, sighing as they found cool comfort. Lewis stepped over broken pieces of stump to see if he could find where the entrance had been and saw a flash of colour. Lifting away a large piece of wood, he found a yellow cloth. It looked like an old handkerchief or scarf, now dotted with holes. Lewis felt it had been important to Eddie somehow and shoved it into his pocket. Then he walked over and sat down beside his uncle.

"Where's Abel today?" he asked. Abel had gone to day school with Alphonse and now stayed with him for weeks at a time.

"He's getting diesel from the Falkland garage." Alphonse scooped a handful of sandy gravel from the river to rub over his feet. He laughed. "I think your grandma would 'preciate me doin' this. She always said I had the smelliest feet around. Hope I don't kill off too many fish downstream."

Lewis tossed a stone into the water. "So what about those white guys that shot the padlock off our gate?"

Alphonse shook his head. "I don't know. That's got me stumped."

"I thought you would have found something out by now. They talked about building a shop and moving in down there."

"Maybe they're natural gas workers and they're gonna build a pumphouse for their gauges?"

"Those guys didn't look like any workers I saw before. The one guy looked like a wrestler on TV and the other one looked like a Hells Angel."

"We're all going down to the field for the big burn tonight. I'll have a look then."

Alphonse lifted a butt cheek and let out a loud, snapping fart. Lewis ducked away, but the rotten smell hit him like a slap to the face. Pinching his nose, he jumped to his feet and ran for home, chased by his uncle's laughter.

Isabel was at the table, working a batch of dough in the bread bowl, her cheeks reddened by the hot stove. He went by her into his bedroom. She had come for a visit two years ago, with her husband, Ray, on the very day Eddie was taken to the hospital. Lewis doubted his mother would have handled the lonely days and nights without having Isabel for company. For the first month after Eddie was gone, Grace hardly ate, but Isabel slowly coaxed her back to health. All his mother would say about Isabel moving in was that having extra hands meant a lot less work for her, but Lewis knew it was more than that.

In his bedroom, Lewis tucked the yellow cloth under the mattress. Then he went back into the kitchen. "God, it's hot in here. I thought you weren't going to use the wood stove for long today."

"I know how much you like fresh buns, and Alphonse shot a rabbit this morning while we were all snoring, so your mom made stew. There's a lot to eat and tomorrow we won't even need to make a fire."

As Lewis watched her work the dough, he couldn't help but notice her breasts moving under her blouse. "Where is she?" he asked.

"Grace went to town to see the Indian agent. She wanted to know what's taking so long to get the work on the house started. When she got back, she didn't look happy and she went off to see Alphonse."

Lewis sat down at the table as she upended the bowl of dough onto the floured tabletop. She began cutting off fist-sized chunks, which she made into buns and laid in neat rows on a blackened bread pan. He said, "Boy, you really know what you're doing."

"Not my first batch," she said. "Don't you have anything better to do than sit around in a hot house?"

"I was going to ask Mom something."

"What do you wanna know?"

Lewis hesitated. "That's okay. I'll wait until she gets back."

Isabel put the last piece of dough on the pan. "It sounds like you got yourself a real head-scratcher of a question there, but you know what your mom is like. So go ahead and ask me. If I think your mom can help, I'll tell you."

Lewis felt strangely bashful about asking a question she might think was stupid.

"Come on, slowpoke. I can hear the dough rising. What is it?"

"Eddie told me a long time ago that when he was in grade three, he woke up one morning so sick with the flu he was puking his guts out. He wanted a drink of water, but Mom was down at the toilet or somewhere. I don't know. So when he was getting himself a cup of water, he looked in the mirror and saw his face was white as a sheet. When Mom came back, Eddie said he told her he wanted to go to school and she said, 'You're not going anywhere but back to bed. What's wrong with you?' He told me he wanted to go to school because his skin was so white he looked like his classmates."

Isabel rubbed bits of dough from her hands and covered the pan with a towel. She filled a glass with water from the pail, pulled out a chair and sat down across from him. "He told you that? Poor guy."

Lewis nodded.

"Lewis, I don't know what to tell you. He only wanted to fit in, but they wouldn't let him. You should be proud of how your brother handled himself. The way I hear it, he was a real scrapper. I bet a lotta boys who crossed him have a scar somewhere to prove it."

She thought for a moment, then said, "And the other thing, Lewis, your skin *is* lighter than his. Didn't you ever wonder about that?"

Lewis stared at the tabletop. "I heard that on my very first day at school. A girl on the school bus said that I prob'ly have a different dad, and her friend said, 'They all do.'"

Isabel shook her head. "Those bastards. That's what the *summas* say because they think Indian women screw every guy they can. But your mom only had one man in her life. And that was your dad, Jimmy. But he was no good. When she kicked him out, I thought she finally had him figured out, but what did she do? She let him right back in the door again. I read in a magazine that some people call that passion. I call it stupid. Look what happened. Even when they were broke up, she tried to rip his head off right on the main street in Yakima when she saw him with another woman. He was damn lucky his car didn't stall at that traffic light or she'd a scratched his eyes out."

Lewis said, "I know. I was just a little kid, but I was there, remember? I never seen her so mad. I was so scared I started crying. Jimmy used to beat up Eddie too, until Alphonse came along."

Isabel said, "Your mom told me what he did before he took off the last time and I couldn't believe it. He punched her in the stomach and killed the little girl she was carrying, and he stole the diamond ring that was going to give you kids a better life. Then he left and never came back. So don't be surprised if one day they find him up on the range somewhere, hog-tied to a tree, naked, his body covered in pork chops. If he shows his face around here again, he'll end up bear bait, that's for damn sure. Women are tired of being punching bags, and some of them are starting to do something about it. Who knows how many assholes are buried in the hills above the reserve. I'd be careful if I was you, because you never know what could happen if you treat a girl bad."

Lewis laughed. "I'll try to remember that. But tell me this. If Jimmy is my dad and Eddie's too, why am I so white?"

Isabel stood and walked over to where the broom leaned against the wall and broke off a straw. When she sat back down, she used it to dig dough from under her nails. "You're lighter-skinned than Eddie, sure, but it's not because your mom screwed around. It's because Jimmy's great-grandfather was white. It just shows up once in a while. That's what I heard. And so the other kids treat you like a *summa*. But, Lewis, you shouldn't feel bad about the way they went after Eddie but not you. There was nothing you could have done. This happens to all Indians one way or another. And don't talk about this to your mom. You know what a hothead she is. If you want to ask these kinds of questions, you come to me."

CHAPTER 3

GRACE RAPPED ON THE WINDOW of Alphonse's house and leaned in for a look. When she saw no one, she swung the door open and yelled, "Hey." Hearing no answer, she pulled the door shut, angry with her brother for not picking up the mail on Friday like he always did.

Earlier that morning she had been at the Indian office to ask why there had been no progress on the house renovations. Mr. Cooke, in his ugly tie and short-sleeve shirt, his stick-like arms making bony gesticulations, told her, "I already mailed you the papers. You should have them by now. All you have to do is sign them and bring them back and the work will start. It's not my fault you lost them." She had left quietly, humiliated. All because of Alphonse.

Walking up the road, she turned her mind to the changes coming soon to her home, the indoor plumbing, the new rooms. Maybe she would get a brand-new electric stove put in, and a better wood heater for the living room–bathroom addition, and a fold-out leather chesterfield where visitors could spend the night. It was satisfying to think she would soon have what she could only dream about before. That is, until she remembered Eddie and the sick feeling in her stomach returned. When she was haunted by his memory, she had to get out of the house to walk around and hear the birds and look at the clouds.

She came to the hill that sloped down toward the river and remembered the one winter of his childhood when it was so cold it took her breath away. She'd watched the boys sliding down the icy hill on shovel heads, their hands gripping the handles as if riding in a rodeo, legs spurring madly. Halfway down, they flew over a jump they made from a car hood they found in Alphonse's scrap pile. They landed so hard on their behinds they winced in pain, but they shuffled right back up the hill, red-cheeked and laughing, to do it again.

Now a bulldozer had cleared the trees and smoothed the ground down to the flat spot where the new pumphouse stood. As she looked down the hill, graded smooth and free of stumps and rocks, she thought how much the boys would have loved to slide down it now.

She walked over to the wide clearing in view of the highway. Off to her right was the well-used path leading toward the bridge that Eddie and Lewis had crossed every day to catch the school bus in the morning and come home again in the afternoon. She saw the stretched square of the page-wire fence they crawled through and where they would stop to check for traffic before racing across to the other side of the bridge. She could almost hear their voices.

This was the place her sons called the picnic grounds because its lush grass and bushes reminded them of a park in Vernon. How they had begged her to come with their grandma to roast hot dogs on a fire, but not to tell Alphonse because he was too grouchy. Grace thought how wonderful it would be now to have a cup of tea up here with her mother and boys. They wouldn't even talk–just being together would be all she needed. Her mother thought a lot of the boys, especially

Eddie, and Grace couldn't remember her ever saying an unkind word to him. Maybe it was a good thing she died before learning her favourite grandson was missing. Her "pardner," she called him.

Grace wandered up the path to a snowberry bush, pulled off a handful of berries and kicked them into the air one at a time just as her boys had done, and she laughed at how good it felt to do such a silly thing. Then she stopped at the end of the trail by the chokecherry bush to pluck a hard little orb off a branch. Even though she knew it wouldn't be ripe until late summer, she popped it into her mouth. When she was little, she had gorged on them once and the bellyache and throwing up that followed was how she learned never to eat green fruit again. She crushed the berry with her teeth, immediately puckering up, and then spat it out.

She walked back to the clearing close to Alphonse's driveway, brushed the dirt off a stump and sat down. Pulling a flattened pouch of Vogue tobacco and papers out of her jeans, she rolled a cigarette, struck a match and held it to the end. She took a long drag, leaned her head back and exhaled.

All makes and colours of vehicles zoomed past. Watching the flow of traffic calmed her and she took her time to enjoy her cigarette. Then she stood, dropping the butt and grinding it under her heel. She folded her arms and walked to the highway in time to see the mail lady's car pull out from the school bus stop and head back toward Falkland.

Grace had made a point of staying away from the mailbox, which was just above the Cluff farm. For the two years since the death of the Cluffs' daughter, Eva, Eddie's sweetheart, she only went for the mail when Alphonse was sick.

When she came to the bridge she waited for a gap in the traffic, then took off running. Just as she reached the other side, a horn sounded behind her and a pickup sped past. A man stuck his head out the window and yelled, "Nice ass."

Grace didn't know whether to scream at him to piss off or blow him a kiss.

The heavy curtains on the Cluffs' picture window were wide open but she couldn't see anyone inside. The yard looked immaculate, with no dead cars anywhere to be seen. Beyond the arched-rafter barn at the back of the farmyard lay vast green fields. Chickens pecking at the ground in front of the barn door and a Jersey milk cow eating hay in a corral was like a photograph out of the *Star Weekly* magazine. She saw that the house had the same cheap asphalt siding as hers. Grace hurried past, hoping no one noticed her.

In a way she felt responsible for Eva's death because her son had been with the girl on the horse. She knew that if the tables were turned and Eddie had been the one killed that day, she might put the blame on them.

Alphonse had witnessed the accident. He was on the way home from hunting when he saw the two riders racing up the shoulder of the highway. When they turned onto Range Road, the girl had stood in the stirrups to haul back on the reins, but the horse wouldn't stop and tried to jump the cattle guard. They didn't make it.

Grace had been splitting firewood when she heard a loud gunshot and Alphonse frantically calling. She took off at a run. When she saw them lying on the road so still, she was certain both were dead.

When she reached the mailboxes at the bus stop, she smelled freshly cut alfalfa and looked over to the field to see Mr. Cluff on his tractor, cutting hay. Just before he made a wide turn to go back the other way, he spotted Grace watching. For a few seconds they stared at each other, both uncomfortable, as if sharing the same thought. *Do we ignore each other because it's easier to do nothing, or do we recognize the pain the other is feeling?*

Then Mr. Cluff tipped the brim of his hat to her, and she gave a short wave back, letting out a breath she didn't know she was holding. As she watched him drive up the field with his mower clacking and rattling behind, she was relieved, knowing she wasn't hated.

Her mailbox was stuffed with flyers and the letter from the Indian office. She pocketed the mail and turned toward home. Alphonse's driveway, with all the ruts and holes, made reading impossible. She stopped to study her letter and didn't see her brother coming up from his house.

"Hey there," he called.

Grace jumped. "Jeez, you scared the shit outta me."

"What are you doing?"

Grace pushed the flyers toward him. "I went to get the letter you were supposed to give me last week. Now I gotta run to town again. You think I got nothing better to do?"

Alphonse took the flyers. "I was on my way to the mailbox right now."

"What's wrong with you lately? You don't get the mail when you're supposed to, and when Isabel tells you to come for supper, you don't bother to show up."

Alphonse laid his hand against his chest as if in pain. "I caught something. Could be plursee."

"Pleurisy my ass." Grace wanted to let loose on this man who always tried to make a joke after being caught in a lie. But a loud car slowed on the highway just then, and soon Abel's car pulled up behind them. Alphonse went around to the passenger side. "If I'm feeling better," he said, "we'll see you later when we go down to the new field and do that burn."

Abel smiled at her. "I got everything we need."

With her hands on her hips, Grace watched them drive away, and then she started for home. She walked between the twin tire tracks where wilted dandelion plants had gone to seed, their heads quivering in a waft of air that released their silken parachutes and sent them floating. When she was a child, she enjoyed gently breaking off a stem and blowing, then watching the fluffs bob and weave away from her. Suddenly, she was struck by a memory so real she had to stop. One day when the boys were little, Lewis was napping on her bed and Eddie was playing outside by himself, and she decided she had enough time to make bread. After the dough had risen, she fried some up and called Eddie inside. Though he was hungry, he wanted to get back to playing, so he gobbled down the fry bread and asked to go out again. She let him, saying, "Don't you go anywhere, you hear?" Eddie flashed a smile at her and took off running.

When the smell of baking bread began coming from the stove, she smiled to herself, knowing there would be enough food for her boys for days. Pulling out a chair to sit down, she glanced out the window to the yard. Eddie was nowhere to be seen. She went to the door and called for him. Hearing nothing, she walked down to the outhouse to find him, even though she knew he would be embarrassed. When she saw the toilet was empty, she went back to the house and climbed the ladder to the attic, but he wasn't there either.

In a panic she asked Alphonse and her mother to help her search. Thinking the worst, they went down to the river, but he wasn't there. Grace ran toward the highway. And that's where she found him, walking back down the road toward home holding a fistful of dandelions. When he reached her, he held out his bouquet and said, with such a lovely smile, "Do you love these, Mom?"

She took his flowers, pulled him close. As they neared the house, she smelled something burning and ran.

The oven door dropped with a bang. Coughing, she pulled out the smoking loaves and threw them on the table. When Eddie appeared in the doorway, she couldn't stop herself. Picking up the whipping stick from the woodbox, she marched over to him and struck him repeatedly for scaring her and for ruining good food.

She couldn't forget the sound of her terrified child wailing or the way his eyes filled with tears as he looked up at her, pleading for her to tell him why he was being punished. She saw him now as clearly as if he was standing in front of her, and it made her feel ashamed.

Tears stung her eyes and rolled down her face. How could she have done such a terrible thing? When the tears finally stopped, she brushed her face with her hands and looked around to make sure no one was watching. After taking deep breaths to calm herself, she cut across the brush over to Range Road, bypassing the cattle guard. She climbed through the fence to go the long way back. She didn't want Alphonse to know that she had finally understood that her precious son was dead and wouldn't be coming home.

CHAPTER 4

IT HAD BEEN A HALF HOUR since the sun went behind Blue Grouse Mountain and there was still no sign of Alphonse or Abel. Grace, feeling less annoyed by her brother, was looking forward to cleaning up the new field. Everyone had worked so hard to get it done and tonight they would celebrate, sitting around the fire and bullshitting over a beer or two.

Finally, she spotted the bachelor pair coming up the small hill above Alphonse's house, chuckling like schoolboys on a Friday afternoon.

Even in his work clothes Abel always looked clean. He had narrow shoulders and was thinner and shorter than Alphonse. Not only was he always well-shaved, he pressed his overalls so that sharp creases ran from his chest to his pant cuffs. He was pleasant to be around, never cussed in front of her, no matter how angry he was. Grace thought the best word to describe him was *decent*, but people said he was a penny-pinching skinflint. Including Alphonse. "Abel's tighter'n a duck's ass, and that's watertight."

Grace, along with Isabel and Lewis, hurried out of the house to see Alphonse lifting a heavy jerry can onto the truck bed as Abel loaded a pail, water slopping over its side. "What you got there, Abel?"

He grinned. "It's in case we get thirsty."

"I didn't know they put water in those brown stubbies," Isabel said.

Abel shook the pail and the bottles of beer clinked inside.

Grace drove with Isabel up front. Lewis, Alphonse and Abel sat on the sides of the truck box, cool wind blowing into their faces as they rode down toward the newly cleared field. Today they would finish gathering the limbs and broken trees into a pile and set it on fire.

As she pulled up to the wire gate, Lewis jumped down, lifted the loop off the post and tossed the gate to the side.

"Where's the chain and padlock?" Grace asked. When no one answered, she drove through and switched off the motor. "Alphonse, where's the padlock? You and Abel been down here lately?"

Alphonse nodded to Lewis. "No, but he saw some guys go in here a couple days ago."

Grace slid out of the truck seat. "Why didn't you tell me, Lewis?"

Her son was busy packing a jerry can of fuel to the bulldozer. After lifting the can onto the dozer track, he looked back at her. "I saw two white guys park here and walk down to the river."

"And you forgot to tell me?"

"I told Alphonse. Before we said anything to you, we wanted to find out who they were or if they came back. That's all."

"Was it the Indian agent sneaking around? It better not be that skinny bugger."

"It wasn't him. I don't know who they were."

Alphonse crouched on his heels to examine something on the ground. "Grace, come over here. Take a look at this." He picked up a cigarette butt, turning it over in his fingers. "Somebody likes Lucky Strike smokes. The closest place you can get these is down in the States, at Ben Prince's in Oroville. And one of them was wearing cowboy boots. The pipeline workers don't wear shit-kickers."

Isabel had come over to join them. She said, "Almost everybody from the reserve goes across the line for cigarettes and stuff. You just came back yourself, Abel. These aren't yours, are they?"

"No sir. Never use 'em."

Alphonse stood and dusted off his hands. "So we'll put another lock on the gate and keep an eye out. No point in standing around here worrying about it. Let's get this stuff lit up while it's cool so we don't start a forest fire."

As Abel emptied the fuel into the bulldozer, Lewis had a look around the new field. Alphonse and Abel had cut down all the trees, delimbed them and sawed them into eight-foot lengths. Stud logs they were called because they would be made into two-by-four studs for building homes. Alphonse said they would bring a good price at Hoover's sawmill on the reserve.

Abel's old bulldozer was a Field Marshall. For years he had kept an eye on it as it stood abandoned at the edge of a white farmer's field near the town of Armstrong, poplar saplings sprouting between its tracks. At a young age Abel had been a mechanic in the army and he was confident he could get it going again, so he approached the farmer to ask if he wanted it fixed. "That machine's been broke so long it'll never run again," the farmer said. "Give me fifty bucks and I'll haul it anywhere you want. The wife will be happy to see that eyesore the hell outta here."

It took Abel two years to strip down the motor and jerry-rig the broken and missing parts. But the machine was still a finicky piece of equipment. Just starting the engine was a hit-or-miss event, as Abel was about to show. First, he rotated the flywheel with his foot until a cylinder was beginning its downstroke. Then he lit a match to a piece of paper on the end of a rod and placed it inside a hole in the engine. Alphonse waved Lewis over and spoke into his ear in a low voice. "That paper there's got saltpetre on it, so you don't wanna get any on your *spalq*, cuz if you do, it won't get hard no matter how many times you pull it or stretch it or slap it around."

Lewis blushed, forcing a laugh.

After Abel placed a shotgun shell in a chamber on the side of the motor, he screwed a cap with a pin sticking out of it back in place. After making the sign of the cross, Abel struck the cap with a hammer and the motor came to life, chugging out thick smoke. A big cheer went up.

"Hey, Abel," Grace yelled. "Can I give it a try?"

"I don't know, Grace. This here old girl is a bit touchy."

Alphonse laughed. "Abel, you better let her do it. This old girl can be pretty touchy too."

Abel didn't look pleased, but he threw up his hands. After he showed Grace how the lever worked to raise and lower the blade and how to steer with the brakes, she revved the motor then drove toward the scattered roots and boughs, tracks creaking. An hour later she had all the broken wood pushed into a tall pile. With a rake and shovel, her ground crew rounded up the rest, tossed them onto the mound and stood back.

Alphonse doused the pile with diesel and threw in a match. The fire started slowly, licking at the bottom of the pile, and then grew hotter. Flames and smoke rose high into the sky, and the wood popped like gunshots, spitting out sparks and embers that curled in the air and drifted to the northeast. It was dark when the fire had died down enough that they could sit, staring into the coals. Alphonse and Abel pulled up blocks of wood while Isabel, Grace and Lewis sat on a log. No one spoke. Abel popped off the beer caps and handed the bottles around, even to Lewis, who was soon taking sips from the first beer he ever had in the presence of his mother. She warned, "Just don't let me catch you drinking with these two guys."

Alphonse burped and nudged his friend. "Abel here knows more stories than anybody. Best bullshitter I ever knew. Go on, Abel, tell the kid a story. Tell him the one about how the chipmunk got his stripes."

Abel guzzled the rest of his beer, wiped his mouth with his sleeve and cleared his throat.

Alphonse pointed, grinning. "See how he drained that bottle without stopping, Lewis? Maybe someday you'll be able to do that."

"Hah," Grace said.

Abel set the empty bottle down and began. "This story's been around a long time. Dunno where it came from. First time I heard it was around a campfire just like this.

"Well, long time ago when all the animals in the bush could talk to each other, a bear was walking down a trail minding his own business. And because he was so big he thought he was the meanest one around. 'There's nothing I can't do,' he said loud enough that a chipmunk stuck his head out from his hole in the ground.

"'Zat so?' the chipmunk asked. The bear looked down and said, 'Damn right.' Then he rolled over a big log. 'See how easy I done that? I'm the strongest sumbitch in the world. That's why all the other animals hide when they see me coming.'

"The chipmunk asked, 'Can you stop the sun from coming up in the morning?'

"'Sheeeeit, I just told you, I can do anything.'

"'You sure about that?' the chipmunk said in a smart-ass tone.

"'The sun will not rise. I said so,' the bear answered.

"But first thing in the morning the old sun come up just like it always did and that bear, he ain't happy, 'specially when the little chipmunk started dancing and running around in circles singing a song. 'The sun come up, the sun come up, and the bear is a big fat liar.'

"The bear shot out a paw and pinned that chipmunk to the ground quicker'n Gene Kiniski the wrassler. That's when the chipmunk started suckholing. 'Okay, okay, you're the strongest and quickest animal—I was only teasing you. You can kill me if you want, but let me say a prayer to the Creator before you do.'

"'Okay, say your prayers, you little bastard.'

"'Bear, I can't. You're pressing down on me so hard I can barely squeak. Just lift your paw a little and I'll say my prayer. Then you can eat me.'

"Bear lifted up his paw just a bit. That's all Chipmunk needed. He squirmed out and took off running like a bat outta hell. He was just about to scoot down his hole when Bear reached out to grab him. But he missed and his long claws scraped Chipmunk's back, leaving three long scars. So to this day all chipmunks wear those stripes to remind them what happens when you talk smart-assed to the wrong guy."

CHAPTER 5

AFTER BREAKFAST, Lewis climbed the ladder up to the attic and sat down on the ledge. He had a pocket book Western to finish and return to his uncle, but there was nowhere else to sit alone without being bothered. At first he wasn't impressed with the book, but soon he became caught up in the story. As he turned the last page, he finally found out what the cowboy did to the man who killed his brother. He closed the book, satisfied revenge had been done.

After easing down to sit on the ladder's top rung, he leaned back against the house wall. The sun felt good and he looked up at the clouds slipping across the sapphire sky. They looked clean, white and perfect, as if someone on the other side of the mountains were making snowballs and placing them up there, one by one. He followed a cloud with an unusual shape that seemed to take forever to make it across to the other side of the horizon, but minutes later, when he looked back, it had travelled to rest above the high blue hills at the back of the range.

He heard a loud cawing of crows. Shielding his eyes, he spotted them in the treetops at the edge of the new field, see-sawing up and down on the ends of the boughs, their feathers black as old motor oil. Their cries were directed at a lone hawk drifting on a rising pocket of air. Lewis thought of Eddie then and longed for the two of them to be up in the sky with the hawk, gliding shoulder to wing in wide circles, watching their shadows on the ground below.

He was imagining the places they would go, the things they would see, when the crows dropped from their perch and rose, heading straight for the hawk. Lewis heard a desperate screech within the army of squawks, then all the birds were gone and it was quiet again.

In the centre of the field a dust devil stirred to life by a rush of wind floated across the ground, picking up weeds and dirt, a piece of paper caught in the upward spiral. And then, as quickly as it had started, the whirlwind collapsed, and the debris drifted back down to the ground.

Even though the bulldozer had cleared away the trees in the new field, plenty more grew along the river. At times the fir forest, with tall cottonwoods, poplar and birch lining the shore, was so thick that a person looking for a place to fish needed to get into the water to make any kind of headway along the bank.

And all the way from the river through the middle of their land, including the new field, the government had cleared a right-of-way and dug a trench for a natural gas pipeline. After the pipe was laid, workers filled in the trench. It stood out like a scar on the land. Lewis followed the pipeline to where it crossed Range Road and came to a stop. That's where he saw, a half mile away, a backhoe parked in the shade. Then sunlight glancing off glass, the mirror or windshield of a vehicle hidden in the trees, flashed in his eyes. Soon a car drove up and people climbed out and approached the backhoe. Lewis crab-walked down the ladder, ran around the corner of the house and swung open the kitchen door. "Mom, something's going on down at the range."

Grace, Isabel, Alphonse, Abel and Lewis all climbed in the old truck. When they drove across the cattle guard and turned up the hill, they saw a police car parked alongside pickup trucks and cars that were lined up like they were at a drive-in movie. Grace turned off the road and parked and they walked toward the crowd that had gathered around the backhoe. Everyone was staring down into the trench. An arm reached up out of the hole and grabbed a canvas tarp from a person standing at the edge.

"Francis," Alphonse called. A man in the crowd looked back and walked over to them. "What's going on here?"

"The backhoe dug up a body that was buried on the edge of the hill above the road. Somebody called the police. When they came to see if it was somebody that was murdered, they got a hold of Lawrence, our heap big chief, and he told a few of us councillors we had to get out here. The rest of the people here are pipeline workers. The guy in the coveralls is an archaeologist."

"Jesus," Grace said.

"The body was all wrapped up in birchbark. But the backhoe made kind of a mess. When we saw the bones, we were all a little spooked. See old Percy Mackie over there?" Francis pointed to an elderly man clutching the elbow of the woman next to him. "He said it's probably a chief because he had a grave all to himself with a good view of the lake. There was a spear and other stuff in there with him. The archaeologist is taking samples to send away so he'll know how old the bones are. Look, they're bringing it up now."

Several men carried the tarp-wrapped bundle from the edge of the trench and laid it on the grass. The archaeologist kneeled and pulled back the canvas. Lewis saw a skull and curved rib bones, and an icy chill went through him. He had always wondered how a person looked after being buried in the ground a long time.

The man pulled a pair of scissors from his pocket and cut away a square of birchbark that he placed in a plastic bag. Then he reached for the spear.

"Leave that alone," Percy Mackie shouted. "Just leave that where it is and get away from there."

The archaeologist looked up at him and gave a weak smile. Then he folded the tarp back around the bones and wrapped the bundle with a white cotton rope.

"What's going to happen now? What are they going to do with that . . . thing?" Grace asked Francis.

"We're not sure. We could take it down to the boneyard at Head of the Lake and bury it there or put it somewhere close to here. We'll mark where it was dug up, though. Somebody said we should make a cairn. That's a fancy name for a pile of rocks. Hell, we got cairns all over the place."

Lewis watched as the tarp-covered body was wrapped in thick blankets and more protective coverings for the rough journey ahead, then placed in the back of a pickup. After slamming the tailgate shut, the chief and the archaeologist drove the truck away, other vehicles following behind like a funeral procession.

A strange feeling of wonder came over Lewis after seeing the remains of a once important Indian buried long ago. It was mystical, almost holy.

"Hey, Lewis, are those the guys that shot the padlock?" Alphonse pointed to a pickup coming down the right-of-way from the river. They watched it turn toward the closed gate below them.

"Yep, that's the truck I saw," Lewis said.

"Let's get down there and find out what they're up to." Alphonse and Abel turned to go back to the truck.

"Wait a minute," Grace said. "Let's see who they are first. What if they're just pipeline workers? Before you go running off, I'll ask these guys if they know."

She hurried over to the men gathered around the backhoe. Lewis, Alphonse and Abel watched a large man Lewis recognized immediately step out of the truck and open the wire gate. After the truck drove through, the man closed the gate. Feeling eyes on him, he looked up and saw he was being watched. He waved, then climbed back into the truck, and it sped off down Range Road.

Grace came back. "Nobody knows who they are. Let's take a drive down to the river and see what they were up to. It could be a couple of dumb fishermen."

"I can tell you this, Grace," Alphonse said. "If they were pipeline workers, they'd have had their hard hats on. And those ain't any fishermen I seen before. You shoulda seen the size of the one guy."

When they came to a stop close to the shore, they all exited the truck and stood looking at the scene in front of them. Four wooden pegs had been positioned in a square on the flattest piece of ground. Grace walked over and stood at its centre. "What's going on here?"

Abel walked back up the road. When he returned, he pointed to a rise in the land. "I thought that hump was just an easy little slope, but from a hundred feet back, you can't see a thing down here. This is a good place to stay outta sight, that's for sure."

"When did you first see those guys, Lewis?" Grace asked.

"It was Friday, the last day of school."

Grace turned around slowly, her eyes fixed on the ground. "What the hell is going on here, anyway?"

Abel cleared his throat. "I'd say somebody is planning on putting up a shed or a shack."

Alphonse looked confused. "So what are they, squatters? I heard people do that sometimes and they don't get caught for years."

"What are we going to do?" Grace said.

Alphonse yanked out a peg and threw it into the bush. "I think we keep an eye out down here. I'll put up a no-trespassing sign. For all we know, them buggers could be birdwatchers, or nudists even."

Later that afternoon Alphonse and Abel nailed a board to the gate post: Step Across on This Land Here and Get Your Head Shot Off.

CHAPTER 6

THE NEXT DAY Lewis climbed the ladder to the attic and sat gazing up at the burial site on the range. The backhoe and the work crew were gone. Only a day ago they had opened a door to a dark, mysterious world, and when the tarp was pulled back from the bones, he and everyone else went quiet; even the pipeline workers stilled their non-stop banter. The eye holes gazed up vacant, expressionless, until someone pulled at the wrapping and the skull fell to the side, looking directly at Lewis in a wicked leer. How many times had he and Eddie walked close to that very spot, not knowing what was buried under their feet.

The sun bearing down on the house released a skunky perfume from the asphalt siding, and the ladder under his feet ticked and cracked with the rising temperature. He was about to climb down when he heard a whistle and saw two people coming out of the trees at the pipeline right-of-way. Shading his eyes, he couldn't make out who they were. He felt a mounting dread that it might be the white strangers. As they came closer, he was relieved to see it was his cousins, who lived a mile downriver, and he hurried down the ladder to meet them.

Marvin was seventeen, a year older than Lewis but inches taller. When he approached Lewis, he pulled the .22 rifle off his back and drew back the bolt. When the shell flew out, he caught it in his palm and slipped it into his jeans. Rosalyn was eighteen and wore a wide hat that shielded her face from the sun.

When they heard laughing and talking, Grace and Isabel came outside. Grace said, "Well, look what wandered outta the bush. We were just going to have dinner, so why don't you guys come in and have something to eat."

"We got buns and canned salmon," Isabel said. "There's a cold jug of Kool-Aid in the fridge too."

Uncle Ned, Aunt Jean and their three children had moved back to the Okanagan Indian Reserve two years ago, from Lillooet. Alphonse and Grace were brother and sister to Jean. Uncle Ned had come first, with a friend who'd served with him in the Second World War. Together they built a log barn for the family to live in while work began on a house. Lewis, Alphonse, Isabel and Grace had visited them many times, but hadn't been back as the house came closer to being finished.

When they were all settled around the kitchen table, Marvin asked Lewis, "What are you doing for your summer holidays?"

Before he could answer, Grace spoke. "Helping the carpenters. The Indian agent said they'll be starting work on the house soon and it'll take around six weeks. We're putting in a new addition with a bathroom and toilet and a shower. When school starts this fall, we'll have what other people have—power and water and a real home, just like you guys."

Lewis said, "Yep, that's what I'm doing."

"When did you guys move into the house?" Grace asked.

Rosalyn said, "A couple weeks before summer holidays started."

"It must feel pretty good to get out of the barn. When me, Alphonse and your mom were kids, we lived in a two-storey log house right beside a creek. We used to play until dark, making toy boats out of sticks and running down to watch them crash over little falls. That creek was louder than the river, and we could jump across it in places. And now here we are, all living close to water, just like we're kids again."

Lewis noticed that whenever his mother spoke about her time as a little girl, she always had a smile on her face.

"Who built that house?" Rosalyn asked.

"Our dad."

"Mom tells us stories about Grandma and you and Uncle Alphonse, but never about our grandfather. Whatever happened to him, anyway?"

Lewis was interested to hear what his mother would say. Whenever he asked her about his grandpa, she just gave a grunt and continued what she was doing.

Grace said, "One day he was just gone. We never did find out why. Hey, Lewis, why don't you tell them about the Indian chief they found."

Just then they heard a car coming down the road. Grace turned in her chair to look out the open door. "It's the Indian agent. Wonder what's wrong now. The only time he comes around here is to give me bad news."

Grace left the table and went outside as a tall, skinny man with thick glasses stepped out of the car. He had a small ball-shaped head perched on a long neck, and he held both hands toward Grace as if in surrender. Eddie had nicknamed him the Buzzard.

None of them could hear what he was saying, but as he spoke Grace tilted her head and placed her hands on her hips. Lewis knew it was only a matter of time before his mother became so riled up that something bad would happen.

"I better get out there," Isabel said, and left the table.

Grace spoke in a voice loud enough for all to hear. "Jesus, Cookie! Do you lay awake all night thinking up ways to make my life miserable?"

The agent cleared his throat. This time they could hear him. "It's Mister Cooke, please. And like I said, not all the money for the work to your house came through. You're a couple hundred dollars short, so you better get a move on and find some work somewhere or the house won't get done this summer. They're coming out first thing tomorrow."

Grace jabbed her finger in the man's face as she shouted, spit flying, "The last time you were here, you told me everything was ready to go. Now you're saying I have to give you more money? You just keep asking for more and more and more. I don't think you know how to add. Why do you keep fucking things up?"

Isabel stepped between them and the Indian agent retreated to his car and drove away. Grace shook her head and watched him until he was out of sight. When she returned to the table and picked up a bun, Lewis saw her hands were trembling. "All that guy is good for is making me mad." Crumbs fell to the table.

"Pass me the butter, please," Marvin said as he split open another bun and reached for the jar of salmon.

Everyone went back to eating.

After a time, Grace said, "Sorry for blowing up like that. I don't want that idiot to ruin my day, so right after we eat, we'll drive you kids back home and have a look at that new house of yours. I can't wait to see it."

After the dishes were washed, Lewis and his cousins climbed into the back of the pickup, and they rode up the dusty road toward the highway. As they crossed the bridge, Lewis glanced at the Cluff farm. The first day he went to catch the school bus after the accident, he remembered, he'd been nervous about being confronted by Eva's brother, Albert. He was ready for anything and was surprised when all the big farm boy did was nod at him.

When Grace slowed down to turn onto Salmon Valley Road, the truck backfired and the cousins laughed. As they came out of the trees that lined the driveway, Lewis saw the new house was on a hill above the hay barn, facing down to a long field. A big chicken coop stood close to the barn, with a woodshed attached to the side. Everything looked neat and orderly.

The dog, Mitzi, began barking as Aunt Jean, Uncle Ned and Lewis's younger cousin Cora came out onto the porch and waved to them. Ned stilled the dog, patting her on the head. Isabel was out of the truck before Grace turned off the motor. Grace stepped out and shut her door. Shielding her eyes, she studied the house. "So this is what brand new looks like. You should build these for a living, Ned."

"If people are anything like your sister, I'd prob'ly quit."

"Oh, don't listen to him. He just doesn't like taking orders from a woman," Jean said. "Come in and I'll show you around."

Isabel and Grace walked up the steps as Ned stepped aside. "I had the tour already."

Lewis sat down on the porch steps beside Marvin and Mitzi. Ned studied the two boys. "Just look at the long hair on you two. I'm itching to get out my old hand clippers and give you both a quick trim. If you were in the army, there'd be a pile at your feet so deep you couldn't see your boots."

"The girls like it, Dad. That's all that matters," Marvin said, and elbowed Lewis in the ribs. "Let's go up the hill before we get scalped. I wanna show you the view from up there."

When Lewis and Marvin jumped off the stairs, Mitzi barked and was about to go after them, but Ned grabbed her by the collar. "No, you stay here, old girl, and keep me company. You're too old to go running up and down them hills."

At the top of the steep hill, Lewis's legs felt like rubber. He and his cousin leaned against a tree, breathing hard. After a minute, Marvin pointed. "There's the road that goes to the store. See how small the river looks from here? It's like a little creek." The house, barn and chicken coop, with the pigpen carefully hidden out of sight, lay beneath Lewis's feet, arranged like a picture on a puzzle box. Two weeping willow trees stood like guards at the back of the house. A large garden was planted between the east side of the house and the steep hill where they stood.

"This is what a hawk would see," Lewis said.

His eyes followed the Salmon River as it looped around a thick stand of trees, curving toward the field below the house. Where the river turned back sharply to the right, he noticed a sandy island beside a deep hole that would be a good place to swim. The sunlight off the water glinted like pieces of broken glass. Cars and trucks coming and going on the road looked like Dinky Toys.

A horn honked. Lewis looked down to see Isabel and his mother waving for them to come back. On the way down, he felt like a skier slipping down a dusty slope. When the boys reached flat ground, they needed to outrun an avalanche of dust rolling across the ground behind them.

His mother waved him over. "Lewis, it looks like me and Isabel are leaving for the States right now. I need to make that money fast, and Isabel knows so many growers down there, she can find us a job as soon as we get across the border. The carpenters will have to get along without you, because I had a talk with your Aunt Jean and you're going to stay here for the summer and work for them. That way, you'll get to spend time with kids your own age. She reminded me about Mom dragging us all over the place, making us work like we were in a chain gang. We never got to go anywhere or do anything."

Lewis couldn't believe what he was hearing.

"Don't look so surprised," his mother said. "We want to get outta here right away and hope to be down there before dark. When I'm packing, I'll gather some clothes for you, and Alphonse can drop them off in the morning. Jean said all you need is swim trunks and underwear anyway."

She placed a hand on his shoulder. "I'm glad we're going. I really don't want to be around with the carpenters sawing and banging all day. Neither do you. So have fun. We'll see you a couple weeks before school. Just look after yourself and listen to your aunt and uncle."

She smiled and walked to the truck. Isabel grabbed Lewis and hugged him hard, then went after Grace.

He watched them drive away, Isabel waving out the window on her side and Grace waving out the other, hand like a bird taking to the air. When the truck turned the corner, the trees seemed to fold together behind them like a curtain.

Lewis listened until he couldn't hear the rattling and banging when the truck hit a pothole. His mother was leaving him, and he was going to have the best summer of his life.

Marvin punched him on the shoulder. "Come on, Lewis! Mommy will be back before you know it."

CHAPTER 7

JUST BEFORE BEDTIME, Jean approached Lewis and Marvin, pointing to the bathroom. "You boys need a shower. I saw how you both came down that hill, and you're not getting my sheets dirty. Lewis, you go first and leave your clothes outside the door so I can wash them. Marvin can find stuff for you to wear to bed. He'll give you a hand."

Marvin joked, "What do you mean, like wash his back?"

"No, I mean get some of your things for him to wear." She went into the kitchen, grinning. "Wash his back."

Lewis stepped into the bathroom, stripped down and tossed his dirty clothes in a heap outside the bathroom door. He stepped into the shower, pulled the plastic curtain shut and turned on the taps. When he pulled up the shower knob, the force of the water stung his face and chest. He retreated to the back of the tub and slowly inched forward into the spray, then grabbed a white bar of soap and covered himself with lather from his head to his toes.

After he was done, he smelled clean and his skin squeaked. Having a shower was so different from taking a bath in the old tin tub at home. He dried off, then wrapped himself in the towel and hurried into Marvin's room. As Marvin took his turn in the shower, Lewis pulled on a clean pair of underwear and slipped into the double bed. After Marvin was done, he crawled into the other side of the bed and the boys chatted until a loud *shush* came from his aunt and uncle's bedroom. Lewis rolled over on his side and listened to the wind through the screened window until drifting off to sleep.

When he woke, it took him a few moments to remember where he was. Marvin was still fast asleep, so he slid out of bed, dressed and went into the bathroom. Just as he was about to have his morning pee, he remembered what Marvin had told him: "Mom wants us guys to sit on the toilet to take a leak so the seat and the floor don't get all wet and pissy-smelling."

Lewis had used many bathrooms before, at school, the bus depot or a café in town, but there was something about doing it in this brand-new one that didn't feel right, as if the smell had no way of escaping. So he stepped out on the porch and eased the door shut behind him. Pissing outside in the fresh air, in the bush or behind a tree, taking aim at a fly on the bark, was the way to go, and the ants didn't care if you got any on their floor. He ran down the steps and broke into a sprint for the river. Mitzi, who had been lying under the back porch, sprang to her feet and raced past him in an orange blur, leading the way.

Lewis stepped off the path and pushed aside the boughs of a low-hanging cedar until he came out at a clearing by the shore. The faint aroma of cedar clung to his clothes and hair. Spring floods had made many changes since his last visit. The river was twice as wide here and slow, where back home the water ran deep and fast. The logjam that he remembered looking like giant pickup sticks was gone, purged by the runoff. He noticed what looked like raindrops breaking the smoothness of the water at a quiet spot upstream, but there wasn't a cloud anywhere to be seen in the sky. Looking closer, he saw trout surfacing to feed on a new bug hatch, their tails flicking water in the air, making rings that spread out in connecting circles before drifting downstream.

Lewis stepped behind a tree and relieved himself, gave a shake, then zipped up and went out to join the dog. He followed Mitzi through a maze of trails until they stumbled onto a cow and calf lying in the shade. The dog and boy turned away to leave them in peace and walked along the riverbank toward the swimming hole. When Lewis came out into the open, he saw his uncle Ned standing with his fedora in his hand, looking out at the water.

"There you are," his uncle said. "I figured you were down here someplace when I seen your bedroom door open and Mitzi was gone." He drew a hanky from his pocket and wiped his forehead.

"I wanted to have a look around," Lewis said, leaning down to scratch the dog behind the ear.

"You remind me of me. My mom used to almost have to tie me up to keep me away from the water up in Lillooet. The Fraser River is a dangerous place for kids, but I knew all the spots to stay away from and I liked to be out by myself, swimming, fishing or just lying on the rocks and falling asleep. Dad didn't mind, cuz he knew that's the only way you learn. My mom, though, she didn't like me to go by myself. If she went outside and hollered for me to get home and I didn't answer, she'd come looking for me. When she found me, she'd kick me in the ass."

Ned pulled a stalk of grass and put it between his teeth. "Marvin will show you all the places on the farm you're gonna like. On the other side of the river, up a little ways, we found arrowheads and sharp stones chipped out of a black rock that looks like glass. Obsidian, it's called. Jean said her mom told her the place was an old fishing camp. Indians travelled there from a long, long ways away. At one time this reserve started at Douglas Lake and stretched all the way down to Omak in the States. That's over two hundred miles. And they didn't have cars them days. They rode horses and met up here to catch fish in the fall salmon run. But nobody goes there anymore because the land belongs to a white man now. You know how *summas* ended up with it? The government just handed it over to them."

Ned pulled the stalk out of his mouth and threw it on the ground. "I can feel the steam coming out my ears when I talk about stuff like this," he said. "Good thing I can take it out on all them hay bales." He looked up at the sky. "Weatherman sez it's supposed be clear, so make sure you have a good sleep tonight. You know what? Let's get back up to the house before them hungry buggers eat all the cornflakes and mush."

Lewis kicked a rock and it skipped twice on the water.

"Maybe you and Mitzi should go on ahead. I have to take a quick count of the cattle. We can't afford to lose a single one or the Indian agent will have a fit. I'll be up in a minute."

Lewis wanted to ask why the Indian agent would be angry about missing a cow, but Ned pointed up the trail to the house. "Home, Mitzi. Go home." She turned and ran up the trail with Lewis beside her, her long coat brushing his hand as they raced through the cool darkness of the woods. Out in the open, a bee sprung from a purple thistle head and sailed into the air in front of them. Mitzi jumped to grab it, but missed, her teeth snapping together.

At the house, the dog raced up the steps then turned to him, her breath hot on his chest. Lewis could see the hay bales stacked in bunches in the field, lined up like soldiers at attention, waiting. He gave the dog a pat on the head and went inside.

"Morning, Lewis. You sleep okay?" Jean asked when he came into the kitchen.

"I sure did."

"Don't them sheets feel good on your skin after a shower?"

"Yeah, I like how the pillowcases smell like snow when they come in off the line."

His uncle came in the door and hung his hat. Then he turned on the kitchen tap and washed his hands. When he finished, he left the water running and motioned for Lewis to do the same. By the time Lewis dried off, his cousins were seated around the table. He took the chair between Cora and Marvin. It felt good to be at the table with his cousins, talking about things he knew, and he wasn't shy about adding his own opinion.

While he was chewing, he looked around at the room. The electric clock on the wall swept soundlessly in circles, and the polished black-and-white floor tiles looked like a checkerboard. There were no fly catchers hanging from the ceiling and no mousetraps in the corners.

When breakfast was over, Ned tipped up his cup of coffee and swallowed noisily. Springing out of his chair, he grabbed his hat off the wall peg. Just as he was about to walk out the door, he stopped and asked, "What are you guys gonna be doing today, Jean?"

"Some weeding and watering. We'll bring in some rhubarb and some early strawberries. I can't wait to start filling up that big freezer."

"I better get going before you find something for me to do." He donned his hat and walked out the door.

Lewis and Marvin followed. "Need a hand, Dad?"

Ned looked back. "I'm cleaning up a mess I made yesterday. I think your mom's got something planned for you both."

The two boys leaned against the outside wall of the house while Mitzi dozed on the top step of the porch, her head resting on her paws, occasionally snapping at a fly buzzing around her ear. Suddenly she jumped to her feet and began barking. Soon a vehicle without a muffler could be heard coming their way. Lewis knew it was Abel's car long before it came around the bend of the road. When it hit a rut, the heads of the two men inside shook like bobblehead dolls. The car rocked to a stop in front of the porch.

After the car was switched off, the motor gave a long moan. Abel and Alphonse climbed out, dark sweat stains spreading from their armpits. The springs squealed with the unburdening and the roof lifted higher. Then the motor sputtered and coughed as if trying to restart and Alphonse walked behind the car and gave a hard kick to the bumper. It became still. "Damn thing never learns."

Jean came out and leaned on the porch railing. "Morning, Abel. Morning, Alphonse."

"Haloo," said Alphonse, followed by a "Howdy" from Abel.

"Come on in and I'll put the coffee on."

"You guys came along at the right time," Ned called, walking up from the barn. "You gave me a good excuse to stop working."

As he walked past, Alphonse grabbed Lewis and tickled his armpit. "Hello, squirt!"

Lewis and his cousin followed the visitors inside. They all wiped their feet on the door sill and let the screen door bang shut behind them. Alphonse and Abel pulled out chairs and sat at the table.

Ned said, "Jeez, Abel, I thought for sure you woulda ditched that car by now. How do you keep it running?"

"Binder twine and haywire," he answered.

"That right, Alphonse?"

Alphonse shook his head. "I never been in such a loud, smoky piece of junk in my life. The steering is so bad it's like herding a cow down the road. Coming up St. Anne's Hill, it was hard to see the road through all the smoke. We had all the windows rolled down, our heads sticking out like dogs."

Ned said, "That's not like you, Abel. You're pretty fussy about your machines. Why are you hanging on to that thing?"

"I'm gonna run it until it quits before I get my good car on the road."

Alphonse added, "That bugger can squeeze a nickel until the beaver shits."

"Okay," Jean said, "you kids don't need to be sitting around here listening to a bunch of old farts, so Rosalyn, you and Cora go ahead and get started on the garden. And take these two boys with you."

Jean placed the coffee pot on the counter and plugged it into the wall outlet, then set cups on the table, a can of milk and a bowl of sugar, followed by a tin of cookies.

Rosalyn took two large bowls out of the cupboard and handed one to Marvin. "You and Lewis pick the peas while Cora and I get some strawberries."

Half an hour later the pickers sat on the porch steps shelling peas, listening to the stories and laughter drifting outside. Alphonse talked about the Indian bones found wrapped in birchbark and Abel joined in with his version. Jean shushed them both when a disagreement over the facts broke out. It wasn't until the pot of coffee was emptied that the visitors placed their spoons in their mugs and pushed back their chairs.

Alphonse came out the door, stopping to speak to Lewis. "Come down to the car, I got somethin' for you."

Lewis followed his uncle.

"Here's the clothes your mom sent." Alphonse handed him a box. "Listen, and don't tell your aunt this, okay? Me and Abel, we got us a couple queens lined up tonight. We're gonna have a little party, just the four of us. Abel's bringing the beer and I'm bringing the Mazola. Maybe you can get away and join us and we'll see if we can get you that first piece of tail, eh?"

Lewis shook his head and laughed. "You're making that up."

Alphonse winked.

CHAPTER 8

IT WAS STILL DARK when Lewis was awakened by a rooster's cry that sounded as if it came from under his bed. He got dressed just as Marvin began to stir and went to the kitchen, where a large breakfast had been plated and laid out on the table. A single plate was already scraped clean, left without a crumb. Two others were loaded with ham, eggs, fried potatoes, toast and pork and beans. He doubted he could eat it all.

His aunt laughed. "You better get that all down, Lewis. You're gonna need it when you get out there and start throwing them bales."

Marvin came out of the bedroom, tucking in his shirt, and settled in his chair. The food was so good that in no time at all Lewis and Marvin were rounding up the last bits with their forks just as the tractor pulled up to the front porch.

"Better get a move on, you two. Ned's ready to go," Jean said.

Even in work gloves, a long-sleeved shirt and a pair of Marvin's haying jeans with a thick patch sewn the length of both legs, Lewis felt the chill in the air when he stepped outside. Marvin jumped onto the trailer and grabbed the headboard like an old hand. Lewis climbed on and almost fell when his uncle pulled away from the house. It looked like there were a million bales in the field.

Both boys jumped off the trailer and Lewis picked up the first bale he had ever handled and tossed it onto the deck. *This is gonna be easy*, he thought. But in no time, he was arm-weary. Then he noticed how his cousin used his knee for leverage, and soon the bales went flying. After the trailer was covered with scattered bales, Marvin jumped up and began stacking. Ned stepped off the tractor to help until he saw Lewis was able to keep up. After the load was high enough, Marvin checked all the corners, making sure the bales were stacked tightly. "Climb on up, Lewis. We can have a rest on the way back to the barn."

Lewis was only too happy to climb up top. It felt cooler there, and he was able to brush some of the prickly hay off his arms and shake the bits out of his shirt.

After a long morning of loading and unloading bales, Lewis saw the station wagon pull up and park in a shady spot under the trees that edged the hayfield. His aunt, Rosalyn and Cora stepped out of the car as Ned pulled the tractor alongside then switched it off.

Jean lowered the tailgate and slid out a cardboard box of food, unpacking hard-boiled eggs and a plate of roast-beef sandwiches. Rosalyn produced a jar of lime Kool-Aid and a cooler filled with water and ice cubes. A cake with pink icing under a tea towel had already been cut into squares.

The three workers pulled up hay bales for chairs, filled their plates and balanced them on their knees. Lewis couldn't remember being so hungry. He took large bites, swallowing noisily. The sandwiches and eggs were soon gone. When the cake pan was almost empty, Ned drank half a glass of ice water and tipped the rest on top of his head.

"What do you think, Ned?" Jean asked. "Any idea when you'll be done?"

Ned wiped his mouth on his sleeve. "Rain is forecast for tomorrow afternoon, so we have to get this field all cleaned off by then. But these guys are making it easy for me. By the time I back into the barn and get off the tractor, they're having a race to see who can unload the fastest. I just stand back and watch. I think we should kidnap our nephew and keep him," he said with a smile.

Lewis grinned.

The three worked as a team, one driving the tractor, one loading the trailer and one stacking the bales. As the sun beat down on them all afternoon, they poured water onto their heads; even though the ice cubes were long gone, the water still gave lukewarm relief. Hay chaff made their eyes burn and itched at hard-to-reach spots on their backs. Marvin wasn't shy about shaking out his shirt or pulling down his pants and flicking the stuff from inside his shorts. The fingertips on their gloves had turned rock hard and needed to be cleaned out often.

The next morning, they were back at it. Ned kept an eye on the rain clouds flirting at the edges of the mountains until an east wind cleared the sky. After the last load was safe in the barn, the hayers lounged on the trailer, letting the breeze blow over them. When the sweat dried, the boys took turns rubbing the chaff off each other's back with their shirts. Ned backed the tractor and trailer behind the barn, and with the help of Rosalyn and Cora, chased the cattle out of a large corral into the empty field to feed along the grassy edges and in the trees.

Lewis was the first one down to the river. He kicked off his runners, swam across and was sitting on the end of the log before his cousins even made it to shore. On this side of the river, there were no rocks to hurt your feet or cow pies to watch for, because the cattle stayed well away.

Rosalyn waded across with a towel on her shoulder and a book in her hand, with Marvin and Cora trailing behind. All three joined Lewis on the log. He pushed his feet up to the ankles in the warm sand and looked around. He said, "I wish I had this at home."

Cora spoke up. "It took us a long time to clear this place, almost a whole day. I didn't think we'd ever finish."

"This is my beach," Rosalyn said as she stood and laid her towel on the ground. She sat down. "To me there's nothing better than lying on the sand and just reading. Sometimes after I finish a good book, I'll close my eyes and think about the story. Once I fell asleep and dreamed I was in a place where it didn't snow and I picked a coconut from a palm tree."

"What are you reading?" Lewis asked.

"This one is by Jane Austen. It's my favourite—*Pride and Prejudice*. I can't even count how many times I read it. Even though it's the early 1800s, it feels so real, especially Mister Darcy. I'm in love with Mister Darcy. Someday I'll marry a Mister Darcy and I'll live in a huge home and wear nice clothes. I'll have servants to boss around and they'll have to gather the eggs and rake up the chicken shit."

Cora giggled then went to join Marvin, who was throwing rocks downstream.

"Mom said you like to read," Rosalyn said. "Who do you like?"

"I dunno," Lewis answered. "Uncle Alphonse reads Westerns and comics, and he gives them to me when he's finished. At school I go to the library and get anything I want. But there's not a lot of other books around at home."

"I have a bunch in my bedroom you can have. I read them all when I was younger, but you might like them. There's *Swiss Family Robinson*, *Treasure Island* and *Little Men*."

"I read those a long time ago in school," Lewis said.

"There's a lot more. Go through them and take the ones you want."

"What about you, Marvin? Do you read much?" Lewis called.

Marvin came back to the log. "Dad keeps me pretty busy, but I do like to sit and read with the girls when I have time. I'm like you, mostly Westerns and comics, and sometimes I'll find a good story in *Playboy*."

"Sure you do," his sister said. "That's what he calls 'reading with the girls.'"

Lewis watched Cora as she copied the way Marvin flicked pebbles into the water with his thumb. She was such a happy little girl that even her failed attempts to get the stone airborne made her laugh. He thought about her in her new house, opening the refrigerator and using the bathroom, and how safe she must feel, which made him remember how he felt when his classmates wanted to drop him off at home. "You guys have a brand-new house with hot and cold water, a bathroom with a shower and that big radio in the living room. I never saw so many new things. How did you get so much?"

Rosalyn folded the corner of the page, closed the book and set it on her lap. "Mostly because Dad was in the Second World War. He heard other soldiers talking about a government grant they would get after the war was over, and they would have enough to buy a farm and build a home for their families. But the soldiers telling these stories were white."

"What do you mean?"

"When Dad applied for the same grant, he didn't hear anything for years. Finally, he met up with a man he served with, a white man, and he helped Dad get some of the money. Not all of it but enough that when we came to live on Grandma's land, they could build this place. Dad and his friend did all the work."

"This was Grandma's land? I didn't know she had so much."

Rosalyn thought for a moment. "Your place is on her land too, you know. But after she died it went to your mom, I think. I am not really sure how that works. All I know is that now we're neighbours. Thanks to Grandma."

As the days of summer grew longer and hotter, Lewis and his cousins' time at the river began earlier and lasted longer than it had the day before. Every morning the rooster's crow echoed off the high hill while it was still dark, pulling Lewis and Marvin away from their dreams. But they always fell asleep again until Aunt Jean's voice became like a bothersome feather in their ears.

"Let's get going, you guys, time to get a move on," she'd say. "You can sleep all you want when you're dead."

One of their chores was to go down to the basement to empty the mousetraps, rebait and reset them and then toss the little corpses in the bush. Even though there were two cats patrolling the house and outbuildings, there were always a few unlucky ones in the traps, looking up with dead, unblinking eyes. At least in this new house the mice stayed in the basement.

Lewis collected the eggs and made sure the chickens had water. He checked for the tracks of predators looking to get inside the coop, while Marvin helped his dad put away tools and sweep the shop floor. Rosalyn and Cora weeded the garden and picked anything that was ready to eat, can or put in the big freezer.

After dinner, when the temperature reached over one hundred degrees, Lewis and his cousins walked in single file down to the river, wincing and stepping lightly as their bare feet touched the hot baked trail. One evening, Jean called after them. "Wait up, you guys. I'm going with you."

Cora ran back to her mother while the rest went on ahead. Lewis was already treading water in the swimming hole when Cora and her mom reached the shore.

Jean called, "Don't you guys go looking at me until I get into the water, you hear?"

Marvin twirled a finger and both boys turned away.

"What's that all about?" Lewis asked.

"Did you ever see your mom in a bathing suit?"

Lewis understood.

When they heard a loud gasp, the boys turned back to see Jean dog-paddling toward them. She splashed and played with Cora for a little while, and then she told the boys to look away again as she hurried out of the water, wrapped herself in a towel and sat on the sun-soaked log. Everyone else swam until they were cold, then joined her.

Lewis saw Mitzi poke her head through the bushes on the other bank of the river, and then his uncle appeared behind her in a pair of swim trunks, packing a bar of soap. His uncle's red neck and the triangle-shaped patch of skin where he left his work shirt unbuttoned made it look like his head was on the wrong body. He tossed the soap over to Marvin and waded out to where the water was deepest and dove under. Cora splashed him when he surfaced, and he staggered and stumbled on the slippery rocks, scooping handfuls of water over her, making her shriek happily. Then he called for the soap and lathered himself up before slipping down into the deep hole. When he surfaced with a loud whoop, he splashed the bathers sitting on the log beside Jean. When the water came too close to her, she shook a warning finger at Ned. He floated on his back, letting the river carry him downstream. Before reaching the shallows, he turned over and went under. Lewis could see him clearly as he worked his way along the bottom, searching for a perfect stone.

Mitzi paced on the other side of the river until Marvin whistled and called for her. When she joined them, she shook the water from her coat, showering them with spray that carried the odour of dirty dog.

One evening after supper, everyone sat in the living room listening to the combination radio–record player. It was a new experience for Lewis to hear the clear notes of a piano wafting through the room, the voice of a crooner, the scratchy swish of a metal drum brush and an upright bass producing notes so deep he could feel them in his chest. It all sounded so different from the tinny noise from the little radio at home.

His uncle liked to play with the shortwave dial, finding foreign languages. "That's a Dutchman talking," he'd say. As he turned the dial, the speakers whistled and beeped until he came across another country whose language he recognized. "Now, that's Italian."

But at seven o'clock he always switched back to the Vernon station, CJIB, that played the Country Hit Parade. He usually dozed off within minutes, but no one changed the dial.

CHAPTER 9

LEWIS HOOKED THE FENCING TOOL over the barbed wire, leaned back and pulled as Marvin plucked the taut line with his hammer handle, making it vibrate with a low hum. "You want it pulled as tight as you can. Listen to the sound it makes when I sink in the staple."

He positioned the staple on the side of the post and tapped it lightly with his hammer to get it started. Then, holding the fence post in one hand, he struck the staple hard and the wire tightened, humming at a higher pitch with each swing. "Like tuning a piano."

Lewis said, "That's what I like about working with you. You don't make it feel like work. It's like you're having fun."

"The work doesn't get any easier if you think about how hard the job is."

"Is that it, then?"

"Yep, all done. Dad's gone for a while, so let's find a cool spot under a tree and take it easy. Or do you want to lay out in the sun and work a little on that tan of yours."

"What?" Lewis asked.

Marvin put an arm beside his. Lewis pushed him away, laughing. "That's just dirt on your arm."

They found a spot to sit under the wide boughs of a fir tree.

Marvin held out a cigarette to Lewis.

"You go ahead," Lewis said. "They make me sick."

Marvin snapped his lighter open just as Mitzi began barking. The echo coming off the hill sounded like two dogs. They saw a new green Jeep pickup come around the bend with a large dog in the truck box, its big head pivoting, its wet nose twitching and sniffing the air, noticing everything.

"Jeez, that looks like a moose in the back," Lewis said.

"Why the hell is he here?"

Lewis recognized the man Alphonse had talked about. "That's Norris Husk. He lives across the river, down below us."

"I know who he is. He thinks he's so tough with that dog at his side. We better go see what he wants."

The two hurried through the gap in the fence as the Jeep pulled up to the porch. Mitzi kept up her yapping until the big German shepherd gave a single woof, sending her under the porch. The boys watched Husk, tall and thin and grim-looking, climb out of his truck, leaving the door open as he went up the steps. When he came to the front door, he didn't bother to knock or wipe his feet on the sill; he just walked in.

Marvin said, "Let's wait here and see what happens. Mom can handle him. She wouldn't like it if I ran in there and started something."

They heard low voices but couldn't make out the words. Then Husk came back out, got in his truck and drove away, the dog staring back at them.

Jean poked her head out the kitchen door and spotted them. "Come here, you guys."

Lewis and Marvin hurried over.

"The cows got into Husk's damn field, so you gotta get them outta there and fix the hole where they got through. Make sure you do a good job—I don't want to see that man in my house again."

The boys drove the tractor and trailer to where they had been working and gathered up the roll of barbed wire, the hammer and fencing tool pliers, along with the pail of staples, and loaded everything onto the trailer. They set off. It wasn't long until Marvin spotted where the cattle had crashed through the fence, leaving the bottom wire stretched. He stopped the tractor.

"I'm going to cut the fence then go across and round up those cows. You go downstream a bit and I'll send them this way. They should go back in where they got out, but don't let them get past you."

After chasing the cattle back into the field, Marvin spliced lengths of barbed wire onto the breaks, then searched the trees for sturdy sticks to use as supports. With Lewis's help, he threaded them through the wire. As they climbed up on the tractor to leave, they noticed Norris Husk watching from across the river. Looking back over their shoulders as they drove away, they saw him wade across to the repair, then pull and push the barbed wire, testing it for tightness.

Marvin yelled, "What are you doing, pulling your wire? Can't you wait until we're gone?"

Norris glared at them as Marvin laughed.

"What did you say that for?" Lewis asked. "Isn't that going to make him mad?"

"I sure hope so. I'd love to see him try to do something about it."

Lewis glanced back and saw Norris standing motionless, staring at them.

Marvin backed the tractor behind the barn and they unloaded the trailer. By the time they came into the kitchen, Ned was back, seated at the table, talking to Jean. "How did it go, boys?" he asked.

"All done," Marvin said. "He would never have a problem if he just got off his ass and looked after his own fence. Who does he think he is?"

"He came over and checked our work when we were done," Lewis added.

Ned took off his fedora and ran his fingers through his hair. "Did he, now? Jean said he walked in the door like he owned the place. Didn't knock or anything. It's good you fixed it up quick but, boy, I'm glad I wasn't here when he showed up."

Aunt Jean boiled the kettle and made tea. Marvin took the Kool-Aid pitcher from the fridge and poured a glass for himself and Lewis.

His eye on his son, Ned said, "I can tell what you're thinking. And yeah, I could go over there right now and tell him off. But I gotta be careful. The Indian agent and the cops only see things his way, and I could end up in big trouble and who knows what'll happen then. This is the way it goes and there's nothing we can do about it."

CHAPTER 10

THE LOW MORNING SUN was so bright Lewis needed to cover his eyes with his hand. Swallows heard him coming and flew out from the eaves of the hay shelter, surprising the cat and sending it scrambling away. Lewis opened the gate of the chicken coop and grabbed the rake leaning against the fence. He collected the manure into a mound and then carried it over and dumped it onto a pile that would become fertilizer. The air was still and the smell of the pigpen on the other side of the coop was strong.

When he unlatched the door to the hen house and swung it open, excited cackling and beating wings made him duck as two chickens sailed over his head out to freedom. White feathers floated in the air, circling around his hand when he tried to swat them away. Eight of the nine setting hens, with vacant, blinking eyes, jabbed a beak at his hand when he dug in the straw under them for eggs that were warm. In the back corner of the top row was the best layer in the coop, who kept popping out double yolks. She was the only hen that didn't peck at his hand when he moved her aside, as if the greater pain had already been suffered.

On his way back to the house, Lewis glanced toward Blue Grouse Mountain and noticed a small herd of six deer wandering among the dry hay stubble as a large buck kept watch. And it reminded him the time when he and Eddie spotted a single buck below their house in an opening in the trees. When they ran to tell their mother, she lifted the rifle off the wall and opened a box of shells.

"Is he still there?" she asked.

Eddie watched the deer from the porch. "Yeah, but he's going into the trees."

Grace shoved a shell into the gun and jerked on the lever, ramming a bullet into the firing chamber, then hurried down the steps. Eddie stayed where he was, but Lewis trailed after her. When she heard him following, she took one hand off the gun and flashed her open palm at him behind her back. Lewis looked back at his brother. Eddie shook his head. Lewis returned to the house.

She wasn't gone long before they heard a shot and then heard her calling. His brother, who always knew what to do, grabbed potato sacks from the woodshed, along with the swede saw and a coil of rope their mother had braided together from twine taken off posts at the Cluff farm. The brothers had watched how she spliced the lengths together with small, tight knots that would never come undone.

Lewis followed Eddie to where they found her gutting the deer. After she removed the hide, they took turns sawing the carcass into quarters. Stuffing the meat into potato sacks, they packed it back to the house. Fresh meat didn't keep long, so she gave some of her kill to Alphonse and to their grandmother. After she decided what she and her boys needed, Alphonse took the rest to give to relatives down at Six-Mile, the reserve hub.

Since Isabel had moved in with them, hunting for deer wasn't such a big part of their lives anymore. She did her share of the cooking and always found ways to save money on food.

She bought sacks of culled potatoes instead of the knob-free No. 1's, and though they still ate fish and grouse, there was more beef on the table now, especially hamburger, which she cooked as spaghetti or meatloaf or hamburger stew. Instead of going to town for hamburger steaks at a restaurant, Isabel would cook up a big meal for them at home. She was always busy dusting or sweeping the floor, then giving it a good washing. She made sure all the spiderwebs in the ceiling corners were pulled down and the windows were clean. And his mom, who still had occasional moments of sadness and misery, became easier to live with.

Lewis walked into the kitchen just as his aunt and uncle sat down at the table. Their three children were too busy loading their breakfast plates to notice him.

His aunt said, "Good morning, Lewis. You're up bright and early."

Lewis placed the bowl of eggs on the sink counter. "I don't know how you guys can sleep with that rooster screaming his head off."

His aunt said, "I guess we're so used to it we don't hear him anymore."

Lewis washed his hands and sat down beside Marvin. He picked up his fork and stabbed at the stack of pancakes and laid a couple on his plate. Then he picked up the dish of eggs and slid two on top and finished them off with a generous amount of golden syrup. He stuck his fork into the yolks and they began to spill over the sides of the cakes. "There's deer in the field. Six of them. A big buck too."

His uncle looked up. "They're back, are they? Let me have a look." Ned pushed back his chair, walked over to the gun rack and grabbed a pair of binoculars. He pushed the screen door open and stepped out onto the porch. Lewis left the table to join him. Scanning the field, Ned soon focused on the deer. "Oh yeah, there they are. Boy, a couple nice ones too. Here, have a look," he said, handing the binoculars to Lewis.

Lewis turned the knob until the blurry bumps became clear. The way their tails twitched when they walked and their noses moved when they chewed reminded him of rabbits. Suddenly the deer jerked up their heads and looked down toward the river. Then the buck leapt into the air and bounded toward the trees, and the small herd followed.

"Are you going after them?" Lewis asked.

"No. I got tired of eating *mowitch*. That's why I raise cattle. Now we always got meat in the freezer. There's always deer passing through here on the way to the water, twice a day sometimes. Once in a while I'll shoot a small one just to have a taste again, but I haven't done that in a while. Some white farmers sell all the beef they raise and eat cheap cuts they buy from the supermarket, but not me. I like to spoil myself."

When breakfast was done, Rosalyn and her mother began to clear away the dishes while Ned picked at his teeth with a broom straw. "Is there any chance of us getting out of here today?" he asked.

"The weeding is done for now," Jean said. "Why?"

"There's a ball game on the reserve down at Head of the Lake. Starts at noon. You guys wanna go?"

Marvin turned to Lewis. "You ever been to a ball game on the reserve before?"

"No."

His cousin leaned closer. "It's like the whole reserve shows up, and you never seen so many pretty girls."

An hour before the game was due to start, Ned brought out a cardboard box and set it on the table. In the time it took to make hard-boiled eggs, the box was filled with a picnic lunch. Ned took the water cooler down from the top cupboard, filled it with Kool-Aid and banged ice cube trays on the table to loosen the cubes and dumped them in. The sound of them cracking and rattling together in the sweet drink made Lewis's mouth water. Jean poured hot coffee into a tartan-patterned Thermos and sealed it with a cork. Ned placed it in the box, laid a thick towel across the top, folded the flaps together and carried it out to the car.

"Can I ask Loretta to come, Dad?" Rosalyn called after him. "She just got back from being up north with her dad. I think she'll want to get out of the house."

"Sure, why not. We got lots of room."

"Good, I'm going to run over to her place. I'll meet you at the gate."

After washing and changing out of their work clothes, Lewis and Marvin took turns in front of the mirror, running a brush through their hair and checking angles to make sure everything was in its place. Then they all streamed out of the house and piled into the large station wagon. Ned turned the key and revved the engine.

"Bye, Mitzi," Cora shouted out the window as the car pulled away.

Ned turned down the driveway and gunned the motor, and the rear of the car swung out. "Oops," he said.

Cora looked up at her father. "Daddy, you always do that."

"He's just an old teenager," Jean said.

Lewis looked back at the two plumes of dust rising from the rear of the car as they merged into a single cloud that fanned out into the trees. A figure appeared out of the dust. It was Mitzi. Her tongue flopping out the side of her open mouth made her look like she was smiling. Ned spotted her in the side mirror and sped up, and she ran even faster. When they stopped at the end of the driveway, Marvin stepped out to open the gate. Mitzi sat down beside the driver's side window, panting as she stared up at Ned, drops from her red tongue landing in the dirt.

Ned reached down and patted her on the head. "Where are you going, you silly girl, huh? Boy, just looking at you is making me too hot. You get on home now to that shady porch."

Lewis looked over to the house where Rosalyn's friend lived. He'd passed it many times before and hadn't given it much thought. A screened-in porch ran its length and a line of huge weeping willows bordered one side, with lilac bushes around back. A corral stood a short distance away but looked unused. Thick grass grew inside the rail fence.

The screen door opened and banged shut behind Rosalyn and another girl who looked like she could be Rosalyn's twin. They both had their hair in a ponytail and wore cut-offs, sandals and a baggy T-shirt that showed the straps of a bikini top underneath. They ran across the road and climbed in the back seat beside Lewis, the girl leaning forward to speak to Aunt Jean and Uncle Ned. "I'm so glad you asked me to go to the game. I miss doing stuff like this. Spending time with my dad is a little boring after a while."

Aunt Jean turned to her and said, "Glad you could come along. How's your mom?"

"Oh, she's okay."

Rosalyn noticed Lewis staring. "Loretta, this is our cousin Lewis. He's staying with us for the summer."

Loretta turned and smiled. "Hi, Lewis."

"Hello," Lewis said. The girl's almond-coloured skin made her teeth look even whiter. Her black hair looked so soft, he wanted to reach over and touch it.

"Okay," Marvin yelled, banging the hood. "Let's go."

Ned drove through. Marvin swung the gate shut to keep the dog on the other side, then placed the metal hoop over the post. "Go on, Mitzi, get home now," he said, pointing back up the road. When Mitzi didn't move, he picked up a rock and tossed it over her head. Mitzi looked sad as she turned and trotted home.

As Marvin slid into the back seat, the two girls moved over to make room, squeezing Lewis into the corner. Ned turned onto the road, then over the wooden bridge, the loose boards on the deck thumping and banging. When they turned left at the store, the rear tires gave a short squeal on the warm asphalt.

Up ahead on the side of the road was a figure that looked like a scarecrow. As the car came closer, Lewis recognized the old man wiping his face with a hankie. It was Abraham Jenkie, who lived in a house close to the river that Lewis walked past every day on his way to the school bus. It was already warm and he looked overdressed. His black wool pants were held up by wide suspenders over a thick sweater buttoned up to his neck, and he sported a ten-gallon hat that had long since lost its shape. Everything about him made Lewis feel hot and itchy. Then he noticed a rifle butt sticking out by Abraham's hip, the barrel disappearing into a hole in the thick pants, the gun hanging from a leather strap looped over his shoulder. Ned pulled the car over, stepped out and walked back to the old man, who peered at him under a hand he held up to block the glare of the sun, his eyes disappearing into the deep fissures lining his face. Ned bent down and said something and the old man shook his head. Ned walked back to the car and got in.

"Who was that?" Rosalyn asked.

"That's Abraham Jenkie. He's the old guy that lives across the highway from the Cluffs. He's over eighty years old and he's half blind. His eyes are white as ping-pong balls and he's deaf as a stump, but he still walks to the store every week for his chewing tobacco."

"How do you know him?"

"Everybody around here knows old Abe. I'll show you where he lives. You should see the car he has. It's a 1949 Chevy torpedo back. His brother bought it brand new and never drove it anywhere except home from the car lot. The morning after he bought the car, he had a heart attack and died."

Marvin spoke up. "Why don't we buy it off him? I could use a good car, and it sure wouldn't go to waste if I had it."

Ned laughed. "If we had the money, maybe. People been after that car for a while now, but he won't sell it. He brought it with him when he moved here from the coast. Poor guy wasn't living here very long when folks started complaining about his driving. Ever since he was a teenager, he worked for the railroad. He started with offloading box cars and ended up as an engineer. He drove trains for so many years that sometimes he'd hang his head out the window of his car so he could watch out for animals on the tracks up ahead. He'd be going twenty miles an hour, with a long line of cars behind him beeping and honking, and then he'd pull out all the knobs on the dash, like he was in the train again, and the car would die in the middle of the road. It wasn't long before the police took his licence away. The Cluffs take him to town for groceries and a bottle of brandy once in a while. Maybe it's a good thing he won't sell that car, because it sounds like it's cursed."

Lewis asked, "Was that a gun in his pants?"

"It sure is. He takes his shotgun everywhere he goes cuz he's on the lookout for wolf. He got stopped once by the police for carrying it and now he figures he outsmarted them by hanging it down his pants."

"But there's no wolves around here," Marvin said. "Up in the high hills, maybe, but not down here."

"Everybody tries to tell him that, but he won't hear of it. He thinks there's a grizzly bear behind every tree too. When he moved here, he bought himself some ducks. He figured he could make some good cash selling the eggs and meat. One night something got into the pen, and even though he's hard of hearing, he heard them ducks making one hell of a racket. By the time he got out of bed, it was too late. Every single one of them was dead. He said he saw a wolf running away with one in its mouth. People tried to tell him it was a coyote, but he's got it in his head that it was a wolf. Now every time he goes to the store, he takes his gun. The old man says if it's the last thing he ever does, he's gonna find the wolf that got his ducks."

A mile later they came to the main highway. Ned pointed across the road. "There it is."

They all looked at Abe Jenkie's car, backed into a shed at the bottom of the drive, still looking brand new.

CHAPTER 11

AS THEY DROVE DOWN Highway 97 around the base of Blue Grouse Mountain, Lewis felt good being back in familiar territory. Across the valley he traced the path of the dirt road that made its way around the small lakes on the basin floor, all connected by a single stream. Early that spring after hearing dynamite blasts rolling through the hills, he went down to Heart Lake to see what was going on. A man in a Fisheries Department truck told him the stream needed to be reopened because beavers had blocked the flow of water. The range loomed large and wide above the lakes, dotted with a dark speck he knew was the turret of a military tank abandoned on the army training grounds.

On a long, straight stretch up ahead was a small, shimmering lake that Lewis knew was a road mirage. A truck coming toward them seemed to drive right through its middle, and he could see its reflection in the water that wasn't there.

Soon the car turned off the highway onto a dirt road riddled with potholes. Dust bit at Lewis's nose. Up ahead were the baseball diamond and the old church. A half circle of Okanagan Lake peeked out from behind the large hall a short distance away. The sod roofs of the team dugouts were nothing more than small hills to the children running up and down them, two fat puppies nipping at their hands and pants. The backstop was lined with more children with their fingers looped through the wire screen, their faces eager and wide-eyed. Cars had parked on both sides of the backstop behind a low railing that circled the ball field.

Across the road from the church was the cemetery, its leaning crosses scattered throughout the grass and weeds. Faint depressions in the earth showed anonymous resting places. In the newer section, crosses stood straight and the plastic flowers and wreaths placed on the sinking mounds seemed to wilt in the heat.

"Can you pull up by the graveyard for a minute, Ned?" Jean asked. "I want to have a look where Mom is. I always feel so bad because I didn't make it for her funeral." She looked down at Cora beside her. "My little baby was so sick." She pointed to a grave only a few feet from the fence. "There's where your grandma is buried."

"Why doesn't somebody pull out all the weeds? It looks horrible," Rosalyn said.

"That's a question that takes me way back," her mother responded. "Me, Alphonse and your aunt Grace once went with Mom to a funeral, and I remember somebody said the same thing about how bad the place looked. And Mom told us that a long time ago some young people had complained about the graveyard, saying it looked like nobody cared about all the relatives and ancestors buried there. So they planned a cleanup. About a dozen people showed up and worked for hours, pulling up all the weeds and raking the grass. Then a car drove up and parked right where we are now. The driver went around and helped an old woman in her nineties out of the car and she waved everybody to come closer and started talking to them in Syilx.

"She asked, 'What's going on here? You shouldn't be doing that. Get out of here and leave things alone.' She pointed to the pile of debris. 'What are you going to do with that?' she asked.

"'Burn it,' she was told.

"'Didn't your mothers tell you you're not supposed to light a fire in a graveyard? If you do, it'll start to rain, and that's the only warning you're going to get because it's just gonna get a lot worse after that. You'll see.'

"Some of the young people smiled, while a few wondered if they really were doing something wrong. They all stood there, and the old lady turned away from them, muttering, 'This isn't a *summa* playground in town.' The driver helped her back into the car and drove away.

"After she was gone, the kids carried on. By the end of the afternoon, a large pile of old boards, sticks and weeds sat in the centre of the graveyard and the young people felt good about what they had done. They stood shoulder to shoulder around the pile as one of them set it on fire. In seconds the fire burned so hot they had to step back. And then the fire began to hiss. They looked up to see black clouds in the sky above them and were surprised they hadn't noticed them before.

"Then the rain really came down, dousing the flames, and the wind scattered everything over the ground. Nobody said a word. They just gathered up their tools and left. Ever since then, nobody says the graveyard needs to be cleaned."

Ned did a U-turn and parked where he had a clear view of first base. White players on the visitors' side of the field tossed the ball back and forth, warming up. They sported cleats, new gloves, new pants and fresh jerseys with the name "Mustangs" across the chest. Their red socks matched the uniform's pinstripes and the brims of their caps.

"That's the Falkland Mustangs. Those guys are the best team in the league," Ned said. "Gonna be a tough one for our boys."

More cars parked behind them. People greeted each other as they stepped out of their vehicles while children ran off in all directions. Some older boys threw rocks at the free-roaming horses grazing just beyond the playing field. The horses took off, then settled down under pine trees beyond range of the boys' arms. They rested weary heads on each other's backs, swishing their tails and occasionally lifting a hoof to brush away a horsefly or bee. A small concession stand set up to sell candy bars, potato chips, chewing gum, pop and penny candy stood between four his-and-hers outhouses, standing just out of nose's reach. The banging of the outhouse doors was constant.

Marvin wandered off somewhere while Rosalyn and her friend stayed in the car chatting. Lewis sat on a front fender, beside Cora and his uncle. Jean was one car over, talking with a woman wearing a wide-brimmed hat that flapped like wings with the slightest movement of her head. Her laughter sounded so much like a scream that each time it happened, players on the field looked her way to see what was wrong.

An inning went by and the visiting players filed into their dugout while the home players took to the field again. The pitcher was tall and skinny, with both of the *S*'s missing on the word *Scouts* on his jersey.

"Hey, Bill, you old coot," the lady with the wide hat yelled, screeching a laugh. When a foul ball sailed high in the air and came down to land on the roof of the car beside them with a loud bang, a chorus of "oohs" sounded. Children raced to find the ball and return it to the home dugout so the coach would give them a nickel.

At first the horns honking at good plays or hard hits by the home team were exciting, but Lewis was hungry and the game seemed to drag on. Finally, his aunt brought out the picnic lunch and the family sat on a blanket on the ground in front of their car. Lewis concentrated on eating, but when he looked up, he saw Loretta watching him.

With his stomach full and the hot afternoon sun beating down, Lewis lay down, turned over on his stomach and closed his eyes. It wasn't long before he fell into a dream that he was lying in a cool, shady spot under a tree by the river, far away from all the noise. Then he dreamed he was taking a leak into the river, his stream making the pleasing sound of small bells as water fell upon water. It became so powerful that when he aimed at the trunk of a tree, it ripped the bark away. Forcing himself awake, he sat up and looked down at his pants, relieved to see he was dry. Lewis stood and spotted Marvin and a girl sitting on the fender watching the game. He waved Marvin over.

"What is it?" his cousin asked.

"Want to go for a leak?" Lewis asked.

"What, you want me to come and shake it out for you? You get going. Nobody's gonna bite you." Marvin went back to his girlfriend.

As Lewis walked down the line of cars and trucks, people he didn't know stared at him, so he walked faster. Then he saw his classmates Roland and Clay leaving the concession stand, each with a pop and a bag of potato chips.

"Hey, Lewis," Clay called. "A bunch of us from school are down by the fence at third base. Why don't you come sit with us?"

Lewis had no desire to sit with them. "What, you guys miss each other already now school is out?"

Roland answered. "Safety in numbers, my dad said."

"Come on, join us," Clay urged.

Lewis shook his head. "Not today."

"Who are you cheering for, anyway?"

"Yeah," Roland added, "for Falkland, or for the Indians?"

"I'm not cheering for anybody. I'm only here for the girls."

Roland had his familiar grin, which had always bothered Lewis. "You just don't want to see what we're gonna do to your team. Isn't that right?"

Lewis had important business to take care of and couldn't be bothered chatting with Roland anymore. "You better watch what you say. You're in Apache territory now," he said, and walked away.

He came up behind an old man hobbling down the path to the toilets with a cane in each hand. The straw cowboy hat tipped back on his head exposed a pale forehead, and his clean white shirt and red tie looked out of place at a ball game. He slowly worked his canes across the ground; if he made a single mistake as to where he placed a cane, he would topple over. Lewis was stuck behind him until they came to the toilets. Then the old man went inside the only vacant one. Lewis shifted his weight from one foot to the other as he tried to hold off the smallest dribble—if it started it would be like opening a dam.

Three Indian boys his age came around the corner of the toilets. They looked surprised to see Lewis, but then their attitude changed—they were bored and now some entertainment had been provided. One boy shot a long stream of snuff juice between his teeth and said, "What are you doing here, *summa*? Huh? Cheering on your team?"

Another boy dropped the cigarette he was smoking, grinding the butt out with his shoe, and stepped toward Lewis.

"Hey, Salmon River, these guys looking for trouble?" a gruff voice asked from behind Lewis, and the boys walked away.

Lewis turned around to find a heavy-set man standing too close to him. He took a step back. The man was not only big, he was tall, with a huge barrel chest. The squashed nose pushed to the side of his face gave him a menacing appearance.

The man saw Lewis's discomfort and gave a lopsided grin that was meant to put him at ease. It didn't. "You're Lewis, right?" he asked.

"Yeah, but how do you know me?"

"I'm Hank. I played pool with your brother, Eddie. He was my good-luck charm. I was just talking to Mabel over there about him and then you come along, and she told me who you were." Lewis looked over to a pickup, where a woman he didn't know waved at him.

"Did he come home yet?"

"Who?" Lewis asked.

"Your brother."

"No."

"Can't say I'm surprised," Hank said. "I seen the way he was around that girl of his. After the way she died, he prob'ly just wanted to get the hell away from here. I bet he saw her everywhere he looked and couldn't stand it no more. I done that a few times in my life. Just packed up and left."

"He didn't pack up anything," Lewis said sharply. He wished people would stop asking about his brother.

The man's face changed. "Oh, you don't wanna be taking that tone with people, young feller," he said. "Not around here."

Finally, one of the toilet doors opened and a man came out. Lewis hurried inside. He let the door bang shut and turned the wooden peg lock. It was hot and stinky inside and somebody had peed all over the seat. A ribbon of smoke drifted up through the toilet hole, and when he looked down, he saw a smouldering cigarette perched on top of the pile of soggy toilet paper and multicoloured waste. He took aim, and the cigarette went out with a whisper. It felt like he peed for a good five minutes. When he stepped outside, Marvin was waiting for him.

"I thought you fell in the hole or something. What took you so long?"

"I dunno, just talking to a guy. Why?" Lewis asked.

"There's only two innings to go and Dad wants everybody to be back at the car as soon as the game is over so he can get us outta here before the big traffic jam."

The two boys were making their way back to the car when Marvin grabbed Lewis by the arm. "Hey, there you go. It's Loretta."

She was standing by herself at the concession, sipping a Coke through a straw. Lewis thought she looked different away from Rosalyn. With her silent smile, she watched the people go by, studying them with an air of confidence that kept all these strangers at arm's length. He always felt uncomfortable around strangers, *summas*, but he found it a little terrifying to be in a crowd of his own people who had no idea who he was.

"The way she looked at you when we were having lunch, I think she's kinda sweet on my haying cousin. You better get over there before somebody beats you to her. Go. Make your move."

"Why don't you go?"

Marvin chuckled. "If I didn't already have a girlfriend, I would. I could have her knocked her up just standing here looking at her."

Lewis pushed him. "Stop saying stuff like that."

"Whoa, touchy, are we? I was just joking. Who do you think I was with at the car? That was my Jenny. Now don't be such a chicken and get over there."

Lewis shook his head. "I don't know what to say to her."

"Just talk to her about anything you want. It doesn't matter what. Or just listen. You can do that. Don't ask me why, but women really like that shit. And here's a buck so you can buy something at the concession. Pay me back when Mom pays you. Get some bubble gum or whatever you want, then just sort of bump into her and say something like 'fancy meeting you here.' Or–"

"I'm not gonna say that. She came here with us. That sounds stupid."

Marvin looked down at the ground as if in great thought. "Okay. How about . . . too bad we couldn't get some rum for that."

Lewis was puzzled. "For what?"

"Her Coke," Marvin said impatiently. "Jeez, pay attention, will you."

Lewis shook his head. "Forget it. I'll talk to her on the way home."

"Come on, Lewis. Just ask her if she's having fun and then just agree with everything she says after that."

Lewis looked over at Loretta. He wanted nothing more than to go up to her and do as Marvin said, but he didn't have the courage. Then she saw him and smiled.

"There you go," Marvin said. "This might be your only chance with the lovely Loretta. So get in there."

The next thing Lewis knew, he was standing in front of her, completely unsure of what he should say.

"Enjoying the game?" she asked.

"Yeah, you?"

"I love coming to stuff like this. Are you going to buy something?"

"Sure. Maybe I can get some rum for that," Lewis said, nodding at the Coke in her hand. He instantly wished there was a deep hole somewhere he could jump into. But Loretta put a hand on his elbow and laughed. Lewis became oblivious to all the people coming and going around them. When someone rushed past, banging into his shoulder, he barely noticed. He wasn't even sure what Loretta was saying to him but nodded anyway. She talked, he listened.

Then Loretta pointed at the woman in the pickup truck. "Somebody is calling you. I'll get back to the car now, because your uncle wants to get out of here soon as he can. I'll see you there, okay?" Loretta said.

"Hey, come over here," the woman called.

Lewis pointed to the concession and bought himself an Oh Henry! chocolate bar and a pop and then walked over to the truck.

In a soft voice, she said, "Hello there, Lewis, I'm Mabel. Mabel Harvey, your cousin. What do you think of the ball game?"

"It's okay."

She said, "Baseball is the last thing on your mind, isn't it? I seen you talking up that pretty little Ryder girl. Is she your girlfriend?"

"No. She's my aunt and uncle's neighbour. I better get going. They're waiting for me."

Mabel dug into her purse and brought out a quarter and held it out to him. "Have something on me."

"I got money," Lewis said, and turned away. Then he stopped and looked back at her. "Thanks anyway."

By the time he made it back, every car and truck seemed to be honking its horn. The home team were jumping up and down, clapping each other on the back. They had beaten the mighty Falkland Mustangs. Lewis couldn't care less about baseball, but he found himself smiling when he thought of Roland and Clay.

CHAPTER 12

THAT NIGHT LEWIS SAT in a chair in the living room with a book Rosalyn had given him, *To Kill a Mockingbird*. He was so absorbed in the story that when he looked up, everyone had gone to bed except for him and his aunt and uncle, though his uncle was sleeping in his chair. "You tired, Lewis?" Jean asked.

"Not really."

"I bet it was that snooze you had at the ball game."

Lewis closed the book. "I met a woman there. Mabel Harvey. She said she was my cousin."

Jean put down her magazine. "She calls everybody cousin. I don't know if she's related or not. You remember Ray, don't you? Isabel's old man? She's Ray's sister, and she was Gregory's aunt. Gregory lived with Ray and Isabel. Do you remember him at all? Gregory?"

Lewis was barely four years old when his family went to the States so the grownups could find work picking fruit and vegetables. The boy Gregory, who Ray and Isabel looked after, was the same age as Lewis's brother when he drowned in the swamp behind their picker's cabin, the shack where they stayed until the job was done. But he did remember. When the ambulance men opened the sheet wrapped around the body so Ray and Isabel could see, Lewis had been standing by himself at the side of the house. At that time, he didn't really understand what was happening, but he never forgot the sight. Seeing the dead would become a common though always disturbing occurrence for him. Next was his grandma, then others at funerals, casket open so people could see for themselves, as if they needed confirmation. And just weeks ago, the bones of the old chief.

"You're so different from Mom," Lewis said. "She always says you aren't supposed to say the names of dead people."

"According to some of the old folks, that's right. They also say you have to burn all their clothes after they're taken away from the house, and you're risking your life if you get caught standing on a grave. Once the priest was giving a prayer beside a new grave and without even looking around to keep an eye on where he was, he took a step back right onto an older one. The coffin must have rotted from being so long in the ground, and he fell through up to his hip. He scrambled like a dead person had him by the ankle and was pulling him under. An old lady started wailing and that made it even worse. People were too scared to watch, let alone help. Finally, two guys ran up and got him outta there. After that, the priest always made sure where he was standing.

"That's the difference between Indians and white people. Indians, especially the old ones, treat the dead different. They have a lot of respect for the dead and they show it in their own way. They dig the graves themselves and bury the coffin too, while the *summas* let somebody else do it. And they brush the grave with a sweeper made of the plants and weeds that grow there, like they're welcoming the dead back to the earth."

Jean took a drink of water and set the glass down. "I could talk to you all night about funerals because I know you haven't been told much by your mom. Don't blame her for that, though.

Your mom saw things when she was young that nobody else should ever see, no matter how long they live.

"I know Ray told his sister stories about Eddie and Gregory, how they were like twins and couldn't stand to be away from one another. Mabel said to me once that every time she saw Eddie after that, she couldn't help but think of Gregory. Maybe you remind her of Eddie. You do look a lot like him, you know. So be nice to her when you see her. And talk to her too. You'll make her feel good even if it doesn't look that way."

His aunt picked up her water glass and stood. "It's time for bed. Oh, just look at your uncle snoring with his mouth wide open like he's trying to catch a fly ball. I better get him to bed or tomorrow morning he'll wake up with a big knot in his neck."

Lewis lay awake for the longest time thinking about Eddie and Gregory. He didn't want to believe that one was just as dead as the other, but Eddie had been gone for so long now. What else was he supposed to think?

He stared up at the ceiling, listening to the creaking radio antenna pole rubbing against the house. The night sounds of whirring insects, hooting owls and a cat meowing outside seemed to become louder. He rolled over to stare out the window at stars that were brighter than usual tonight—he could even see the rings of Saturn. Then the sounds coming through the window screen went quiet, like the silence when creatures in the bush became aware of his presence.

A shadow floated across the night sky. At first Lewis thought it was from a passing cloud, and then he saw it was a man at the window, his hands cupped around his eyes so he could see inside the dark room. Lewis sat up. The man's eyes found him, and Lewis felt ants crawling on his skin. He reached over and shook Marvin, but his cousin only moaned and slept on. Suddenly the room lit up as if a full moon had come out from behind a cloud, and the man scratched at the window screen with long, thin fingers. Lewis, mesmerized by his piercing neon eyes, couldn't move. Marvin was now groaning so loudly, someone would surely hear and come to see what was wrong. But no one came. The air grew so cold he could see his breath. He went to pull on Marvin's shoulder to wake him, but he was completely covered by the blanket. Lewis grabbed at the cover. When he touched the material, it sagged and collapsed on the bed. Then came a clicking sound like shaking dice. He yanked away the cover and a skeleton's face looked up at him, shivering.

Someone shook Lewis so hard he opened his eyes to see his aunt's concerned face. "Hey, wake up, you're having a bad dream. You're okay now. Come on, look at me."

She was so close Lewis could feel her breath on his wet eyes.

Marvin woke. "What's the matter, Mom?"

"Go back to sleep. Nothing's the matter."

"What's wrong with Lewis?"

"He was fighting the bad guys."

Marvin sighed, rolled onto his side and pulled up the covers.

"I'll be right back," Jean said.

He heard her go into the bathroom and turn on the tap. When she came back, she sat on the edge of the bed and wiped his forehead with a warm cloth. Her voice barely a whisper, a gentle breath on his cheek. Lewis closed his eyes and then he was asleep again.

CHAPTER 13

MARVIN AND LEWIS CLIMBED onto the roof of the barn, looking to find a cool spot under the overhanging poplar tree. But the shade had moved onto the nearby chicken coop, and the roof was unbearably hot. They jumped across and the sudden thunderous noise on the roof caused the chickens below to squawk wildly. When the hens calmed, Marvin lit a cigarette. The cousins lay back, each with an arm behind his head, watching Marvin's smoke drifting up toward the buzzards circling above them against a backdrop of clouds.

"Wonder if they think we're dead?" Marvin pondered.

"What if they know something we don't?" Lewis said. "Maybe they're a little early."

From below them came a loud *buk-buk-bagawk*.

"Sounds like another egg," Lewis said.

"Did you ever hear 'Heart Full of Soul' by the Yardbirds?" Marvin asked.

"I love that song."

"Know what a yardbird is?"

"No."

"A chicken."

They both laughed.

"Really? Chickens? That's funny," Lewis said.

Marvin blew four smoke rings in a row. After he smoked his cigarette down to the filter, he flicked the butt into the mud of the pigpen behind the coop.

"So what are you going to do with yourself, Marvin? Are you planning to stay here on the farm?"

Marvin scratched behind his ear. "I got it pretty good here, but I been thinking that when summer is over, I'll see if I can get a job at Hoover's sawmill."

"What about school?" Lewis asked.

"I'm done with that. I told Mom and Dad I'm not going back. They didn't say much. I want to get a few bucks saved so I can get my own car, but I'm in no hurry to get out of here. How about you? What are you going to do?"

Lewis paused, then said, "I think I'll keep going to school and I'll see what happens when it's over. But you got it made here. Where else can you get a job with a good boss like your dad?"

Marvin wiped at his forehead. "Boy, it's getting hotter by the minute. Let's go down to the river."

"We swim every day. Why don't we try something different? How about we go tubing? You ever done that?"

"No. The river is different at my place. The trees go right down to the shore and there's rocks and fast water."

"Well, what are we waiting for?" Marvin slapped Lewis on the back.

Lewis grabbed him by the leg and they wrestled briefly, which sent the hens squawking again. Then they slid off the roof and ran down to the shop and found Ned sharpening a scythe.

He looked up. "What you boys up to?"

"We're gonna float down the river. Are there any tubes we can use?" Marvin asked.

"Look under the workbench. There's a pile there but every single one has a hole in it. I got a new patch kit sitting on the window ledge. Fix them up and they're all yours."

Lewis and Marvin were sorting through the tubes when Rosalyn and Loretta walked into the barn.

"What are you guys doing?" Rosalyn asked.

"We're going tubing."

"Can we come? We were just saying how we were so bored."

Marvin looked to Lewis. "Yeah, I guess. What do you think?"

"Sure."

Rosalyn jumped up and down in little hops. "Oh, this is gonna be fun."

As Rosalyn turned to leave, Loretta asked Lewis, "Did you like the ball game?"

"I sure did. It was the best sleep I had in a long time."

When Loretta laughed a little too long, Marvin glanced over at his sister, who raised her eyebrows and smiled.

"Come on, Loretta," Rosalyn said. "Let's get outta these cut-offs and into our bathing suits."

After scuffing the surface of the rubber with the lid of the patch kit, Marvin spread smelly glue around the hole, lit it with a match, blew it out and covered the hole with a patch. He placed the tube on the workbench and rolled a steel bar back and forth over the patch a few times. When he had four tubes mended, they took turns working the hand pump to fill them with air. After bouncing them on the floor to test if the patches held, they picked up the tubes and went for the door.

"Marvin, hold on a minute," his dad called. "I don't know if Loretta is a good swimmer, so watch out for her. And don't you go on Norris Husk's land. You'll be looking for trouble from that guy if you do. Okay?"

"We won't,' Marvin said. "And don't worry about Loretta. If she starts to drown, Lewis can give her mouth-to-mouth."

His uncle laughed. Lewis felt his face flush.

"Remember now, old Norris, he don't own that river. It's a neutral zone, like Switzerland. He can't touch you if you're in the water. Have fun, now, and see you at supper."

Marvin and Lewis walked side by side through the field, with Rosalyn and Loretta following. Each of them carried an inner tube over one shoulder. It didn't take long before the tube became so hot it burned their skin, and each of them needed to constantly switch sides.

"It's so hot it feels like we're walking through fire," Rosalyn said.

She was right, Lewis thought. Each step felt hotter than the one before. The dry hay stubble crunching under their old running shoes teemed with golden grasshoppers that hurled themselves into the air as they passed. Only Marvin looked as though the heat didn't bother him. When they came to the fence, he held up the top strand and pushed the second one down with his foot. When they were all through, Marvin threw his tube into the water and, with a running jump, somersaulted into the river with a splash. Lewis tossed his tube, took a deep breath and ran. When he hit the water, he felt as if he had fallen through the floor of one world and crashed through the ceiling of another. The deeper he sank, the cooler the water felt. When his feet touched bottom, he resisted the urge to return to the surface as streaming sunbeams swirled like northern lights.

All around him, everything looked different. River stones looked like boulders in a wide valley. Water weed clinging to sticks were green flags bending away from a bubbling wind, and the reeds by the shore were trees that grew so tall they poked up through the ever-moving sky. Bubbles that had followed him down drifted up toward what looked like two tubes stacked on top of one another, which was his own tube's reflection. Lewis noticed shadows coming out of the gloom that transformed into the legs of a giant, whose shuffling gait raised great clouds of dust. The giant stopped in front of him and a large hand reached down. Lewis burst out of the water. "Boy, you can really hold your breath, Lewis," Marvin said. "But let's get going."

The four lay stomach down on their tubes, paddling with their hands out to the middle of the river. Lewis caught up to Loretta, grabbed her by the ankle, pulled her back and skimmed past her, laughing. The four tubers floated downstream, hostages to the whim of the current.

Where the river narrowed under a thick stand of cottonwood, they drifted past uninterested, cud-chewing cattle lying in the shade, looking down at them from the bank. Then they came out in the open again, where a wider stretch of water slowed the current. Wavelets slapping the tubes rocked them up and down. Rosalyn and Loretta, busy chatting over the sound of the tumbling water, were missing the sights. But Lewis eagerly took in the landscape, which changed with every turn. From inside a thick growth of cedar trees, they heard birds they couldn't see, whistling and calling. The trees looked impenetrable, and he wondered if anyone had ever wandered inside and not come out.

Then, on the left side of the river, the brush ended in a line as straight as a trimmed hedge. He heard irrigation sprinklers knocking in a field and then he saw a man in hip waders piling rocks around a pipe that ran from the river up to a pumphouse perched above the shore. It was Norris Husk.

Husk straightened up. He wore a flat-brimmed cap, a tan long-sleeve shirt over a white T-shirt. The whiskers dotting his chin and cheeks gave a granite-like quality to his face. He drew on the rolled stogie hanging from the corner of his mouth as he watched them float closer. His large German shepherd came around the corner of the pumphouse, barking loudly at the interlopers until Husk called it to heel. After they passed, Lewis looked back. Husk had his eyes focused on Rosalyn and Loretta.

"Look at that dirty old bastard," Marvin said. "His property goes all the way from just below where you live down to our bridge, including where that old Indian fishing camp was. But Husk won't let anybody go onto his land to have a look at what's there. There's a spot up ahead where me and Dad found all kinds of stuff.

"He comes and tells us we have to patch our fence when he doesn't keep up his own fence along the river at all. Nobody likes him. The only people that'll put up with him bitching and hollering are his old lady and the storekeeper, because he thinks that's how he'll get Husk to spend some of his money. Dad says Norris stands there in the store and bitches about Indians all day." Marvin spit out onto the water. "Dad also says that any guy that has a mean dog like that around them has a dink the size of a peanut."

When Rosalyn and Loretta laughed, upstream the dog barked.

The river turned a corner. Marvin pointed. "There it is. That's where all the good stuff is. Why don't we have a quick look and see what we can find."

Rosalyn warned, "Remember what Dad said."

"We'll be quick. Husk is too far away to see us anyway."

Lewis and Marvin dropped their tubes on the gravel shore. Marvin picked up a stick and they climbed the bank. In the centre of a ring of trees, he began scraping away the top layer of soil. Then he dropped to his knees, scooping up the dirt, letting it fall through his fingers. "Hey, I found something."

Lewis came over as Marvin brushed off a flat rock on his cut-offs. Marvin handed it to him.

"Holy cow. It's a real arrowhead." What Lewis held in his hand was a relic from an ancient time, and he was giddy at their find. He imagined the people arriving, and the pack horses, after being unloaded, rolling in the grass to scratch their sweaty, itchy hides. He wondered if the men actually wore feathers in their hair. "Just think of all the Indians that were here, fishing and visiting. And they came from all over . . . ."

"Hey," a voice called. It wasn't the pleasant sound you hear when a friend spots you in a crowd, but an angry shout demanding instant attention. "You sons-a-bitches."

They looked up and there was Norris Husk and his dog, running toward them from the edge of his field. Husk shouted at the dog and it ran even faster.

Marvin yelled to the girls, "Grab some rocks. If he comes at you, bounce one off his big head."

"Whose head?" Rosalyn asked.

"The dog's."

The two girls, waiting on the shore, dropped their tubes and scrambled to find rocks as the tubes floated downstream. Marvin and Lewis rushed over to join them. They waded out to the middle of the river, each with a rock in hand, elbows bent at the ready to let it fly. Husk called to the dog and it stopped, barking loudly. Lewis felt his heart pounding inside his chest.

Husk came to stand beside his dog, hushing it to silence. "Caught you, didn't I?" he yelled, the stogie held in his mouth as if glued there. A thread of smoke drifted past his eyes. "You were all trespassing, and stealing too. I saw you. I got a mind to phone the Mounties. You people just don't listen, do you?

Maybe I should let my dog eatcha. Whaddya think about that?"

Ned appeared out of the bushes on the other side of the river. "What's all this hollering, Norris? What's the problem?"

"These four were trespassing. Can't they read?"

"Read what?"

"The sign."

"What sign?" Marvin shouted.

Husk pointed to a nearby tree. The board that held the notice was facing the road, away from them.

"How are we supposed to read that?" Marvin asked with a smirk.

Ned said, "Listen, Norris, it won't happen again. I know we don't see eye to eye on much, but Jesus, this is just boys showing off to girls. It's not World War Three."

Husk looked from Ned to Marvin. "These boys are damn lucky I didn't have my gun."

"Or what, you'd shoot us?" Marvin shouted. "You better not miss or I'll take that gun away and shove it up your ass and pull the trigger."

"Marvin," Ned shouted. "Don't you say another word."

Lewis had never seen his cousin so angry. His fists were clenched so tight his knuckles were white.

"It's my fault, Mr. Husk," Lewis called. "My mom told me about the old fishing camp, and I asked Marvin to show me where it was. He told me we weren't supposed to go on your land, but I kept bugging him. It's my fault. I'm sorry."

Lewis wondered if anyone heard him, because no one moved a muscle. Four people up to their knees in the water, with one man on one bank and the other on the opposite, all standing their ground like gunfighters. Even the dog stood waiting, panting loudly as saliva oozed between its sharp teeth.

"Go on, then," Husk said at last. "Get the hell outta here and don't let me catch you on my land again. And hand over whatever it was you found."

Lewis dug into his pocket and tossed the arrowhead to him. Husk caught it and rolled it over in his hand, examining it. Then he turned and threw it into the trees.

"You better tell that boy of yours to watch his filthy mouth," Husk yelled at Ned. "Come on, Max," he said, and they walked back the way they had come.

Ned shook his head. "Thanks a lot, you guys. The last thing I need is to get into a war with that bastard. It's lucky for you I was checking your fence work or Christ knows what mighta happened. But that was smart thinking, Lewis. Good for you." He turned his eyes to his son. "What did he mean about your filthy mouth? What did you say to him?"

"He thinks I'm dirt, so every time I see him I let him know how much I hate him. What's he going to do? Go to the cops? They'll just say sticks and stones, sticks and stones."

Ned shook his head and turned toward home.

After the girls found the tubes trapped in the branches of a fallen tree, they continued their journey. A half hour later they came to their swimming hole and threw the tubes on the sand. They sat quietly until Loretta spoke up. "I never saw anybody as scary and mean as that man and that dog. All you did was go on shore and dig up a rock. A rock to him, anyway, right?"

Rosalyn nodded. "He hates Indians so much he doesn't care if we live or die, so you never know how far he'll go or what he'll do. To him we're nothing but a bunch of boozehounds sniffing around for a bottle of cheap wine or beer or even vanilla. He doesn't know a thing about us." She sighed. "It makes me so mad. Where do *summas* think we came from? And how many books are there about our history? I sure can't find any. Mom knows a lot more about our history than any teacher I know. If you told Norris Husk that Indians gathered here on his land for hundreds and thousands of years before he was even born, do you really think he'd believe it . . . or care? What about the Romans? Where are they? Gone, like our ancestors, but the difference is their history was saved and studied, and people like Norris Husk just threw ours in the bush."

Loretta said. "I never thought about it like that. But I'm still shaking. And I don't know if it's from the water or that horrible man. I'm going home—I'm getting hungry anyway."

Rosalyn stood and brushed sand off her bathing suit. "Don't go yet, Loretta. We were having fun until that bonehead showed up. Come up to the house with me and we'll bring some dinner back here. I think there's wieners in the freezer." She turned to Marvin and Lewis. "Why don't you guys make a fire. I'll bring my radio too, and we can have a beach party like in the movies."

Marvin had a small fire going soon after the girls had gone.

Lewis poked at it with a stick. "What happened back there, Marvin? I remember what you said to him when we fixed the fence, but did something else happen between you and him?"

"The first time I went to the store to get some groceries for Mom after we moved here from Lillooet, he was there. When he saw me, he gave me a look I don't think I saw before. He didn't blink or say a word, just stared at me with pure hate. Every time we meet up, it gets worse. I'm waiting for him to say something to me when it's just the two of us so I can punch his lights out. And I don't care what Dad says—I'm not going to stand there and do nothing. I'll kill his dog right in front of him, then he'll have to fuck his other bitch. I don't care if he calls the cops. Going to jail will be worth it."

Uncomfortable with his cousin's anger, Lewis looked back at the fire. The two sat quietly until the girls came wading across the river carrying a small box and a radio. Cora had come along, smiling and happy to be included.

They roasted and ate hot dogs and drank Kool-Aid as the sun dipped behind the mountain, the light from the fire giving their faces an orange glow. When they were done eating, they tossed the papers and bits of food that had landed on the ground into the fire and sat cross-legged on the sand and stared quietly into the flames. When a catchy song came over the transistor radio, Rosalyn and Loretta clapped and sang along. Soon Cora joined in.

Lewis looked over at his cousin. Marvin had his legs drawn up, with his jaw resting on his knees, silently watching the red-hot coals.

CHAPTER 14

IT WAS GOING TO BE ANOTHER HOT DAY. Lewis looked forward to swimming with the cousins, but it wasn't meant to be. Marvin talked his dad into letting him have the car so he could spend the day with his girlfriend, and Rosalyn was on her own, down at the sandy island in the river, with the book she was looking forward to finishing. She believed that a book ending was a big deal and that she needed to be away from the family so she could enjoy it in peace. Ned, with Mitzi at his side, was about to walk the fence around the farm and check on the cattle. He wanted to make sure they had enough salt blocks and the gate wasn't left open and a tree hadn't fallen across his fence. This was something his uncle liked to do every Sunday.

Just as Lewis was about to ask Cora if she wanted to go with him to the store to get a pop or an ice cream, his aunt came out onto the porch. "Hey," she called after Ned, waving him back. "Take Cora with you, okay? She's grumpy and needs a good long walk."

Ned hollered, "Cora!"

The little girl pushed through the screen door.

"Wanna come help me?" her dad asked.

Cora ran down the steps to join her father. She placed her hand on the dog's back and they strolled down toward the gate to the field. Cora beamed as she looked up at her dad, the audience she was always seeking. The way they smiled and laughed with each other made Lewis feel like he had been deserted, and he decided to go to the store on his own. He followed the road through the trees, the fir, cedar, poplar and birch crowding against the riverside. Around him was a din of whistling, rasping birds. Honeysuckle and Saskatoon berry bushes sprouted wherever there was space.

Beside the driveway a flicker entered a small hole in an old cedar, kicking out sawdust, housekeeping. When she heard his footsteps, she stuck out her head for a look. The bird stayed stone still, owl-like, studying Lewis as he walked past.

At the bottom of the drive, a car sped past on the road to the store, disturbing his quiet world. He glanced toward Loretta's house, hoping she'd be outside. Seeing no one, he went through the gate, then toward the store, a youth accustomed to and comfortable being alone.

He ducked a locust snap-snapping past his ear and walked across the bridge, which was so hot in the sun the timbers and decking gave off a tarry reek. On the bank above the water, the dry leaves on the poplars hissed like quivering tambourines in the slight breeze. Soon the store was close enough he swore he could smell the candy. And then a girl came around the lilac bushes at the side of the store, a shoulder bag at her side, a Coke in her hand and a bag of chips under her other arm. When he saw it was Loretta, he stopped. In her short sleeveless yellow dress and flip-flops, she looked more like a model than the cute girl next door. Her nose was perfect, unlike his own, which stared back at him in the mirror, all bumpy and sporting a pimple in the middle. Her big dark eyes, her hair, everything about her was flawless. Lewis shook his head and hurried toward her. She hadn't seen him yet–a cat across the road had her full attention. Soon Lewis was close enough he thought he should say something. He opened his mouth to speak just as Loretta stuffed hers with potato chips. "Hello, stranger."

Her head flew up and she dropped both the bag and the pop, the straw shooting up like a rocket when the bottle hit the ground, foaming and spinning.

Lewis stooped to retrieve the bag. "Jeez, Loretta, I didn't mean to scare you. I'll get you another pop." He held the bag out to her and she took it from him, still chewing and unable to speak. He picked up the bottle, pouring out the last of the liquid. "I'll be right back," he said.

The cowbell above the door rattled like a tin can as he yanked the door open and entered. Minutes later he returned with a Coke for her, a cream soda for him, along with other treats inside a paper bag. "Here's your pop."

She said, "You didn't have to buy me a new one–I already drank half of it. But thanks."

Just then a car turned down the road. The driver was so short Lewis couldn't see his arms. His hands looked fixed to the steering wheel like bizarre driving knobs. In the passenger seat was a hefty woman who jiggled and bounced with each bump of the road. She stared down her pointy nose at Loretta as if aiming down the sights of a rifle. She had the whitest skin he had ever seen, the red rouge on her cheeks making her look like a freshly painted corpse. Her nose wrinkled, then the car sped past and was gone.

Lewis said, "That old bat."

Loretta seemed to collect herself, then smiled at him. "Sure hot out, eh?" she said. "I know a place down by the river where we can sit and visit and cool off a bit if you want?"

Lewis didn't want to sound too eager, so he simply nodded.

They walked across the bridge and took a path behind her house that ran along the river. When they came to a sandy shoreline, they kicked off their shoes, sat on a log and put their feet in the water. Loretta ate her last chip, folded the empty bag and tucked it in the side pocket of her dress. Lewis watched the river curl by them in circles and swirls that changed shapes as they spilled over smooth stones. Judging by the many jumping trout, it looked like a good spot to throw in his line.

Turning to look upstream, he spotted a woman standing in the shadows of a tree, watching them. A prickly feeling went through him, but he stared past her toward the mountains as if he hadn't noticed her. He whispered to Loretta, "I hope I'm not seeing things but I think there's somebody in the trees watching us."

Loretta pulled a compact out of her shoulder bag. She opened it and, looking into the small mirror, ran her fingers around the edges of her mouth as she angled the compact until she could see the person, then she snapped it shut.

"That's Mom. I should have gone into the house and told her where I was going. She always has to know where I am. Just ignore her. When she sees I'm all right, she'll leave."

"What's she worried about?"

"Nothing. It doesn't matter."

Lewis had no idea what he should do or say, so he stood, picked up a flat stone and whipped it across the surface of the water. Loretta walked over to where he was gathering more stones and watched how he skipped them expertly, four, five, six times. "Do you have any brothers and sisters at home?" she asked.

"I have an older brother—had an older brother—but he disappeared two years ago and we don't know if he's dead or alive."

"Oh, that must be so awful," Loretta said. "I'm sorry I asked."

Lewis shrugged.

"About my mom . . . she's not crazy, but sometimes, not all the time, she watches me like a hawk. Do you remember those two girls who were murdered over at Mabel Lake four or five years ago?"

"Yes," Lewis said. "That was something. Everybody at school talked about it."

"That really bothered Mom and she felt so bad for the parents. It wasn't long after that happened that my brother, Vincent, left home. He told me he just couldn't put up with her anymore, watching over us and making up rules. Now, when Mom hears terrible news on the radio, like a boy or girl being kidnapped and murdered in Vancouver, she relives what happened to those sisters all over again. Sometimes I really want to get away from her, but I know I shouldn't because she'll just worry herself to death. Once she realizes you aren't going to run off with me, she won't be so bad. You're not, are you? Running off with me, I mean."

Lewis's face warmed.

"Are you blushing?" she asked, smiling.

He turned away and pulled one of his favourite treats, Lucky Elephant Popcorn, from the bag. The pink puffy kernels tasted so good with cream soda that he seldom bought one without the other. He hoped to change the conversation, so he opened the box and offered it to her. "Want some?"

She shook her head. "I'm pretty full."

He tipped the box to let the pink kernels tumble into his mouth, and he chewed and became lost in the sweetness and crunch.

Loretta said, "Do you know you close your eyes when you eat that stuff? You're making me want some."

Lewis held out the box and she reached inside and came out with a handful. A popcorn dropped on the ground.

"Oops," she said.

"That's okay. Watch what happens."

Lewis kicked the popcorn into the water and they both watched as it drifted downstream, dipping with the current. Then it vanished underwater, only to bob up with a piece missing. "The fish have bigger eyes than their stomachs," Lewis said. He held up a single piece of popcorn. "Hey, can you do this?"

He flicked it six feet into the air. When it came down, he caught it in his mouth.

"Look at you," Loretta said. "Bozo the clown and his circus act."

"Let's see you do it, then."

Lewis tossed up another piece just above her head. Loretta leaned back, her mouth wide open, but the popcorn bounced off her nose. She laughed so hard she staggered and tripped on the log, landing on her back. "Help me up," she said, still giggling.

"Hang on a minute." He circled the log. "It's hard to hurry with these big clown shoes."

"Just help me up, you donkey."

Lewis grabbed her by the elbows and pulled her up. Loretta was now laughing so hard Lewis couldn't help but smile. When she calmed down a little, she leaned back as if to have a better look at him.

"Oh," she said, meeting his eyes. Lewis pulled her against him, and her brown eyes eased shut.

CHAPTER 15

LEWIS AND MARVIN stepped outside on the porch. Black clouds darkened the land and heavy rain covered Blue Grouse Mountain in a misty cloak. All the birds that normally would be singing and carrying on had fallen quiet as wind pushed the storm nearer and nearer. A curtain of rain swept across the hayfield, the patter of small drops soon drowned out by a deafening deluge pounding the barn roof like a mighty drum roll.

"Jeez, look at that," Marvin said. "I feel sorry for anybody caught out in this. I guess we won't be going fishing."

"Damn. I don't want to sit around the house all day doing nothing. Why don't you guys have a television set, anyway? On days like this, I like to lay on the couch and just watch whatever is on, even Mom and Isabel's soap operas."

Marvin nodded toward the steep hill. "That there's the reason. It's in the way. We tried everything. Dad heard if you connected the antenna wire to the barbed-wire fence the picture was supposed to be perfect. That didn't work."

Lewis said. "I don't believe you can't get reception. Did you try putting the antenna on top of the hill?"

"Tried that too. Now we got a big spool of useless wire in the barn. It wasn't cheap, either, and the TV's gone back to Bennett's

Hardware. Dad heard they might be putting a booster around here somewhere but until then he won't bother trying again."

Lewis had perfected the reception at home by holding the antenna pole and walking around the yard until Isabel yelled that the picture was better. So he considered himself something of an expert. "If you still had the set, I bet I coulda got it working. I play with ours all the time."

Marvin said, "Maybe next time you visit. Why don't we go down to the basement, and I'll show you the arrowheads we found."

They jumped off the porch, ducking their heads in the rain, and ran around to the basement door. In a corner behind the wood furnace, Marvin moved boxes until he found a tin case on top of an old trunk. It rattled when he picked it up. He pried it open and handed it to Lewis. Inside were seven pieces that at first glance looked like any flat stone from the banks of the river. Lewis picked up a piece that was as black and shiny as if it was underwater, and he could see where the edges had been chipped away. He realized he was holding a genuine arrowhead in his hand and set it back down carefully. Another caught his eye.

"What's that?" he asked, pointing to a large, flat one.

"Dad said it was used like a knife for cutting meat or scraping hair off a hide." Marvin picked it up and rubbed the edge of the stone across the corner of a box. The stone sliced through the cardboard easily. "See that? It's still sharp even after being in the ground all that time. Dad said the rock probably came from up above Westwold, just north of Falkland a few miles. His war buddy grew up there and he showed Dad a place where he could stand in the middle of a small volcano and see the ridges and circles of other volcanoes all around him."

Marvin handed it to Lewis. "Here, you keep this one."

"Oh wow," Lewis said. "This is like finding a fossil, except a fossil is like a photograph of something and this is the real thing. What else do you have? What's in this big trunk?"

"War stuff," Marvin said, opening the hasp and lifting the lid.

He took out a Hudson's Bay blanket that gave off a faint perfume of roses and spread it out on the floor. Then he lifted out a Belgian chocolate box and set it down on the blanket. Inside were old photographs. A sepia-toned picture showed a soldier with an arm around another man's shoulder. They looked like brothers. It took Lewis a moment to recognize his Uncle Ned. Both men carried backpacks, and each had a rifle draped over his back and helmets fastened by chinstraps. "That's Dad and another Indian he met when they were getting ready to march into Holland. They were both so glad to run into each other, Dad asked somebody to take a picture of them."

As Lewis continued to study his uncle's face, Marvin picked an envelope out of the chocolate box that was full of currencies from around the world: German marks, Dutch guilders, Italian lira and Belgian francs.

"Too bad they're not worth anything now," he said. He put the envelope back and picked up a folded cloth. Inside were medals with colourful ribbons.

Lewis ran his thumb over them. "What are these for? Do you know?"

"No. I've never asked, because I'm not sure if Dad likes me looking at them." Marvin rewrapped the collection carefully and put it back exactly where he had found it.

Above them, they heard knocking on the kitchen door– Uncle Alphonse's signature *shave and a haircut, two bits.* Then a thump as the door was shut.

Marvin put the rest of the stuff away and they ran up the stairs and outside. The rain, which had come down with such force that garden flowers lay bent or broken, had stopped. They pushed through the kitchen door just as Alphonse draped a raincoat and cap on a wall peg.

Ned was already sitting at the table. "That's a handy coat for being out in this. Where'd you get it?" he asked.

"Rummage sale." Alphonse pulled out a chair and smiled at his nephew. "Hello, squirt."

"What are you doing here?" Lewis asked.

Alphonse lowered himself onto his chair with a groan. "What am I doing here? Well, that's a fine howdy-do. I came to check on you."

Marvin and Lewis both sat. Lewis asked, "Did you get any mail from Mom and Isabel?"

"I did get a letter. Grace said they got a job at the big packing plant in Oroville and found a nice house to rent too, but they can't wait to get back here. She said to come see if you were okay."

Lewis grinned. "Sure am."

Ned stood and filled the electric kettle, plugged it in and set the cookie tin on the table. By the time he brought down the teapot and dropped in two tea bags, Alphonse had finished off three cookies. He rounded up the crumbs into a pile, swept them into his palm and dropped them back into the tin. "Damn that Jean. She can cook and drive a tractor too. Just like Grace. Except the cooking, maybe. Where is my little sister, anyway?"

Ned said, "She's in town with the girls. What are you walking around in this rain for?"

Alphonse gave a little shiver. "Well, my buddy Abel, the lovesick pup, he moved in with a woman up in Williams Lake and left me all by myself, so I thought I'd take a wander over here so I at least had somebody to talk to. There wasn't another *skin* over there at all. I was the last Indian west of the Pecos."

After filling the teapot, Ned picked it up and gave a gentle swirl. "Can you grab us some cups, Marvin?"

Marvin went to the cupboard and brought out four mugs. As Ned poured, Alphonse gazed at the rising steam as if he were being warmed up and dried out just by looking. He raised the mug and blew at the hot liquid and took a noisy slurp.

"On my way over, I saw Norris Husk's missus, Ruth. I never saw her up real close before. She was trying to dig holes by the road with one of them well diggers. You know the kind with two shovels you jab into the ground and squeeze together to trap the dirt? I watched her for a minute but she ain't making no headway cuz she's holding it wrong, so she threw that thing down and cussed. That's when she saw me coming down the road. As soon as she laid eyes on me, she looked scared.

"I said, 'Not havin' much luck with that, are you?' She didn't say nothing, so I picked up that thingamajig. 'This here rig is good for planting daisies but not much else.'

"Then I stabbed at that ground and be damned if that thing didn't go in four inches. I said, 'Boy, this is good bottom land. It's all soft dirt. No rocks atall. I guess it wouldn't hurt to use this.' I dug down about two and a half feet, then I hand it to her and turn and walk away, and she still hasn't said a word. Not a thank you or a go to hell.

"When I was a ways away, she hollered, 'Thanks.' I gave a little wave of my hand without looking back and kept going."

Ned picked up the teapot. "Anybody want some more?" After he refilled their cups, he said, "I never met her. What's she like?"

Alphonse shook his head. "She's okay. She's a hard worker cuz I seen the calluses on her hands. And anybody that can live with that bastard should get a medal. And even though she's old and a little wrinkly, she has the one thing that's important in a woman."

Ned looked confused. "What's that?"

"She got a nice big ass."

Ned, Marvin and Lewis laughed, then Ned grabbed Alphonse by the shoulders and gave him a shake. "I knew you couldn't go long without saying something like that."

Alphonse grinned as they drank their tea. Then his expression changed. "When I got to the store, I seen Norris's truck parked to the side, and when I walked past it, that damn dog of his jumped right at me. Jeez, I thought for sure that was it for me, but he reached the end of his logging chain and I just got hit in the face by dog spit.

"At the door I look in the window and see Norris at the counter, yapping and shaking his head. So I put my ear to the door crack and I hear him say, 'I made that Indian patch a big hole in his fence and two hippie Indian boys chased the cattle back onto his land. I stood and watched them to make sure it was done right.'"

Alphonse looked at Marvin and Lewis. "Hippie Indians? I guess that's you two long-hairs."

Marvin flung his head back and tossed his shoulder-length tresses. Lewis tucked his behind his ears.

"When I pushed the door open and went in, those guys looked like two cats got caught shittin' under the bed. Delbert, he started wiping dust off that clean counter with a rag and tried not to look me in the eye when I asked for tobacco and papers. After I paid and went to the door, I looked back at those fools, and I said, 'You know, both of you should be careful what you say about my brother-in-law and his family. In the war he didn't have time to stand around chatting like old women. He was too busy picking off the enemy. And him being a sniper, he could shoot off a person's ear a mile away. And another thing, Norris, how is it an ugly bastard like you can end up with a woman like Ruthie?'

"His face turned red he's so mad. And then he says, 'Fuck you.' So I walk right up to him and I said, 'You'll never go back to women.'"

Uncle Ned laughed so hard he began coughing and it took a minute for him to catch his breath. "Hey, I didn't know I was a sniper in the war. How about that?"

"I just wanted to give them something to think about. I didn't know what else to do."

"There's nothing you can do," Ned said. "You can't make people like that see sense."

Mitzi began barking. Marvin walked over to the window. "Hey, Dad, it's the Indian agent."

Ned gave a low groan. "Aw Jesus." When he stood, it was as if his body had suddenly become heavier. "He comes out here every month to count cattle. I can already hear him when he sees that one a them's missing. Lewis, come along and keep me company."

When Marvin went to follow, Ned said, "You stay here. Last time you got Cookie all riled up."

Lewis asked, "Why is he doing that? Counting cattle, I mean?"

"It's against the law for an Indian to sell cattle without telling him first. A guy can get into real trouble doing that."

"Which way you headed?" Alphonse asked.

"Down to the far end of the field. The cattle like to bunch up under them trees when it's been raining."

"I'm going that way. I'd like to hear what this yahoo has to say."

Ned pointed his finger at him. "Okay, but don't you go jabbing at him with your devil's pitchfork. God don't like to be poked."

The Indian agent stood leaning against the car waiting, clutching a leather binder, his foot bouncing in a restless rhythm.

"That time already, Mr. Cooke?" Ned asked.

"Yep" was all he said.

Ned pointed the way and they walked down the tractor path at the side of the field with Mitzi trotting behind. Ned set a fast pace, his army march, which Lewis knew his uncle could keep up all day long. Alphonse was soon breathing hard, and every so often the Indian agent had to run to catch up.

As they came to the cows lounging under the trees, Ned gave a warning. "Here they are, but keep an eye on that Angus."

The Indian agent said to Ned, "You knew I was coming. Why didn't you put them into the corral?"

Alphonse said in a loud voice, "Quit pissing around and get counting."

Ned looked down to the ground.

Frowning, the Indian agent walked slowly toward the herd, the cows swinging their big heads his way. As he began to count, the Black Angus cow noticed the strange-looking man and began to separate herself from the others. The agent, whose eyes had been on his binder, looked up and saw the cow coming his way. She let out a broken grunt, sounding like a male lion. Mr. Cooke ran behind Ned, but the cow kept coming. Ned didn't move until the cow picked up speed. Then he stepped forward, waving his arms, and she returned to the herd.

Alphonse laughed and slapped his knee.

Ned said, "I'll make it easy on you. There's nineteen cows there and twelve yearlings. Thirty-one in all."

"I'll just make sure, if you don't mind," Cooke said, and began his count again. When he was done, he recorded the number in his binder, compared it with his previous tally, then looked up at Ned. "There's thirty-one here when it's supposed to be thirty-two. Where is the other one? What did you do?"

"One died."

"How did it die? Why didn't you tell me?"

"I just did. I had to shoot one and we butchered it soon as we could."

"How do I know you're telling me the truth?"

Alphonse bristled. "Ned don't tell lies, you little—"

Ned interrupted. "Alphonse, you better get on home."

Alphonse bumped the man with his belly as he walked by.

"Look, Ned. You better prove to me you didn't sell that cow or I'm going to have to write you up."

Ned tipped back his hat and put his hands in his pockets. "When that cow died, I didn't have time to sit around and wait for you. I butchered it right away before all that meat went to waste."

"How do you know it wasn't some disease that killed it? Your family could get sick, and even die."

"Because I'm not stupid. I know what a broken leg looks like. That bull is pretty heavy. When he went to breed her, she broke her leg, so I made her into hamburger and stew meat. It's all there in my freezer. I can take you there and you can see it for yourself."

The Indian agent swung out his arm, gesturing for Ned to take the lead. "Let's have a look, then, shall we?"

On the way back to the house, Lewis noticed the man studying the hayfield. He looked at Ned over the top of his glasses. "You know, it wouldn't hurt to put a little fertilizer on your hay crop, Ned. That and a little water and this field will produce three times what you get now. They sell it over in Grindrod at Sure Crop Feeds."

Ned ignored him, but Lewis couldn't help himself. "What, he should buy water?"

"Fertilizer," the agent snapped.

At the house they made their way down into the basement, where Ned opened the freezer and stood back. It was filled with packages of meat wrapped in butcher's paper, laid out in rows.

Mr. Cooke said, "Next time you tell me right away when you have to shoot a cow and there won't be any problems. By the way, who was that man with us out in the field?"

"My brother-in-law. You seen him before. Now listen, while I got you here, I wanna know about when I'm getting the rest of my army grant money. I didn't get half what the white guys got."

The Indian agent tucked his pen into his binder. "There's no more, I'm afraid, and there's nothing I can do about it. The government said you get less because Indians have an advantage living on reserves."

Ned's mouth fell open. "An advantage?"

"You don't pay any taxes and we can provide you with an agricultural advisor any time you want."

Ned shook his head. "I suppose that was my agricultural advice, was it, the fertilizer and water?"

The agent didn't say another word. He went out to his car, climbed in and drove down the lane with Mitzi chasing after the car, barking. Ned watched from the porch until the car disappeared through the trees.

Marvin came outside. "How did it go?"

"Good," Ned said. "Yeah, it went good." He turned and walked back toward the field.

"Where's he going?" Lewis asked.

Marvin watched his father. "He's cooling off."

That night, just before Lewis clicked off the light and crawled into bed, he noticed Marvin staring up at the ceiling. As if feeling his cousin watching him, Marvin said, "I hate the way Dad lets Cookie and Husk push him around. There's nothing we can do about Cookie because he works for the government and he's got the law on his side, but I gotta do something about Norris Husk. I don't know what, but I gotta do something. That man thinks it's okay to just walk into our house and say whatever he wants. He's gotta be taught a lesson. There has to be a way to shut that big mouth of his."

CHAPTER 16

ALPHONSE RETURNED THE FOLLOWING DAY, driving Grace's truck. He turned the motor off, stepped out and walked over to where Lewis and Marvin sat on the back steps. "I told your mom I'd keep this old thing running while her and Isabel are away, but you can do that. Just take it for a spin up the range once in a while."

The truck was old and rusted but Lewis was happy to have it.

"I need to get dropped off home first and you can have it for the rest of the summer. But I'll drive and you open the gates."

They drove through the trees out into the clearing of the new field. Alphonse, whistling a tune, tapping the steering wheel, turned toward the river. Lewis asked, "Where are we going?"

"You remember those white guys that shot off the padlock?"

"Yeah."

Alphonse gave him a funny grin. "Last night, just when it got dark, I heard a truck go down the road and I wondered if it was them. I thought I better go on down the river to have a look, so I took my flashlight and 30-30. Sure enough, there they were, the two of them, unloading lumber off their truck and laughing like it was their own place. I waited until they finished and then I put a bullet right through their gas tank. There's something about a gun blast at night, you can't see who's doing the shooting. Ghosts, maybe. Anyway, they skedaddled out of there like jackrabbits. I put another shot in the air just to give 'em a little push, and they bounced across that field and took off on Range Road. They prob'ly ran outta gas before they made it to town. I don't think we'll see them again."

He stopped at a pile of neatly stacked two-by-fours. "Let's load 'er up and dump it off at your place."

The back of the pickup hung low to the ground as they drove slowly down the road toward home.

Boxes and packages sat close to the back porch, covered in tarps, and garbage was strewn around the yard. But in what looked like total confusion, the skeleton of the addition had been built and was about to be boarded in. As they stopped the truck, a man passed a sheet of plywood up to a waiting worker, who pulled it onto the roof trusses, flipped it over and nailed it in place. With all the hammering and sawing, Lewis understood why his mother wanted to be away.

A carpenter came over to them just as they finished unloading. "That stuff is a lot better than the cheap shit we had to use. It's cracked and as straight as a dog's hind leg. You can build a new porch with it if you want."

Lewis stood with his uncle watching them work for a while and then he drove the truck back to his cousins'.

After supper, Lewis began to feel restless. Loretta was in town with her mother and wouldn't be back until dark. He had been thinking about the range the last few days, and now that he had the truck, he could go up anytime he wanted. But he wanted to show Loretta. Maybe she was back home by now, he thought, and he rushed out to his truck and drove down to the gate by the bridge. Loretta had just closed the car trunk and was going up the steps with bags of groceries in her arms.

"Hey," Lewis called. He got out and hurried across the road.

Loretta was surprised to see him. "I thought you were coming over tomorrow."

"I know, but I got my mom's truck now and I wanted to take you for a spin up to the range."

"Sure, I'll go. Just wait a minute."

Loretta went into the house. Lewis could hear her mother talking. When Loretta came back out, her mother was with her. Lewis could see she wasn't happy about it, but she watched Loretta go with Lewis, calling after them, "You guys be careful."

They ran across the road. As Lewis jumped in, Loretta tried the door handle but nothing happened.

"Hang on a minute," Lewis said. "It only opens from the inside." He leaned over and pulled up the handle.

Loretta climbed in and slammed the door hard a few times before it stayed shut. Somewhere down inside the door, metal rattled around. "Thanks for rescuing me," she said. "What a day I had."

Lewis started the truck. "I can imagine." He backed up until he came to a wide spot in the road and turned around.

Loretta went to roll down the window, but the handle didn't work either.

"You gotta roll the handle down all the way then push the glass down with both hands. After that, you can roll it back up to where you want it."

Lewis ground the gears into first and the truck jumped. "Sorry about that. Alphonse must have tightened the clutch. It's gonna take a while getting used to it."

Loretta managed to get the window down and the cab filled with cool air. Lewis saw her looking down through a hole in the floorboards at the road passing under them.

"The truck's seen better days. The body is pretty well shot but the motor and transmission work okay. My uncle said it was just sitting there so I might as well use it. Nice, huh?"

"You sure this thing is gonna make it up there?"

Lewis patted the dash. "This old gal? You bet."

At the end of the field, Lewis stopped at the fence, jumped out and opened the barbed-wire gate, leaning it against a post. After driving through and closing the gate, he turned up the trail that joined up with Range Road. He downshifted and the truck bounced over small boulders and potholes until they reached the track leading up to the range. Frightened by the noise, small birds rose up out of the dry bunchgrass like a ragged cloud to scatter away directionless. They hadn't gone far before Lewis swung the truck to the right and climbed a steep hill.

"Boy oh boy," Loretta said. "Sounds like this truck is going to fall apart any minute."

"Hey, don't you be calling down old Betsy." Lewis shifted gears and floored the gas pedal, and the engine gave a loud whine. Finally, they rocked to a stop at the top of the hill overlooking Heart Lake and Lewis turned off the motor.

Loretta took her hands off the dashboard, where she had braced herself. "I rode a Tilt-a-Whirl at the fair once, and this was pretty close."

With outspread arms, Lewis presented the range to Loretta like it was his backyard. "This is one of my favourite places. Even in the dark you can feel how big it is. The sound really carries up here too. If my mom was back right now and hollered for me to get home, we could hear her plain as day. Listen, do you hear that dog barking?"

Loretta stuck her head out. "I wonder how far away it is?"

Lewis cupped his hands around his mouth and yelled out his window, "Shut up."

They both laughed when the barking stopped.

Loretta moved closer and Lewis put his arm around her shoulder, and they looked into each other's eyes and kissed and then rested their heads together, staring out at the stars.

"What a beautiful place this is," Loretta said. "I've never been up here. I'm glad to be anywhere quiet and away from my mom. She is such a pain."

"All moms are. Mine can't help sticking her nose in my business and always has something to say."

"How did your brother get along with her?"

Lewis turned to look at her. "What?"

"You only told me that your brother was missing. But Rosalyn told me all about Eddie and how he disappeared."

Lewis said, "Eddie and Mom never saw eye to eye about much. And now she never wants to talk about him. But you know what, it's too nice up here to be getting all gloomy. Let's just sit and enjoy the quiet."

A half moon beamed down from the star-filled sky. Soon coyotes began yapping, the sound seeming to come from all around them. Wild horses nickered. Then from Heart Lake came an eerie wail.

"What is that?" Loretta asked.

"A loon. You never heard one before?"

"Is that what it is? Then I did hear it before." Then she gave a quick shush. "Did you hear that?"

"I heard something."

The noise came again, loud enough now that they could make it out. "Help me, help," a voice pleaded. The horses took off at a dead run, snorting and neighing.

"Maybe somebody's hurt," Lewis said, starting the truck and turning around. "He sounds pretty close. Just up ahead there a bit."

He toed the high-beam button on the floor and they spotted a person in the distance, waving his arms.

Loretta said, "What's somebody doing out here this time of night?"

When they came closer, they saw it was a young cadet. As Lewis pulled up alongside, the cadet dropped his backpack and came to the window. "I saw you drive up and I was scared you were going to leave before I got to you. I thought I was going to die out here."

"Why are you all by yourself?"

The cadet closed his eyes, head down. "I got separated from my group."

"Don't you have a compass? Didn't they teach you how to read one so you can find your way back?"

The cadet pulled a compass out of his backpack and held it up. "I fell and broke it."

"You're lucky that's all you broke. How long you been out here?"

"Since just before dark. Our group climbed up a mountain and we found some human bones scattered all over the ground. Sarge said animals been at them. Then he called back on his walkie-talkie and told the radio operator to let the police know what we found. After he gave him our location, he said we all had to get back to camp."

Another body found, Lewis thought. *What's going on here? They're popping out of the ground all over.* "Where was this at? Do you remember any landmarks, a funny-shaped tree or anything? Were you on a trail?"

A coyote howled and the cadet spun around.

Impatient, Lewis said, "Did anything stand out near where you found the bones?"

"No. They divided us up into small groups and we had to find our way back. And then it got dark and I lost the other guys." He thought for a moment. "Oh yeah, we passed a big rock that had a lot of quartz in it. The bones were around there somewhere. I love collecting rocks, and quartz can mean there's gold, so I stopped to explore. That's why I lost them."

Lewis said, "Whereabouts is it?"

"It's at the top of a big landslide. And we could see the lake below the highway from there. I thought I knew the way back and was okay until I heard something following me. I never been so scared. This is the second time I got lost up here. Not much of a soldier, am I? Can you take me back to camp? Do you know where it is?"

Lewis pointed back to the truck box. "Hop on. It's just over to the right in that long draw. If you walked up that little rise, you would have looked down at your camp."

With the weary boy perched on the tailgate, Lewis started off slowly so he wouldn't fall off. He said to Loretta, "Now there's a city kid who follows street signs to find his way around. In this country, he might as well be on the moon."

Loretta turned to look at the boy. The red glow of the tail lights showed wet marks on his cheek. "Poor kid."

"Not much of a killer, is he?" Lewis said.

The truck rattled down the long hill to the camp, its headlights picking out an army jeep parked by the side of the road. A soldier jumped out, positioning himself in the middle of the track, clutching a rifle. Lewis stopped in front of the sentry.

"What's your business here, sir?"

"You guys lose something?" Lewis nodded toward the tailgate.

The sentry walked to the back of the truck. "Baker?"

The cadet jumped down. "I got lost, sir."

"You look worn out. Go on and climb into your tent and get some sleep. You're gonna need it."

"Yes, sir." As he walked past Loretta's window, he stopped. "Thanks for helping me."

"Try not to get lost again, okay."

The sentry waved to Lewis to turn around and they drove back and stopped where they had first parked.

"Well, that was exciting," Lewis said. "I guess we weren't all alone out here after all."

Loretta took his arm and pulled herself closer. "I saw how you looked when the kid said they found the bones. What were you thinking?" When Lewis didn't answer, she nudged him with her shoulder. "You okay?"

"You know when you have a good dream, you wake up and still have that good feeling? After Eddie was gone, it felt like every night I was having nightmares. I'd wake up sweating and out of breath. Then every once in a while, I'd dream he was just away somewhere, safe and having fun, and that I'd see him someday. Since they found that old chief's bones at the bottom of the range, I don't have those good ones anymore."

CHAPTER 17

LEWIS SPENT AS MUCH TIME as he could with Loretta. Taking her out for a drive was a treat, but if it rained, they played games at her kitchen table, sitting so close their knees touched, aware that Loretta's mother kept a watchful eye. Lewis began to think she didn't like him and was surprised when Mrs. Ryder asked him to join them on a trip into Vernon for the day.

Lewis showed up right on time to find her standing by her car as Loretta ran back to the house, shouting over her shoulder, "I'll just be a minute, Mom."

Mrs. Ryder shook her head. "Come on, Loretta, we're late already. A minute ago, it was your barrettes." The screen door banged. "I don't know what's wrong with her today. This is all I need." She opened the driver's door, tossed her purse in the back seat and sat behind the steering wheel.

"Good morning, Mrs. Ryder," Lewis said as he opened the passenger door and slid in.

She looked at him. "Every time you call me that, I think of my mother-in-law, and I don't like it. My name is Alma."

Lewis nodded, but he had no intention of calling her by her first name.

Silent minutes ticked by. Even Loretta's old dog gave up waiting in front of the screen door, went to a corner and lay down. Mrs. Ryder turned to Lewis. "While I got you here, I want to tell you something, just between the two of us. I know you like Loretta and she likes you, but that little girl is all I got. So if you ever do anything to hurt her, I swear to god I'll hunt you down and skin you alive."

Before Lewis could say anything, Loretta came out of the house and ran to the car. "About time," Mrs. Ryder said. Lewis opened the door and got out to let her in. After the door was shut and they were settled, Loretta's mom turned the key. The motor turned over but wouldn't start. "Not again. Oh, this damn car." She tried again but the starter began to labour.

Cursing, she stepped out of the car and opened the hood. Then she walked over to a pickup parked by the house and grabbed a small can of gasoline out of the back. She carried the can over to the car, removed the air filter and dribbled fuel down the throat of the carburetor.

Lewis said to Loretta, "Boy, your mom's a real Indian, isn't she. I thought only Alphonse and Mom knew how to prime a carburetor like that."

This time when she turned the key, the motor coughed out flames that shot out of the carburetor with a bang. She revved the engine until it idled smoothly and then got out of the car again, put everything back together and slammed the hood. Dusting off her hands, she slid behind the steering wheel and they were off.

Just as they came to a sharp turn in the road, she pulled out and sped past the car in front of them. Hanging on to the door handle, Lewis leaned over and whispered to Loretta, "We'll be lucky if we don't get killed before we get there. You think it was a good idea to catch a ride with this maniac?"

"Don't be such a scaredy-cat."

As they neared the outskirts of town, Mrs. Ryder slowed down. Lewis relaxed and moved his arm slowly over Loretta's head to rest on her shoulders. She shrugged him off with a warning look.

Ducking into a parking spot in front of the Vernon Medical Clinic, Mrs. Ryder switched off the motor and turned to her daughter. "I got lots to do today. Between going to see the doctor and picking up stuff at the hardware store, I won't be done until around three. So you two got four hours to do nothing but wander around the streets like hobos. You sure you don't want to come with me instead? I could use the help."

Loretta said, "I found this place where they have the best hamburgers and milkshakes, and I really want to take Lewis there. And you've been talking about the big sale today at Stedman's since you heard about it. Well, here's your chance to take all the time you need without me bothering you to hurry up."

"Okay, but you meet me at the Fruit Union just before five. I could use that farm boy of yours to load some things in the trunk for me. Okay?"

Loretta asked, "Is this car going to start again?"

"It'll be fine now. Your dad told me to start it up and let it run once in a while and I forgot."

Loretta waited until her mother went inside the clinic, then reached for Lewis's hand and they set off down the sidewalk.

Lewis couldn't remember seeing Vernon so busy. Main Street was crowded with people. A delivery truck making a left turn had stalled the flow of traffic. Cars honked until traffic resumed. Then all the vehicles came to a stop, waiting for the light, and when it turned green, they rushed ahead like cattle through an open gate.

When they came to the Okanagan Restaurant, they went inside. An aproned lady showed them to a seat and placed menus on the table. Lewis had been here before with his mother and Isabel, who said the place made them feel like high-toned *summas*. But all they'd ordered was coffee and pie.

"What can I get you?" the waitress asked.

"We'll have two deluxe cheeseburgers with french fries and two chocolate milkshakes, extra thick," Loretta said.

While they waited for their burgers, they watched the waitress adding ice cream and milk to the mixer. The machine struggled before it picked up speed. As it gently rocked on its stand, frost appeared on the side of the aluminum container. Then she poured the frothy milkshake into tall glasses until they were so full some spilled over the sides.

Loretta took out her compact and studied herself in the mirror as Lewis glanced around the busy restaurant. Two tables away, an old man sat facing them, his eyes centred on Loretta, as if wondering what she was doing here in this restaurant. His mouth, the corners of his eyes, even the wrinkles on his face pointed downward. Lewis had seen this look before, a face ugly with hatred. His mother and Isabel were used to such people and could give back as good as was given them. But Loretta, protected by her father and hovering mother, viewed the world through innocent eyes. Lewis knew the old man was aware he was a white man in a crowd of his own kind. Safe and untouchable. Lewis pulled a toothpick from the chrome holder, and with his thumb, flicked it toward the man, hitting him on his cheek. The man saw Lewis watching, sat up in his chair and finished off his coffee. He stood, holding on to the chair back, and dropped money on the table. Favouring his left leg, he limped to the door and went out. Loretta hadn't seen a thing.

When their food came, Loretta sucked on the milkshake straw until her cheeks caved in. After they finished the burgers and fries, they noisily slurped the last of their milkshakes, just as the waitress brought them the bill.

Lewis intended to pay for lunch with his hard-earned money, but Loretta grabbed the bill from his hand. "My treat. Remember I told you my dad is hardly ever home because he works up in Clinton? I don't dare tell Mom, but he mails me money whenever I ask. She thinks I make a fortune baby-sitting for the people by the store."

After the bill was rung up at the cash register, Loretta took the change and walked back to the table to leave a tip while Lewis waited by the door. Outside the restaurant, he said, "I'm so full now I could lie down and take a snooze right here under that parking meter."

"You sound like your uncle sometimes."

"Alphonse?" Lewis was surprised.

"Yes. He's funny like you and a bit of a charmer too."

"Charmer? Jeez, I don't think I ever heard anybody say my uncle is charming. Mom said he was always getting into trouble when he was younger. His dad couldn't stand him anymore, so he sent him away to residential school to smarten him up. When he came back, Mom said he was worse. She said he would get into fights and steal stuff from cars in town. I guess old age has mellowed him."

It was Loretta's turn to look surprised. "Old age? How old is he?"

Lewis thought for a moment. "Thirty-eight, thirty-nine."

Loretta shook her head. "Thirty-eight isn't old."

"I guess he has changed. He's a lot different now than he was even when I was a kid. Back then, he didn't have time for me and Eddie. He was always swearing at us when we got in the way, and only stopped when Grandma told him to leave us alone. Still, I think women would have a hard time putting up with him. I see the way he stares at my mom's friend, Isabel, when she's not looking. Boy, if his eyes could pull off clothes, there'd be a lot of naked women walking around."

"Well, he's always nice to me."

Lewis laughed. "You only met him once or twice. If I was you, I'd keep one eye out when he's around just to make sure you're still wearing something."

Loretta linked his arm. "You ever been to the museum?"

"I went once a long time ago. I was a little kid then and I didn't think it was so special."

"Well, you're not a kid anymore and I want to show you something. I think you're gonna like it."

They walked up the street, weaving their way through the crowd. Loretta stopped often to look at dresses on the mannequins in the clothing store windows.

The museum had moved from its location next to the Allison Hotel to a new building complex that held the police station and city hall. Lewis pushed the door open and Loretta followed him in. At the far end of the spacious room Lewis saw a single-horse buggy in a roped-off area and started toward it, but Loretta grabbed his hand and pulled him back. She led him, instead, to a display of local Indian artifacts featuring a beaded buckskin dress, moccasins and other relics. "This is what I wanted to show you." Loretta pointed to a collection of arrowheads. Marvin's was nothing compared to what was arranged inside the glass-covered case. "Remember the one that horrible man threw away? Makes you wonder how many more there are under that ground," Loretta said.

Lewis shrugged. "For all the stories I heard about Indians living here for thousands of years, there's not a lot to show for it, is there? Just a few beads and junk."

"Maybe the historians and archeologists are just getting started."

"I don't know. This place bothers me. Uncle Alphonse knows more about Indian history than these museum guys, but they're not going to listen to a dumb Indian. It wouldn't surprise me if they had a collection of beer bottles labelled 'glass vessels used by the local Indians.' Or 'brownies used by the brownies.' Let's get out of here."

In a window at the Hudson's Bay building, they saw a canvas tent reduced to $9.95 for a quick sale. "That's a good-looking tent," Loretta said. "It even has an awning. Cute."

Lewis agreed. "Wouldn't it be nice if we had that up in the bush somewhere and could hide out from your mom?"

"It'd be just like having our own home."

"Yeah," Lewis said. "We could play house and everything."

"And everything?" Loretta said with a grin.

They went inside the store and Lewis bought the tent. When they walked down to meet Mrs. Ryder, he proudly carried the tent bag over his shoulder.

Loretta's mother asked, "What's in the bag?"

"A tarp for Lewis's uncle," her daughter said.

That evening after supper, they searched for a camping site between the bridge and his cousins' home. Soon they came across a hidden spot close to the water. After sweeping away twigs and stones, they raised the tent and Loretta crawled in and laid a blanket across the floor. After they were both inside, Lewis pulled down the zipper. "Look at this," he marvelled.

"It's only canvas but it feels safe in here. Maybe that's how Indians felt a long time ago when they closed the flap on their own place."

"You're right, it does feel like a home. Did you know the Okanagans used mostly reed mats for their tents instead of hides?"

"No, I didn't, but that's a real coincidence. That's what they used for toilet paper."

Loretta poked him. "Now you're making fun of me."

"I'm not. Alphonse told me it's an old saying. It goes something like this: 'In days of old, when Indians were bold, and paper was un-invented, they wiped their ass with blades of grass and went away contented.'"

Loretta punched him on the arm. Then she handed Lewis a brown paper bag she'd brought from the store. He emptied the contents onto the blanket: bottles of pop, potato chips, a package of peanuts, different colours and flavours of suckers, and a handful of Dubble Bubble gum. Then she pulled a fat orange candle out of her shoulder bag, which she placed in front of the door flap, followed by the game Trouble.

Soon the tent filled with the sound of clacking dice and plastic pegs tapping on the game board. The dice, just like at home, were never kind to Lewis. "How come you always get a six and I don't? You're cheating somehow!"

Darkness came unnoticed, deepening until they couldn't see the dots on the dice. Loretta lit the candle and sat on her knees to stare at the little flame. "This really is the best thing we've ever done," she said. "We can come here anytime we want and talk all night."

Lewis said, "And even if it rains, the guy at the Hudson's Bay said the tent has a waterproof coating."

Loretta let out a breath, watching the candle flame flicker and wave. Lewis could almost see the thoughts going through her mind. Then she looked up at him. "Do you think either of our brothers will ever come home?"

Lewis took his time answering. "I don't know. Maybe yours will, but I gave up on Eddie. How long do you sit around and wait, especially when everybody says he's dead. I just wish we had a tent like this one so we could've gone fishing at a lake up in the mountains. We used to sneak off into the bush and build a fire, and he told me his secrets, especially about Eva. He said he was in love with her, but I didn't understand a thing about that back then."

He reached for Loretta's hand and pulled her close. "But I do now."

They kissed, Lewis's hands moving to her belly then up to her breast. "Wait," she said, stopping him. "I know you wanted to do that for a while now, but you're breathing so hard you're starting to snort like a horse. Slow down. You're scaring me a little."

"Like a stud, you mean?" he said. "I'll show you a stud."

He buried his face in her neck and began neighing. Loretta giggled and tried to push him away, but he tickled her neck with his nose. "Stop it, you cayuse," she said in a fit of laughter.

Then they were sprawled on the blanket, Lewis on top of her, his eyes closing as they kissed, body trembling, his tongue searching for hers. He reached down and unsnapped her jeans and was about to undo his own when Loretta screamed and pushed him off. Flames rose around them in a whoosh. In his urgency, Lewis had knocked over the candle and the tent was on fire.

Loretta grabbed the blanket and began hitting at the flames as Lewis fumbled for the tent zipper, eyes closed against the smoke and heat. He found the metal tab, pulled it open and pushed Loretta out the door. He crawled out after her, ran to the river, and began scooping handfuls of water onto the blaze. Then he saw the flames licking at the nearby brush. "Come on, Loretta, we have to put out those bushes before the fire spreads to the trees. Just do what I'm doing, hurry."

They splashed frantically as if in a water fight. By the time they doused the flames, all that was left of their tent was ashes. Lewis pulled Loretta into the shallows and splashed water onto her hair, greyed with soot. After cleaning themselves, they sat on the ground looking at the remains of their new home.

Lewis said, "I wonder what they used to waterproof this thing, gasoline?"

Loretta used a long stick to pull out their game. The board was burned right up to the plastic bubble that held the dice.

"Look at that," she said. "I rolled a six."

CHAPTER 18

AFTER MARVIN PARKED THE STATION WAGON at the hall and switched off the engine, Lewis heard the clapping hands and stomping feet of the dancers inside, a screeching fiddle, the twang of a guitar, the hollow plucking of a banjo and a lone singer's voice that rose and fell as he sang out of tune. People gathered at the bottom of the steps watched the comings and goings of the crowd, shouting a name whenever they recognized someone. Others filed up the stairs into the building through double doors that were propped wide open, light streaming down on them like a spotlight, cigarette smoke billowing out of the hall as though the place was on fire. Lewis's stomach fluttered.

"Look at all the people. This is going to be so much fun!" Loretta said.

"I heard these Head of the Lake dances can get pretty wild," Marvin said. "Loretta, you stick close to Lewis, and Rosalyn, don't you wander off with a guy. I don't want to have to go looking in the back seat of every car here to find you."

"Piss off, Marvin. You just make sure you take it easy. If Mom and Dad find out you're driving while you're drinking, you'll never have the car again."

They stepped out of the car, slammed doors and went toward the hall, pausing for a minute near the steps.

The eyes of a group of young men studied the faces of Rosalyn and Loretta as they passed, then moved down to dwell on their legs, while girls gave glances at Lewis and Marvin. A large man stepped out of the shadows beside the hall and came toward them. It was Hank, the man from the ball game.

"Hey, Salmon River, you in a better mood today?"

Lewis said, "You bet. Sorry about last time."

Hank laughed and patted Lewis on his shoulder. "I almost didn't recognize you all dressed up. Who's your company?"

"Marvin and Rosalyn, and this is Loretta."

"Your girlfriend?" Hank asked Marvin, pointing to Rosalyn.

"Not on your life," Marvin said. "She's my sister."

Rosalyn ignored Marvin, stepped forward and offered her hand, surprising Hank. He awkwardly reached out his huge fingers, wrapping them around her hand up to her wrist. He stepped back.

"And who are you, little pretty one?" he asked.

Loretta looked up shyly. "Loretta."

"Hello, Loretta," Hank said, then looked around at them all. "Is this your first time at the dance? You guys look a little nervous. Maybe we could use a drink before we go in? I got beer and other stuff. Whaddya say?"

"Sounds good to me," Marvin said.

Hank led them back to his car. When he opened the trunk, Lewis saw it was filled with cases of Lucky Lager beer, six-packs of Coke and boxes filled with bottles of rum, vodka and whiskey. "Name your poison, boys and girls."

Lewis said, "Wow, look at all this stuff. You're not going to drink all this, are you?"

"Jeez, do you think I'm a fish or something? I sell this stuff at dances or jackpot rodeos or wherever there's thirsty Indians. I'm the guy they wanna see."

"What do you want, Rosalyn, Loretta?" Marvin asked.

"We'll have a Coke," Rosalyn said.

"What do you think, Lewis? Can you handle a beer?" his cousin said.

"You bet. I'm so dry I can't even spit."

Hank opened the beer and pop and handed them to his guests. Then he pulled out a flask from his back pocket, unscrewed the cap and took a long swig. "Ahhhh," he said. "There's nothing like a little Scotch to get them dancing legs doin' the twist."

When they finished their drinks, they followed Hank up the steps into the hall. Just inside the door, he leaned in toward Lewis so he could be heard over the noise. "If you want more beer, just look for me. If you don't see me, I'll prob'ly be in the car having a nip. Have fun. And don't worry, nobody'll bother you because you're with me. Okay?"

"Okay," Lewis answered.

Loretta said, "I'm going to the bathroom. Be right back."

Marvin went one way and Rosalyn the other, leaving Lewis standing there all alone. Then a hand clapped him on the shoulder, and he turned to see his uncle Alphonse grinning at him. "What the hell are you doing here, squirt?"

Lewis felt relieved to see him. "I came with Marvin, Rosalyn and Loretta. We were supposed to go to the drive-in, but Marvin wanted to come here instead."

"Where is that girl of yours?"

"Bathroom."

Alphonse grabbed Lewis by the arm and nodded to a woman standing at the bottom of the stairs as she took a light from another smoker in a crowd. "Uh-oh, here comes trouble. And looks like she's loaded for bear."

The woman smiled, showing deep dimples, then shifted her weight to a shapely leg as she brought up the other to give her thigh a quick scratch. Even her knee had a dimple. Lewis saw what his uncle meant. Her tight black dress clung to her perfectly rounded bottom and when she glanced up into the hall, Lewis recognized the self-assured arrogance of a woman who knew she was good-looking and men couldn't help but stare at her, and women too. She had an edge to her, as if she was here for reasons other than to dance. With her nipples poking at the thin material of her dress and threatening to break through, it was obvious she wasn't wearing a brassiere. She wore a silver chain and cross that sat tucked in the valley of her breasts, and her right hand sported a large ring. Lewis wondered how a woman could look so stunning and dangerous at the same time.

"That's Lily Edwards herself, Tiger Lily, heat lightning in a dress. At the start of the night, she can be fun, but all you gotta do is add booze and wait. Then she turns crazy. I know what she can do. Once when I came out of the Kal Hotel, I seen this guy had her in the back seat of his car and was just a'giving it to her. But then he got a little rough. Know what she did? She bit off the end of his ear. He was screaming his head off and she was laughing with blood on her teeth. Looked like a goddamn vampire. I'll bet when you get her bare-assed in bed and ready to go, it's like calling for the chute gate at a rodeo. They say her cherry is pushed back so far she uses it for a tail light. She likes the younger ones, though, so I guess I'll never have the pleasure."

Lily dropped her cigarette, ground it out with a high heel and climbed the stairs. Stepping into the hall, she saw Alphonse and came toward him like a wolf eyeing prey. Lewis felt thrilled and uneasy. "Hello, Alphonse, you old mink. How's she hanging?"

"Fair to middlin', good for diddlin'."

She gave a short laugh, then her eyes fixed on Lewis. "Well," she said. "Look at you."

"Take it easy, Lily. He's just a teenager," Alphonse said.

"That's exactly how I like 'em." She stepped close, and then closer, her breasts bulging as she pushed into Lewis, her nipples digging into his chest. Lewis felt a swelling in the front of his pants.

"Lewis?"

A small voice sounded from behind him. It was Loretta and her eyes went immediately to Lily's chest. "What are you doing? And who is this?"

Lewis stammered. "I . . ."

"She's a friend of mine," Alphonse interrupted.

"I'm no friend of yours," Lily said, "but I sure could get friendly with this boy."

Alphonse pushed his way in front of her. "Okay, you had your fun, now get outta here. Go find somebody else."

"Bye-bye," she whispered to Lewis and walked away.

"Holy cow, Lewis, is that a hard-on?" Loretta asked, staring. People nearby heard her and looked over to see for themselves. She left him standing there with his hands covering his crotch as onlookers and dancers giggled.

Alphonse turned his nephew toward the wall and backhanded him between his legs.

"Ow! Jesus. That hurt for chrissakes!"

"Only way I know how to kill it quick. Boy, you gotta make sure that don't happen again. Pull your shirt outta your belt and let it hang down so nobody can see it. Yeah, like that. Come on, let's go get us a beer and let your face cool down a bit."

Alphonse placed his hand on Lewis's shoulder and walked him to his car. Lewis sat slumped while Alphonse grabbed two beers from the case behind his seat and opened them. He handed one to Lewis, who drank the entire bottle without stopping.

"Boy, I never seen you do that, even with pop. You really are washing your troubles away."

"I didn't know I had a hard-on," Lewis said. "Jeez. What's wrong with me?"

"Tiger Lily is what's wrong with you. She does that to guys. Somebody could park a truck on your pisser and she'd come along and you'd lift that sucker up like a hydraulic jack. You're not the first horny dog this happened to."

Lewis rested his cheek against the cool window.

"Now listen up, lover boy. Your mom is coming back next Sunday, so if I was you, I'd let that beer work its magic and then get right back in there and have some fun while you can. I done a lot worse things than that."

After Alphonse closed the door and walked away, Lewis was thankful to be by himself. He finished off another beer, leaned back against the seat and closed his eyes. Suddenly, he was jerked awake by the sound of someone yelling. When he sat up, he saw there were a lot more people at the dance now—the noise coming from the hall was so loud he could barely hear the music. He wondered how long he had been asleep.

He needed to pee but couldn't face going back inside the hall to use the bathroom. After taking a good look around, he got out and stood behind the open car door so he wouldn't be seen. When he finished, he gave a shiver, pulled up his zipper and turned around. Lily Edwards watched from ten feet away, her hands on her hips, feet planted wide. Light from the dance hall behind her lit her shapely legs and hips through her dress. She said, "I been looking all over for you and here you are in the dark just waiting for me."

She came over to him, pushing the passenger door closed and opening the rear door. "Get in."

"What?"

"I said, get in the car."

"What for?"

Lily grabbed Lewis and pushed him so hard he fell back on the car seat. When he tried to sit up, she climbed on him and held him down by his shoulders. "Now you just stay down there, sunshine. Don't you move now."

She stepped back out of the car and lifted her dress over her head. Her full breasts hung up in the material for a split second, releasing and falling down with a single bounce. All the while her hot eyes were on him.

And Lewis couldn't take his eyes off her. He was seeing what he had only dreamed about. She dropped her dress and panties on the floor of the car, then, working quickly, she unbuckled his belt, grabbed his pants and underwear as one and yanked them down. Then she took hold of his *spalq*, her cool fingers squeezing gently, expertly, stroking him slowly until he was hard. Positioning herself above Lewis, she eased herself down. Then he was inside her. Lewis let out a groan.

"You like that, don'tcha. Now don't just lay there and make me do all the work. Let's see that horse buck around a bit."

As if out of his control, his hips began moving.

"Yeah, like that. Attaboy. Oh yeah, yeah, yeah."

Every story his uncle had told him hadn't prepared Lewis for what was happening now. Not a single naked picture in his dog-eared *Playboy* came close. Alphonse had unloaded all his knowledge about sex on him, whether he wanted to hear it or not, and he could hear his uncle's voice in his head as if coaching him on.

"When you get to the vinegar stroke, you wanna squeeze your ass cheeks together. It'll damn near blow your head off."

Lewis couldn't take his eyes off her breasts.

"Well, don't just stare at 'em," Lily said, grabbing his hands and placing them where they both wanted them to be. "Squeeze them together until the nipples touch and get that tongue going. Do I have to tell you everything?" Lewis had fantasized about having sex with an older woman who would show him all the different methods and positions, and now here he was, a willing hostage, seduced and ridden bareback. Roland and Clay should see him now.

Suddenly he let out a groan as if in great pain and knew he was close to the vinegar stroke. When he came, he felt like he had been jabbed with a cattle prod. His temples throbbed and then a rushing sound like a waterfall boomed in his ears, his toes curled under, and he squeezed his ass cheeks together.

Lily laughed at the faces he made, but continued rocking back and forth, strange animal sounds coming from her throat, her movements becoming faster. Lewis wondered how he could still be hard. Finally, she let out her own long groan, quivered and shook like a wet horse, rolling her hips and pushing her breasts into Lewis's face. Then she bent down and kissed him, forcing her tongue inside his mouth, her sharp nails dragging through his hair. The scent of bare bodies, mixed with the aroma of perfume, stale beer, sweat and ass, bloomed with a sweet and sour funk. She continued to roll her hips and he felt himself rising up to a place even higher than before, and he came inside her again. Crashing down to earth, he realized he had been holding his breath. As he gasped for air, Lily bent down until he felt her hot breath on his neck. Then she bit his ear.

His hand went up. "Ow! What are you doing?" He looked and there was blood on his fingers.

"Marking my territory."

She sat up and leaned to grab her dress. Lifting it over her head, she let it go and it fell down, settling onto her body like a second skin. She backed out of the car, picked her panties off the floor and slipped them on. After adjusting herself under her tight clothing, she produced a pack of cigarettes from somewhere in her dress, opened it and drew one out. A wooden match fell out of the pack to the ground, and she picked it up and lit it with her thumbnail. She took a long draw and released the smoke out her nose. Looking at Lewis, she said, "I don't even know your name."

"Lewis."

"Lewis who?"

"Toma."

"Toma?" she said with a smirk. "You're Jimmy's boy from Salmon River? Grace is your mom?"

"Yeah."

Her mouth curved into a wide smile. For a second she looked as if she was trying her hardest to hold it back, but then she broke into a long fit of laughter.

"What's so damn funny?" Lewis asked, embarrassed she was laughing at him.

When Lily managed to calm herself, she wiped the tears from her face. "I know your dad," she said. "Boy, I don't know why I didn't see it before, but you sure look like him. Maybe I'll come pick you up sometime and we can do this again. What do you say?"

"Mom would whip me first and then she'd come for you."

"I think you're right, Lewis Toma. I think she would."

Then she ambled away toward the far side of the hall, where she vanished into the darkness like a ghost. As he staggered out of the back seat, he heard her laughing.

"Lewis? What the hell. I've been looking all over the place for you. It's time to go."

Turning, he saw Marvin in front of the car. Lewis wasn't sure if he should tell his cousin what happened. Then Marvin began sniffing. "Is that . . . ? Is that smell what I think it is? You been slapping bellies with somebody? Was it Loretta?"

"No."

"Well, who? You don't know anybody here, so what the hell?"

Lewis hesitated, then said, "Lily. A woman called Lily."

"Lily? You nailed Tiger Lily? When I was talking with Hank, she walked right by us and he told me who she was. Holy shit, how in the hell did . . ."

Marvin stopped talking and a look of panic came over his face.

"You can't get into our car smelling like that. I saw a hose and tap at the front of the hall, but we don't have any soap. Damn. We're in deep trouble if we can't come up with a way to get rid of that smell. Let's get to the car. Come on, hurry."

Weaving around the parked cars and trucks, they ran to the station wagon. Lewis looked back as loud shouting broke out at the hall entrance. Rosalyn and Loretta stood among a crowd, watching a young man pummel a bigger man to the ground. Then the young man walked over to Loretta and they hugged and kissed. Lewis took a step toward them, but Marvin grabbed his arm and pulled him back. He opened the door and snatched the tree air freshener off the rear-view mirror.

"What are you going to do with that?" Lewis asked.

Marvin began rubbing it on Lewis's crotch.

"Hey, quit that. Give it here."

After Lewis was done, Marvin took the air freshener from him and shoved it inside Lewis's pants. "There, I think we did it," he said. "But I better check." Marvin dropped to a knee and began sniffing the front of Lewis's jeans. He looked up at Lewis. "You smell like a Christmas tree in a hoor house. I don't know if this is going to work."

"Marvin, what the hell are you doing?" Rosalyn asked as she and Loretta appeared out of the dark.

"What does it look like?" Marvin said, looking serious. "He said he's never had a blow job before."

Lewis pushed Marvin away. "Jesus, Marvin, what's wrong with you? I was having a beer with Alphonse and I spilled some on my pants. We didn't want your mom and dad to smell it, so Marvin had this big idea that his air freshener would cover it up." *Another lie. I'm getting good at this.*

"Well, did it?" Rosalyn asked.

Marvin said, "Smells pretty good but there's still something I can't place. Why don't you take a whiff."

"Don't you dare," Lewis shouted. "Let's get outta here. I seen enough crazy people tonight."

Rosalyn and Marvin laughed but Loretta stayed quiet.

Lewis asked, "Who was that guy you were with, Loretta?"

Before she could answer, a car pulled up beside them and the young man waved out the window. "Bye, Loretta. It was sure good to see you again."

Loretta smiled and gave a small wave back.

Lewis went to get into the back seat with Loretta, but Rosalyn pulled him close and said, "I think you're safer up front. And you really stink. Oof."

As he slid into the front seat, Marvin leaned over and whispered, "A dirty old dog. That's what you are."

Lewis turned his face away as a car started up on the road by the graveyard. The driver floored the gas pedal and the exhaust pipes roared as the car drove up to the dance hall. The hood was painted with flames and ornamented with a naked woman in chrome, her arms reaching out behind her and her long hair trailing off into the wind. The aerial stood six feet above the fender, with a raccoon tail attached at the top. The driver honked the horn, opened his door and stepped out. Even though it had been years since he had seen him, Lewis recognized his father immediately. Jimmy whistled to someone in the darkness, then yelled, "Come on, for Chrissakes. We got a long way to go. I told you to be ready."

A woman appeared out of the darkness. "Don't you whistle at me," she said angrily. "I'm not your damn dog." As she walked into the glaring headlights, hips swaying, Lewis saw it was Lily Edwards. His father stood looking around as though wondering which of his prized possessions the other men and boys admired most, his car or his woman.

Lewis watched Lily get into the car. He rolled down his window to get a good look at his father, and Lily saw him. As Jimmy drove by, she gave a little wave of her fingers and blew him a kiss. He could feel Loretta's eyes on his back.

CHAPTER 19

AFTER WIPING THE CRUMBS OFF THE TABLE, Grace ran the water until it felt warm, rinsed the rag and squeezed it out before draping it over the kitchen tap. She looked out the window above the sink at the telephone poles, their sagging wires cluttering the view of the sky. Rooftops stretched out toward the packing plant where she and Isabel spent each day sorting apples until their backs ached. Because Isabel and her ex-husband Ray had spent their working lives picking fruit, Isabel knew so many people in the fruit business she had no trouble finding them work at the packing plant. Even though they joked and laughed with the other workers every day, it was nice to walk into their little house at night and close the door on the rest of the world.

She slid up the window and propped a stick under the sash. As cool air and the sound of children playing somewhere drifted inside, her thoughts were drawn back to her home at Salmon River. She imagined herself watching the trees along the river moving in the wind and the scent of blossoming Saskatoon and mock-orange bushes coming in her window.

She looked around her temporary home, at the pink bathtub with matching toilet and sink, at the kitchen with its white fridge and electric stove and yellow cupboards. She enjoyed the luxury of it all, but still missed crawling into bed and falling asleep to the swish of the wind in the trees. Even though to some people her house was little more than a shack that couldn't keep out the winter cold or the summer heat, it was where she had raised her children.

Her little boy, Eddie, had loved playing outside and explored every inch of the ground around their home. When he came to the edge of the dark forest, he always stopped, as if deciding whether to go any farther. But his curiosity would eventually win him over and he'd disappear into the woods. She once heard him crying when he couldn't find his way back out, but left him in there a few minutes longer so maybe next time he wouldn't go in as far.

After Lewis was big enough, he and Eddie loved to play hide-and-seek. How they laughed when one found the other. Eddie was so good to his little brother that he would hide in the same place so Lewis was able to find him every time.

Shaking her head, Grace pushed away her memories, shoved the chairs under the table and swept the floor.

Isabel called, "Come on outside, it's too warm in there."

Grace put away the broom and joined her friend on the porch. They sat on two chairs, facing down the path to the road. For a few minutes they made small talk about little things, but Grace couldn't get Eddie out of her mind. She felt sad and before the tears could come, she stood up quickly. "I just have to get moving or I'll go crazy."

Grace went into her bedroom and picked up her purse. As she walked out the door, Isabel called after her, "Want some company?"

Grace looked back. "I'm not running away to do something stupid. I won't be very long."

Isabel watched from the porch as Grace turned a corner and was gone.

Saturday afternoon in Oroville felt like a Sunday to Grace. Boys kicked a ball back and forth as a group of girls played skip rope in front of the small houses that lined the street where fruit pickers or packing house workers stayed until the seasonal work was finished. Their laughter and loud voices filled the air. Just up ahead a young boy sitting in the dirt at the side of the road struggled to put a bike chain back on his upturned bike. He looked up at Grace with a frustrated expression as she came nearer. "I can't do this," the boy said.

Grace stopped. "What's the matter?"

The boy threw a crescent wrench on the ground. "This stupid bike. My grandpa told me I had to fix it myself, but I can't." He rubbed his eyes with grease-stained fists as Grace bent down and placed her purse on the ground. She had no idea what to do, but figuring out how to fix things on her own was something she was used to. The boy picked up the loose chain. "It goes on here," he said, touching the rear sprocket.

Grace fitted the chain on the sprocket teeth and turned the wheel pedal, and the chain clicked into place. "What's your name?" she asked.

"Norman."

"Hand me that wrench, Norman."

The boy picked the wrench out of the dust and handed it over to Grace. She tightened the chain, then stood and flipped the bike back on its wheels. The boy put the wrench in his pocket and grabbed the handlebar.

"This is a funny-looking rig, isn't it?" Grace said.

The boy jumped on the long seat, smiling. "Don't you know anything? It's a banana bike. My grandpa gave it to me."

Grace had a vague recollection that, at this boy's age, Eddie had been after her for a bike. "Can you do a wheelie?"

The boy pedalled away as fast as he could and pulled back on the handlebars, but the front wheels stayed on the road. The boy kept going. Grace heard the grinding chain and the boy's laughter as he turned down an alley out of sight, and she smiled.

Old men playing cards in a small park hardly noticed her as she walked by. When she came to the Ben Prince's store, she opened the heavy glass door with her shoulder and went inside. The space was huge, bigger than any store back in Vernon. There were sale signs everywhere, with shoppers loading their carts and hand baskets. She went to the beer cooler and pulled out a twelve-pack of Schlitz. She recognized two of her fellow workers in the line beside her, held up her hand and rolled her fingers their way. After grabbing a pack of Camel cigarettes off the shelf and placing them beside the beer, Grace paid the cashier and walked out the door.

As she came to their little house, she spotted Isabel still sitting on the porch.

Isabel waved at her. "What you got there?" she called.

"The cure for tears is smokes and beers."

Isabel laughed. "I just boiled water to make tea, but a beer sounds good."

Grace went inside and put the beer in the fridge. She took out two bottles, cracked them open, then went back outside and sat in her chair, handing a beer to her friend. She took a long swallow. "I just saw a little boy who reminded me of Eddie. He was almost crying because his bike broke, so I helped him. I don't know why, but I feel a lot better. On the way back, I thought of how our luck keeps going up and down. When we first came to Oroville, I wasn't sure if we did the right thing stopping here. Then you got us jobs in the packing house and found us this house."

Isabel said, "We make more money here than we would berry-picking down in Yakima. And we don't have to work out in the hot sun all day or come in from the field and cook on a wood stove that heats up the place so bad it never cools down. Down there, you get killed by the heat, one way or another."

Grace sipped her beer. "You're right, Izzy. It sure is nice to get under that shower at the end of the day. I never felt so good in my life. But tomorrow we head back to Salmon River and leave all this behind. Can you imagine if my boys grew up in a place like this? We could walk to the store to get groceries and they could go to the show every Saturday."

"I know, Grace, but we can have all of this up there—that's why we're here. You remember what Cookie said about giving him the rest of the money. Well, we did that and maybe they put the septic tank in the ground and a hot water tank for the bathroom by now. The new addition is all finished and you'll have the plumbing in the new bathroom and a sink in the kitchen with a drain instead of a bowl you have to carry outside to empty. Cookie knows you'll be on his ass all the way to the end, and he's probably hoping you'll leave him alone once the renovations are done."

"Fat chance of that. But maybe the world up there won't look so bad after a good hot shower."

A car stopped in front of the house, stirring up a cloud of dust on the bone-dry road. A woman stepped out and waved. "Is that Mabel?" Isabel said. "Oh no, see that look on her face? Something bad happened and she can't wait to tell us all the gory details. The goddamn grim reaper is what she is and she does it all with that shit-eating grin."

"Come on, Isabel. Be nice."

Isabel stood and placed her hands on her hips. "Hello, Mabel. How did you track us down?"

"I saw my cousin Annie, and she told me where you were staying."

"I hope you don't have bad news. You don't, do you?" Grace asked.

"Nobody died but it's not the best news either. I just came from Vernon. I think you should know what your ex is up to."

Grace took a big swallow of her beer.

"Here, Mabel, sit down and I'll get another chair." Isabel said. "Want a beer or a cuppa tea?"

"Beer? No, I don't drink this time of day. Tea would be good."

Isabel walked into the house, shaking her head.

"What's this about Jimmy?"

Mabel brushed off the seat and sat down. Grace noticed she had her hair permed into tight black curls. Mabel had always tried to look her best in the clothes she bought at the Salvation Army store. But somebody should tell her to wash them before she wore them. She looked nice but smelled musty. "I guess he was down at Six-Mile talking to his cousin, the chief. It looks like he's planning to move onto your place. He said the land is his now by law."

Grace could feel her body tighten but held her tongue and listened.

"The thing is, he's mixed up with some pretty bad people out of Seattle."

"What do you mean?"

"That's what we heard. People are saying he's with these guys stealing cars and selling the parts across the border up into Vancouver. Jimmy is such a good mechanic he can strip a car down to the axles in no time, and he makes good money. They say he's walking around thinking he's king shit, spending money like its water. You should see his car. He put a fancy paint job on it with a big aerial, chrome reverse rims and fender skirts. I don't even know what those things are, but my brother Alfred says they might as well be made of gold. You should hear what all the guys are saying. They think Jimmy's a big show-off."

"I don't care about his car, Mabel. What did you hear about him moving up to Salmon River?"

Isabel set a cup of tea, some milk and the sugar bowl on the table, and Mabel added a heaping spoonful of sugar and stirred. Then she picked up the cup and held it in front of her mouth like a microphone.

"Alfred was sitting in the Kal Hotel having a beer and he heard Jimmy talking to this guy. 'Never mind about my old lady,' Jimmy said to him. 'The chief is gonna take care of that. We can build a shop on that spot close to the river, like I told you, and people won't even see us. I sent my guys up there to get started, but Grace's brother took a shot at them, and now they won't go back until this land thing is done. All I'm waiting on is the chief. He's been working at it for a year now and he said in a month it would be signed over to me. When that's done, we can do the shop and then you can bring me new cars every week and the parts will be there waiting for you a couple days later. Nobody is doing that up here. If her brother shows up, you can put a bullet in him, for all I care. He's your problem.'"

Isabel stood in the doorway watching Grace.

Mabel paused and took a sip of tea. "Alfred said Jimmy told the guy the best way to get the parts into Canada was through the Nighthawk border crossing because the guards go home early and there isn't anybody there at night.

"Everybody knows what Jimmy did to you," Mabel said to Grace. "Now that he has all these scary guys behind him, he thinks he can do whatever he wants. Every Saturday night, him and his woman are at the Pastime Tavern downtown here, buying rounds like big shots, and he walks around like he owns the place."

Mabel finished her tea and wiped a drop from her chin with the back of her hand. "That's all I know, Grace. If I hear anything else, I'll let you know as soon as I can."

She stood to go, then paused. "Well, there is something else, but it's not about Jimmy. It's about his woman, Lily Edwards. People were talking about something that happened at the Head of the Lake dance last Saturday."

"Lily? He's got Lily with him? Jeez, he really must have a lot of money if he managed to end up with her," Grace said.

"Oh yeah and—"

Isabel interrupted. "I don't think Grace needs to hear anything about Jimmy's woman. She's got enough to think about. So come on, Mabel, thanks, but maybe it's time you hit the road."

Mabel stood. "Bye, Grace. Wish it could've been better news but like I said, we thought you needed to know."

"See you, Mabel," Grace said.

As Isabel walked Mabel to her car, Grace went inside. Rinsing Mabel's cup, she heard voices rising and then a loud thump.

"Yeah, see you around Mabel," Isabel shouted.

A car door slammed and the engine started, then tires spun in the dirt.

Grace sat at the kitchen table with her arms folded tightly, her heel bouncing up and down. Isabel came in.

"What was all that hollering about?" Grace asked.

"That woman gets me going every time. I just don't like her and I told her. Jeez, I'm ready for another beer." She went to the small refrigerator and took out two more bottles. The beer hissed when she popped the caps. "Here, Grace. I think we both need this."

Grace took a sip while Isabel drank half of hers and let out a belch.

"Izzy, it seems like every time something good happens to me, Jimmy comes along and ruins it. What did I ever do to deserve that?"

"You married him."

Grace nodded. "I guess that's it. I married him and did all this to myself. It feels so different when you're young and you meet a good-looking guy who can charm the pants off you and likes to dance and is always smiling and makes you feel like you're the luckiest person in the world. How do you know what's coming for you when it starts like that?"

"You don't know, Grace. Nobody does. We were all young and pretty once, and all we wanted was a good time. Look at my ex, Ray, he was the same. God, when he smiled at me, it made me weak in the knees, and then one day, without me noticing, he turned into an asshole that forgot how to smile. It's my own fault for not being smart enough to run for the hills sooner. But what is it that makes guys on the reserve end up so mad at the world they walk around with a miserable face you gotta look at all day?"

"I don't know. Maybe when I'm a hundred I'll have it all figured out. But I can't wait until then to do something about Jimmy. It's hard to believe he could be worse than before, and now he thinks he can just waltz in and take over my place. Well, he's got another think coming. I always wonder if Eddie would still be around if I didn't take Jimmy back after the first time I kicked him out."

Isabel nodded. "Sure, we would be better off if Jimmy hadda dropped dead years ago, but there's nothing we can do about the past. Now is now, Grace. If the chief says he can move onto your land, there isn't much you can do about it."

Grace bit her fingernail. "I know exactly what I should do. Grab my gun and put a bullet right between his eyes, because he's never going to go away and he won't stop until he takes everything from me."

Isabel shook her head. "That's the worst thing you could do. If you did that, you'd end up in prison. Think about Lewis. You won't be around for him when he needs you and then you won't be able to see your grandkids. No, there's a better way—we just have to figure out what it is. Maybe get a lawyer or something, I don't know."

Grace pushed her chair back and rushed to the closet. She searched around inside her purse, cursing and talking to herself. When she came back, she was smiling and holding up a key. "I knew I kept this for a reason. This here is Jimmy's car key—I got a copy made up when we were still together. I got an idea what we can do with it. Mabel said Jimmy and Lily go to the Pastime Tavern every Saturday night, so why don't we get packed up now and head on home tonight. We'll wait outside the tavern and when everybody is inside celebrating with him, we steal his dream car. I'll drive it across the border through Nighthawk and park the car in Kelowna, right in front of the Willow Inn. There's outlaws and car thieves hanging around there, and I'll leave the key in it to make it easy for them. Some guy will think he won the Irish Sweepstakes and he'll drive it away. You just have to drive across the border with all our stuff and pick me up. What do you think? That bastard will bawl his eyes out when he sees his car is gone."

"That sounds like a plan, Grace. But it's only going to put him off for a little bit longer. With the money he's making, all he's gotta do is go buy another one, and then what?"

Grace waved her hands as if shooing away the words. "We can figure that out later. Maybe we tell the cops what he's up to, but first, let's have a little fun. Let's piss him off."

"You can be such a devil when you put your mind to something, can't you?"

Grace laughed. "You bet. And you know what else? I gotta thank Mabel and her big mouth. He would have had that shop up on my land and we'd never have seen it coming. So you know what?" Grace picked up her beer and held it high in a toast. "Here's to you, Mabel, at the same old table."

CHAPTER 20

ISABEL PULLED THE CAR OVER and parked under a tree, just out of the glare of the street lamp. On the sidewalk a skinny cat with a bird or a mouse dangling from its mouth eyed them closely. Then a large truck rumbled past carrying a load of creaking vegetable crates, frightening the cat into a bush. Just down the street was the Pastime Tavern, a neon Olympia Beer sign gracing the large window, the *L* blinking off and on. Whenever a person went in or came out of the tavern, the shouts and laughter spilled out the open door. Grace said, "If there's one thing Jimmy likes, it's attention, even if he has to pay for it. He'll be here."

They watched a man come out of the tavern and turn up the quiet street in their direction. He stopped to take a long drag of his cigarette then flicked the butt onto the road. Jamming his hands into his pockets, he hunched his shoulders and walked with his head still, eyes scanning. He noticed their car in the shadows and slowed for a moment to look it over, then carried on.

"Now there's a jailbird if I ever seen one," Grace exclaimed. "You know who that is? That's Lazar Alexander. Remember him? Looks like he's just out of prison and getting some fresh air before he goes right back inside again. He's a bad one.

I heard somebody owed him some money and wouldn't pay him, so he burned the guy's house down."

"I remember him," Isabel said. "When I was younger, boy, did he ever have a hard-on for me. He was always there at a dance watching me, even when we were kids. He'd look at me with his tongue hanging out, the creep. You remember that, don't you?"

"I sure do. Alphonse said Lazar spent so much time in solitary he got to like it. Sometimes he'll be in there for a month all by himself. I seen that jailbird shuffle before when somebody on the reserve gets out after doing some hard time. They're always on the lookout because they don't trust anybody." Grace lit a cigarette and took a drag. The glowing tip lit her face.

"How do you know so much about people just by looking at them?" Isabel said. "You're like Mandrake. I bet you can almost read their minds."

"Maybe the reserve is my prison and I'm in for life."

The tavern door opened again and this time a woman in tight jeans stepped out. She crossed her arms and looked down the street one way and then up the other. She put her hands on her hips, took a last look around, then went back inside.

"Was that Lily Edwards?" Grace asked.

"That's her for sure. Jeez. No wonder she drives the men crazy. Looks like she's waiting for Jimmy."

"Nothing we can do but wait, I guess. God, I just sounded like my mom." Grace took the spare car key from her purse and turned it over in her fingers. "I sure miss my mom sometimes. She could make me feel safe just looking at me. I remember talking to her before she died about how long it was taking to get the house fixed up, and she said, 'Nothing we can do but wait, I guess.' She was right. But even she would be surprised

I'm still waiting. I know what people mean now when they say they're in the poor house."

"Aw, Grace, we're all in the same boat. That's what living on the reserve does. All you want is a home where your kids are safe and you got enough food to eat and the police watch out for you when some mean guy with a grudge comes along and takes it out on you. But that's just a dream for us. Hell, when I was thirteen, my mom nailed my window shut to keep the men from getting at me. Can you imagine that? And when I was little, she always said to never sit on a man's lap, no matter who he was. Men, hah. They're only good for one thing and they're not even good at that."

"What time is it getting to be? Feels like we been here a while."

Grace pulled a watch with a broken strap out of her purse. "It's nine thirty. If he doesn't show up in half an hour, let's hit the road. We can't wait all night."

Isabel tapped the steering wheel. "Where the hell is he?"

Just then a car slowed down and turned up the street, exhaust pipes snapping. Jimmy's flashy car drove past and pulled into the parking lot.

"Finally," Grace said.

Jimmy stepped out of the car, locked the door and pocketed the keys. He made his way toward the tavern, stopping briefly under a street light next to a little shop to glance in the window and adjust his hair.

"Did you see that, Izzy? He was admiring himself. What a prick."

"What do we do now?"

"After I take his car, we can get out of here."

"I'm scared, Grace. What if we get caught?"

Grace opened the door, got out of the car and pulled the key from her pocket. "All you have to do is get yourself to the Willow Inn. I'll meet you there in two hours."

"Awww, Jesus."

Grace crossed the road, unlocked Jimmy's car and slipped into the driver's seat. When she put the key into the ignition and started the engine, the exhaust pipes barked and growled. She turned to Isabel to give her a smile and a wave that all was going well and saw her friend beating the steering wheel with her fists, mouthing soundless words and pointing at a man casually coming up the sidewalk.

Grace watched him come closer and closer until he walked under a moth-clouded street light. It was Jimmy. When he broke into a run, Grace stepped on the clutch, shifted into reverse and floored the gas, but her foot slipped off the clutch and the car stalled. In a panic, she pumped the gas pedal as the starter rolled and rolled. The engine flooded and the car refused to start. She looked up as a shadow loomed at the window. Yanking the door open, Jimmy reached inside and seized her by the arm. "Jesus Christ, Grace. Is that you? What the hell?"

Grace shook his hand off, slid over to the passenger side, opened the door and stepped out. Jimmy grabbed a lighter off the dash. "Good thing I came back for this, ain't it? Were you really gonna steal my car?"

Grace walked around to the rear of the car and waited for Jimmy. He came toward her with his thumbs hooked into his Levi's, casually chewing gum. A pack of Lucky Strike cigarettes sat tucked in the sleeve of his white T-shirt. When he was three feet from her, he blew a bubble until it popped, then gathered the gum back into his mouth with his tongue.

"I got every reason to beat the shit outta you," he said.

The fear Grace had felt a moment ago left her. "I was going to take your car and set it on fire just to piss you off, but you went and spoiled everything, just like you always do. So why don't you go ahead and show me what a tough guy you are. But this time you're going to lose an eye or I'll bite off that nose of yours. Look at you, standing there trying to look like a teenager. Gawd, I can smell the Brylcreem from here."

Jimmy spit the gum into his hand and tossed it over Grace's head. "Yep, there's that smart mouth of yours. You always kept going at me until you made me so mad I'd have to shut you up. But I'm not like that anymore, so don't waste your time. I don't need to worry about anything ever again because now I got all the money I need."

He pulled out his wallet and opened it so Grace could see the thick wad of bills inside. "That's three hundred and fifty dollars, Grace. You never seen that much in one place in your life, did you?"

Grace harrumphed. "Big deal. You'll never have enough in there for me anyway."

"What's that supposed to mean?"

"You stole the ring that was supposed to get us five hundred dollars that you knew was to fix up the house."

"I needed it."

"For what?"

Jimmy shrugged. "Things. I dunno."

"Things? You really are stupid, aren't you? Do you even know that your son Eddie has been missing for two years?"

Jimmy didn't speak.

"You did know, didn't you?"

Jimmy crossed his arms. "What was I supposed to do? Come up and hold your hand? He probably left because of you anyway."

"You really make me sick, but if that's how you're gonna talk to me, I'll tell you that I promised my dead baby girl that if I ever came across you in a dark alley, I'd kill you. I'm going to keep that promise. Maybe it won't happen here, but I'll find you. You'll never be able to keep me down again."

Jimmy held out his wallet to Grace. "I don't need to stand here and listen to you. If it's money you want, then take everything that's in here."

Grace shook her head. "Why are you being so generous?"

"For Chrissakes, just take the money. That'll square us up and we can leave each other alone."

Grace pointed to the cigarette pack in his T-shirt. "You were up there in my field having a look around, weren't you?"

"So?"

"So stop dirtying my ground and pick up your butts next time. I also heard you're planning on moving onto my land and setting up shop for your crooked friends."

Jimmy grinned and put his hands up. "You caught me. I sent some people up there, sure. But it's not your land anymore, Grace. It's mine. The chief told me the Indian Act sez so."

"The Indian Act? Fuck the Indian Act. If you move up to Salmon River, that'll be the last thing you'll ever do. Maybe I'll wait until you're asleep, then I'll come on in and cut your throat and you won't feel a thing. Or maybe I should just waltz into the Pastime right now and tell all the people you buy drinks for that you're a thief and a baby killer."

Grace heard a car door slam and looked over to see Isabel hurrying toward them. "Come on, Grace, let's get outta here. Both of you should stop talking before somebody gets hurt."

Jimmy said, "I'm trying to help her out, but she don't want nothing to do with it. She's mean right down to her bones. She won't stop bellyaching until we go at 'er."

Isabel tugged at Grace's arm. "You said what you wanted to say. Now let's go."

The noise of a shoe turning on gravel made them look toward the street. A man stood on the sidewalk watching them. "Isabel? Is that you?" he called.

It took Isabel a few seconds to realize who it was. "Lazar?"

His thin, stringy hair hung down past his shoulders, and he was bald from the ears up. He said, "Jeez, it is you. I haven't seen you since I don't know when. Boy, you're looking good." He glanced at the other two squared off facing each other. "What's going on here? Need any help?"

"Grace was just having a little talk with her ex, but we're going now, right, Grace?"

Grace stared hard at Jimmy. He held out his wallet again. "Last chance."

When she reached for the money, Jimmy snatched the wallet away. "Kiss my ass."

She lunged at him, striking him hard on the face. Jimmy staggered back and wiped his mouth with his hand. He took two quick steps and slapped Grace. It was as loud as if someone set off a firecracker. Isabel took hold of his shoulders to pull him away, but his T-shirt ripped. Without looking back, Jimmy threw an elbow to her forehead, dropping her to the ground. He grabbed Grace by the front of her blouse and backed her up against the car as she kicked and struggled. "I tried to tell you to stop. See what happens when you don't listen?"

Eyes narrowed, growling with rage, Grace dug her nails into his face.

"Ow, Jesus," Jimmy said, letting go. She came for him again, and he grabbed her by the neck this time and banged her head on the trunk, once, twice, like he was pounding a drum.

"Stop that!" Isabel was on her feet again, trying to pull Jimmy away.

Then came a loud crack. Jimmy's legs collapsed, and he dropped to the ground. Lazar tossed a heavy piece of scrap lumber into the bush at the corner of the parking lot and stood looking down at Jimmy. He had landed with his legs oddly twisted under him. Lazar reached over with his foot and nudged Jimmy. There was no reaction.

"What the hell, you killed him!" Isabel shouted.

"No. He's just out cold. He shouldn't a' hit you, Isabel."

"He sure looks dead to me. What do you think, Grace?"

Grace couldn't look away from the still figure lying on the ground.

"Is this his car?" Lazar asked, and Isabel nodded.

"Help me get him into the back seat. I'll take him down to the hospital and drop him off. I was looking for a way to leave town anyway–I got a warrant out for me. I'll take his car and dump it somewhere across the line."

Grace, so used to knowing what to do, stood there confused, her brain unable to sort out what had just happened. Isabel shook her by the shoulders. "Hey, we gotta get him outta here." She pointed to Jimmy. Grace forced herself to bend down and take a hold of Jimmy. When Lazar opened the back door, all three managed to lift him inside.

"Just a minute," Grace said. She dug around Jimmy's pockets and pulled out his keys. Then she saw his wallet where it had fallen to the ground, opened it and took out all the cash except for a fifty-dollar bill. She handed the wallet and keys to Lazar. "That's the best I can do, Lazar. Now when you get across the border, you get rid of this car, and I don't want to see you again. Got that?"

Isabel said, "Thanks for helping us out."

"I'd do anything for you, Isabel. But before I go, how about a kiss, for old times' sake?"

"What?"

Grace said, "Oh, go on and do it, Izzy, so we can get the hell outta here."

Lazar's eyes scanned Isabel's body, his hands shaking as if he couldn't wait to touch her. He hadn't shaved in days and the creases on his jeans were black, as if they had never been in a washing machine, and his crooked smile showed horse-sized, shit-coloured teeth.

"All right," Isabel said with a sigh. "If that's what you want."

"When I was alone in my bunk in jail, I used to think of you."

Isabel stepped toward him and closed her eyes. Lazar grabbed her ass and pulled her closer, sticking his tongue into her mouth, groaning. When he brought his hands up to her breasts, she broke away. "Okay, that's enough."

Grace turned Lazar's head away from Isabel so he could pay attention to what she had to say. "If people ask you if you saw us any time tonight, you say you didn't, right? Just do what you said and get rid of this car."

"Okay, he said, his eyes staying on Isabel as the two women dashed across the street.

Inside the car, Isabel shuddered, making a face. "Yuck," she said. "Like kissing ass."

A mile out of town, Grace tossed the spare key out the window.

CHAPTER 21

FOR A WEEK Lewis had found no comfort in his bed and tonight was no different. He tossed from side to side for what felt like hours, with his cousin kicking and elbowing him whenever he rolled onto his side of the bed. "Go to sleep, dammit," Marvin snapped. Lewis eventually fell into a restless slumber.

The next morning, he woke to someone pulling at his shoulder. "Lewis, Lewis. Hey, sleepyhead," his aunt said. "How come you're the last one out of bed? Big day today, so you better get a move on."

Lewis rolled away from her and pulled up the covers.

"Nope, time to get up and get going." She yanked the blankets down to his feet, and cool air from the open window swept across the bed.

"Okay," he said. "I'm getting up."

His aunt patted him on his back. "Attaboy," she said, and walked away.

Yawning, he stretched and sat up. Hearing a raven's croak and bluebirds on the roof chirping loudly, he looked out the window. The world was already in motion and doing fine without him.

It was his last day at his cousins' house and tonight his mother and Isabel would be home again, and he would sleep in his own bed. Maybe they'd bought him new clothes for school. Maybe the work on the house would be done and he'd go home to a place with a shower and an indoor toilet. For a moment he felt better, and then what happened at the dance came back to him. As he rubbed an ache at the back of his head, he caught a whiff of his armpits and unwashed feet.

He called to his aunt in the kitchen, "Can I have a shower before I get dressed, Aunt Jean?"

"Yeah, go ahead. You want to smell good for your mom when you get home."

After he was dressed, Lewis combed his hair and went into the kitchen. His breakfast was sitting on a plate on the table as his aunt put the last of the dishes in the rack to dry. Everybody else was outside except for Marvin, who was sitting at the table sipping hot coffee. "Better dig into them eggs before they go cold, Lewis. You need to get your strength back."

Jean reached under the table with the broom and the boys lifted their feet. She looked at Marvin. "What does that mean? Get your strength back?"

"All week he's been rolling around in bed like a fish outta water. He looks almost as tired as me."

"More bad dreams?" his aunt said.

"I guess so. I don't remember."

Lewis looked out the screen door as he chewed. Rosalyn and Cora were in the garden, each wearing a sweater or light jacket, bent over digging at something. He couldn't tell what. The weeds and bushes on the hill didn't look as green as when he first arrived. The hot weather had taken its toll. But cooler mornings like this forewarned that summer was beginning to wind down. Soon enough, autumn would be in full swing, their warm days swapped for cold winds that ripped leaves off trees and still mornings when thick frost covered everything in feathery crystals.

Lewis felt like the cold had already settled into his body. The night at the dance with Lily Edwards was either a wet dream or a nightmare; he still hadn't decided.

Aunt Jean and Marvin went outside to join the others, leaving Lewis to finish off his plate. He walked to the sink to rinse his plate and looked out the window at the cloudless sky. Blue Grouse Moutain, ever present and beckoning, where rows of trees left behind by a long-ago forest fire stood out on the steep slope like ribs. He looked down to the field and saw a person strolling on the tractor path toward the house. Lewis picked up the binoculars, focused and immediately recognized the unique gait of his uncle Alphonse. Lewis couldn't deal with his teasing today, so he hurried outside just as Uncle Ned called out, "Hey, look who it is."

As his aunt and uncle sat at the kitchen table drinking tea with Alphonse, Lewis went about his morning chores for the last time. In the basement, he checked the mousetraps, which were all empty. Then he carried a bowl to the chicken house and came out with six eggs. He stopped at the foot of the porch, setting the eggs down carefully, and went down to his knees and nuzzled Mitzy's neck. He would miss the old dog. Alphonse came out of the house just as Lewis was about to climb the stairs and go inside. "Hey there."

Lewis shaded his eyes and looked up.

"You okay?" Alphonse asked.

Lewis shrugged.

"Why don't you come with me down to the shop. I gotta borrow a scythe."

Walking away from the house with his uncle, Lewis waited to hear a sarcastic comment about Lily or about how Lewis must have been blessed by the gods to have had her in the back seat of his car. But there was no conversation between them. When they came to the shop, Alphonse found the scythe hanging by a nail, took it down and ran his thumb across its cutting edge. "Boy, Ned, he keeps his tools good and sharp, don't he."

Lewis didn't answer.

His uncle stared at his nephew. "So your sweetheart booted your ass out the door, right?"

"No," Lewis said. "No. I don't know."

Alphonse shook his head. "What the hell is it about you and women? You're a good-lookin' boy who can have almost any girl he wants, like Lily Edwards, for Chrissakes. But now you wanna lay down and die because you lost the first girl you liked? What's the matter with you?"

Lewis didn't have any idea what he should say to this. Ever since he was a little boy, his uncle had always found something in Lewis's misfortunes to laugh about.

"Okay, you don't know whether you lost your girl. What did she say when you went over there and talked to her?"

Lewis looked down. "I'm not going anywhere near her. It's too late now anyway."

"Look at me."

Lewis kept his eyes down.

"I said look at me, dammit."

Lewis jerked his head up.

"That's just chickenshit. I know you're not a coward, so you get your ass over there and take it like a man. After she tells you to piss off, then you can get back to your cryin'."

Lewis stopped at the gate across the road from Loretta's house and leaned on the rails. His knees felt weak at the thought of seeing her, but he steeled himself, opened the gate and stepped through. Pausing at the foot of the steps to the front porch, he took a deep breath and wiped his sweaty hands on his pants. Through the screen door he could see Loretta lying on the living room couch, her feet on the arm. Loretta's mother was there too, ironing as she watched the black-and-white figures flickering on the television set.

Before he could chicken out, he knocked on the door. A feeble bark from a corner of the porch made him jump. It was Duke. The dog lifted his head but stayed on his blanket, too old to even bother to get up.

"Oh, hello, Lewis," Loretta's mom called. "Why are you standing out there like a stranger?"

"Is Loretta home?"

"You coming in or what?"

"Never mind, Mom." Loretta rose from the couch and came to the screen door, where she stood with her arms folded. "What do you want?"

She looked like she was holding herself back from doing the one thing she wanted to do more than anything else: slap his face. When she reached to open the screen door, he took two steps back.

"Can we—" he started to say.

"Not here," she said.

Lewis followed Loretta down the steps, glancing back once to see her mother standing at the screen door, watching them, a puzzled look on her face. It was obvious Loretta hadn't told her yet.

It wasn't until they were on the other side of the bridge that Loretta turned and faced him. Lewis opened his mouth to speak.

"No. You don't get to talk. Just shut up and listen. I've been wondering why I ever trusted you. It's one thing to have a hard-on for that woman at the dance—even I can understand that—but to fuck her in the back seat of a car while I'm looking everywhere for you is as low as you can go."

Lewis was angered by what she said but couldn't think of how to defend himself. Instead, he asked, "Who was that guy you were talking to at the dance?"

"What guy?"

"The guy you were hugging. Looked pretty chummy to me."

"I don't have to tell you a thing. From now on, my life is my business, not yours."

"So you won't tell me who he was?"

"Nope," she said.

Lewis knew she was ready to walk away from him and he had to say something before she did. "Loretta, I never meant for anything to happen. It's just, well . . . my uncle took me out to his car to have a couple of beers after you left me standing there, and I fell asleep. When I woke up, I got out to have a leak. That's when Lily saw me."

Loretta shook her head. "You don't have to tell me—I know what happened. You embarrassed me in front of the whole reserve and now everybody is laughing at me." Her anger left her and she began to cry. "How could you do that to me?"

"Oh, Loretta, don't . . ."

Tears streamed down her face as she turned and ran back across the bridge. Lewis started after her, but then he saw Mrs. Ryder standing on the road with her hands over her mouth, staring at him in shock. He stopped. It wasn't until both women climbed the steps to their house and went inside that Lewis walked back across the bridge then up his cousin's drive.

CHAPTER 22

LEWIS PACKED HIS CLOTHES in a box and went outside to load them into the old pickup truck, but he couldn't see it anywhere.

Just then Uncle Ned came around the corner of the house. "Is it okay if we take you home on the hay trailer?" he asked. "Cora's been after me saying that a hayride home would be fun. We'll wait until dark. Supposed to be a perfect night with the full moon and that warm wind. What do you think?"

"I thought I had to drive Mom's truck back," Lewis said. "Where is it?"

"Alphonse took it back."

"What did he do that for?"

"Because Cora told him what she wanted to do."

"Okay, then," Lewis said, forcing a smile. "A hayride sounds like fun."

Ned patted him on the back and walked down to the barn, and Lewis carried his box back inside.

It was dark when the sound of the tractor starting up signalled the end of his stay at his cousins. He was so sad about losing Loretta he couldn't wait to get away from here.

After everyone was aboard the trailer, they set off. Mitzi ran alongside until Marvin sent her home. Lewis sat quietly, his legs swinging with the bumpy ride, his eyes on the porch light until it shrank to a dot then disappeared behind the hill that cut sharply into the field by the river.

The rumble of the tractor couldn't drown out the sounds of the running water or the wind hissing through the boughs of the trees. The night may have been warm, but it was always cool along here. Lewis's arms became covered in goosebumps.

At the end of the field, Ned stopped the tractor and Marvin jumped down and ran ahead to open the gate while Rosalyn helped Cora get up on the fender beside her dad. Once through the gate, they veered left into a tunnel of overhanging branches so thick and low that Ned and Cora had to duck their heads. The road sloped up toward the huge globe of the moon. Coming out of the lane, a shadow dropped from above, brushing Ned's fedora before fluttering away like a piece of black paper.

Marvin yelled, "It's a bat," and his dad quickly turned to put a finger to his mouth, nodding to Cora.

As they rolled out onto his flat field, Lewis's eye was caught by the moonlight bouncing off the chimney flashing of his home. The warm wind moved through his hair, and he felt a little better being back home.

They drove over the small hump of the gas pipeline and the tractor came to a stop. Ned switched off the grumbling motor and waved his arm around. "Look at this," he said. "It's like broad daylight out here. Let's stop for a bit."

Rosalyn jumped down and set her transistor radio on the trailer. Turning to a rock-and-roll station, she grabbed Cora and they danced in a circle to the music as his aunt and uncle watched.

Marvin sat beside Lewis. "Come on, it's not that bad. Jesus, you did so much this summer. You had a pretty girlfriend who lived right next door and couldn't stay away from you, and you screwed a woman every guy dreams about. You're the talk of the reserve and you're only sixteen."

Lewis shrugged. "Yeah. I can't wait to hear what Mom has to say about it."

"It'll all blow over. It always does." Marvin slapped Lewis on the back. He ran over to Cora and kneeled so she could climb onto his back, then galloped around in the moonlight.

Now Rosalyn came to sit beside him. She put an arm around his waist and rested her jaw on his shoulder. "It's too bad what happened between you and Loretta—you both needed a friend. But why is it you guys are always thinking with that little head of yours instead of the big one?"

Lewis didn't answer, and she bumped him with her shoulder. "Are you listening to me?"

"I'm listening."

"Okay, you better cheer up right now. If Mom and Dad see you moping like this, they won't feel sorry for you, they'll tease you to death. They're already looking at you sideways, so get a new face on because this one's for the birds."

"Time to go," Ned yelled. He grabbed Cora and perched her on the fender, then climbed up and started the tractor. Everyone jumped back on the trailer. When they came to the gate, Lewis was the one who hopped down, unhitched the wire off the pole and swung it open. When the tractor went through and he returned the gate to the post, he jumped aboard and they all held onto the front hay racks as the tractor made the turn onto Range Road, the muffler backfiring as it bounced over the cattle guard. The gravel road felt like a paved highway, and Ned worked the throttle and gears until they were going so fast he needed to put a hand on his hat to keep it from blowing away.

As Lewis's house came into view out of the thin line of poplars by the road, Ned eased up on the throttle. The front door opened and Lewis saw two people step out on the porch, outlined by the light behind them. One of them waved with both arms. The tractor pulled up to the front of the house and stopped.

Lewis jumped off the trailer, grabbed his box of clothes and dropped it on the porch just as Isabel spun him around and hugged him. When Isabel let him go, his mother grabbed his head and pulled it toward her until their cheeks touched, then stood back and looked into his eyes and smiled. Lewis wondered if there was something wrong with her, because she hadn't looked at him that way before. That was the closest to a real embrace from his mother since he was little.

Isabel called to the others, "Are you guys coming in for a visit?"

Ned shook his head. "Not tonight. We hafta get this little one to bed before she falls asleep on the tractor."

Grace hurried down the steps and took Jean's hand in hers. "Thanks for taking care of my boy. How did he do?"

Jean said, "Him and Marvin worked so good together. You shoulda seen them bringing in the hay. Ned just sat on the tractor and drove and watched. Lewis can come back anytime."

Isabel turned to Ned. "You sure you can't stay for a bit?"

"Not tonight." Ned pointed to the house. "When it's all finished, you let us know and we'll be here for the housewarming. With bells on."

Ned started the tractor and they drove up the road, waving and shouting goodbyes.

CHAPTER 23

AS THE NOISE OF THE TRACTOR FADED, they heard a short honk and turned to see the headlights of a car coming down their road. Under the bright moonlight, Lewis could make out that it was a newer car with a flashy grill and double headlights, a show-off car that looked fast idling toward them.

The car came to a stop at the house, dust floating over the brake lights, drifting past the car like a red mist. The dark figure of the driver shut off the engine, opened the door and stepped out, easing the door shut with a click. Then he walked into the glare of the outside light, where moths and bugs circled and banged against the bulb with a ticking sound.

Tightness came to Lewis's throat and liquid blurred his vision. He blinked and stared at the driver as if he were an alien that had fallen from the sky. But Lewis had been tricked before by a teenager on a sidewalk brushing past him, a face at a window or a stranger in a crowd bearing a striking resemblance to his brother. Could his eyes and brain be fooling him again? Because standing in front of Lewis was his brother, Eddie.

He glanced at his mother, who wore a blank look as she waited for the person to say something.

"Mom, it's Eddie," Lewis said.

Then Eddie raised both arms. "Well, aren't you going to welcome me home?"

Grace's hands flew to her face and she stumbled back, tripping on the steps and landing on her backside. As Eddie went to help her to her feet, she looked up at him, stunned.

Two years had changed him. He was only eighteen years old, but looked more like a man than a boy. His face was lean, the soft teenage cheeks gone, and he was taller, with a broad-shouldered build. His hair had grown to his shoulders and a scar below his eye marred his smooth face.

Grace reached up and touched the scar. Eddie stepped back. "I cut myself shaving."

When Grace still didn't speak, Lewis saw the irritated look come over his brother that he had seen many times before when Eddie was dealing with their mother. Eddie said, "Come on, say something just to let me know you didn't lose your tongue."

Grace finally found her voice. "Jesus, Eddie, what can I say? We all thought you were dead. If I was a religious person, I'd say this is a miracle or something. I don't know."

Eddie nodded. "In a way, it *is* kind of a miracle. I never thought I'd see this place again."

Grace couldn't look away from his face. "So where you been? What were you doing all this time? Why didn't you let us know?"

Eddie said, "We can play twenty questions tomorrow at breakfast. On the way down here, I even thought about your mush. I've been living on TV dinners for too long."

Isabel stood back, watching them. When Eddie turned to find her, she hurried over and gave him a long, firm hug, startling him. She placed her hands on his cheeks and stared at him.

"You still making those buns?" he asked.

"You bet I am. Oh Jesus, Eddie. It really is you?"

She hugged him one more time before he gently pulled away from her.

Lewis stepped forward then, uncertain how he should greet his brother after so long a time apart. The brothers shoved both hands deep in their pockets as if afraid they might hug.

Eddie spoke first. "Long time no see, little brother."

Lewis wanted to say so much, but all he could do was smile.

Eddie said, "Soon as we can, right now if you want, let's go up to the range in my car. I bet you got a lot of questions to ask and I'll tell you everything you want to know."

"It's like I'm looking at a ghost," Lewis said.

Eddie laughed. "I can't believe you're taller than me." He lowered his voice. "You got yourself a girlfriend yet, or are you still in love with Miss July?"

Lewis whispered back, "I'll tell you later."

Eddie looked up at the unfinished addition to the house. Tarpaper had been stapled to the outside walls and the siding had been started. And on each wall a glimmering new window had been installed.

"Jeez, this looks nice. It sure makes the old part ugly-looking."

Grace put her hand on the wall to steady herself. "After all this time thinking you were dead and you just show up here and talk like nothing happened. I don't know what to say to you. I have to go inside and sit down—I'm feeling a bit dizzy."

She went up the steps into the empty new room and sat on a box. They followed her into the house. The floor was bare but the ceiling was finished and painted white. Three colours of imitation wood grain panelling leaned against the bare walls.

Grace explained, "They want to know which one we like so they can finish the room."

"I was staying with Aunt Jean and Uncle Ned all summer, and I'm seeing this for the first time too," Lewis said as he opened a door in the corner of the room and turned on the light. "Holy cow, look at this."

Inside the bathroom was a bathtub and shower with gleaming hot and cold taps and a drain plug on a chain. A doorless cabinet with a gaping hole at the centre looked ready for a sink. A toilet sat against the wall, waiting to be plumbed in.

Eddie ran his hand over the toilet water tank. "It looks like this family is finally moving into the twentieth century. Boy, this would have been nice to have when we were kids."

"It's hard to believe they did this all in, what—six or seven weeks?" Lewis said.

"Yeah, how did you get the money to get this done? Either you won a poker game or you're stepping out with the Indian agent," Eddie joked.

Lewis couldn't help but laugh at the thought of their mother being with a man she hated.

"The only time you'd see me holding hands with that guy is if he was hanging off a cliff just before I let go," Grace said. "It was Isabel who really helped us out by finding us good jobs this summer. Nothing would be done if it wasn't for her."

Isabel waved Grace away. "Baloney, we all pitched in."

Grace walked into the old kitchen and patted the new sink. "We only got home late last night and I'm still not used to it. We still only got two bedrooms, Eddie, but you can sleep here, in the new part, when we get a fold-down couch. You'll have the place all to yourself."

"Jeez, Mom. It's gonna look good as any *summa* house in town." Eddie looked at his watch. "What do you think, Lewis? Want to get outta here for a bit?"

"You bet," he said. They walked toward the door.

"Eddie," his mother called. "What the hell. All of us, every single one of us, thought you were dead. Either you fell in the river and drowned, or you killed yourself. Don't you think we have a right to know where you were?"

Eddie turned to her. "I'm not a kid anymore and I'm taking Lewis for a ride. I might be leaving tomorrow, so I really want to see him. Don't bother waiting up for us."

"You just got here and you're leaving tomorrow? Why did you even bother coming back here?"

Grace went to follow her sons outside, but Isabel grabbed her arm and shook her head. The two stopped on the doorstep.

Eddie opened the driver's door then looked over at Lewis. "You wanna drive? Do you even know how?"

Lewis knew how upset his mother was and he wasn't sure what he should do. He stood there until Grace turned back to the house, pushing them both away with a swipe of her hand.

Lewis said, "I been driving Uncle Ned's tractor and the old truck all summer."

Eddie tossed him the keys and went around to the passenger door as Lewis slid into the driver's seat. "Come on, Lewis. Just forget about her. We'll slug it all out another day. Let's you and me get going."

"Something smells good in here," Lewis said as Eddie climbed in and closed the door.

"It must be the Teen Burger I had at the A&W in Kamloops."

"Jeez, what a beauty this thing is. These bucket seats feel great and the tachometer on the dash makes it look like a cop car."

"I got that just for looks," Eddie said. "But it really does come in handy to see the rpms so you know exactly when to shift gears. See that red line? If you go past there, it means you're revving too high and you could blow the engine. So don't you get anywhere near that."

Lewis started the car. When he stepped on the gas, it growled a throaty roar and the tachometer lit up, the needle sweeping halfway up the gauge. "Oh man."

"See those ears on the stick shift? Put your hand on the knob and lift up the ears with your two fingers and put it into reverse."

Lewis did exactly as he was told. After backing up, he shifted into first, the chrome ears clicking as they fell into place. "I've seen some pretty neat cars, but never anything like this."

"You ain't seen nothing yet. Come on, give 'er some gas."

Lewis released the clutch too fast and the car jumped forward. Turning down Range Road, he slammed down on the gas pedal. The car spun and began to drift toward the fence.

"Hit the brakes!" Eddie shouted. The car slid to a stop an arm's length away from a post. "Jesus, Lewis. What the hell?"

"I guess I'm used to driving the old truck."

His brother said, "It's my fault for not showing you how to drive this beast. Take it easy this time. This isn't some old tractor you're playing with."

Lewis laughed. Easing into gear, he said, "Driving anything after this will never be the same. Where do you want to go?"

"Up to that spot on the range above Heart Lake. But take it slow and go the long way around. I don't want the bottom ripped out of this thing."

Minutes later Lewis stopped the car above Heart Lake and shut off the engine.

"Take a look at this." Eddie reached under the dash and flipped a switch. Red lights shone down at their feet.

"Sex lights!" Lewis said. "I heard a guy in school talking about these. Wonder what it would be like doing it with those on?"

Eddie smirked. "Sometimes they were hard to see because of the tits in my eyes." Then he opened the glove box and brought out a paper bag. He opened it so Lewis could see the collection of panties inside. "What do you think of these? It's like a scrapbook. Here, you hold one and try to imagine them sliding down her legs."

"Maybe wash them first. What else you got in here?"

Eddie opened the console, which was filled with a rainbow of coloured plastic cartridges. He pulled one out and slid it into a flap under the radio. When he reached over and switched the key to Accessory, the sound of a piano drifted softly through the back and front speakers. "These are 8-track tapes. I got the Rolling Stones, Neil Diamond—oh, that's a good one—and what music collection would be complete without the Beatles?"

Eddie settled back and looked at the water below. "This is exactly the way I dreamed it would be—a full moon over Heart Lake, with Simon & Garfunkel singing in the background. All that's missing is one thing." He reached into the back seat and lifted the lid off a Styrofoam cooler. Drawing out two beers, he replaced the lid and undid his belt. Using his buckle, he snapped off the bottle caps and handed one to Lewis. "Here's mud in your eye, kid," he said as they clinked their bottles in a toast.

Lewis took a long drink, beer bubbling down his throat. "Ahh," he said. "Damn, I can still smell your hamburger and it's making me so hungry."

Eddie reached into the back seat again and grabbed a paper pail and placed it on the console between them. When he pulled off the lid, the car filled with a mouth-watering smell. "Kentucky Fried Chicken," he said. "You ever had it?"

"No." Lewis dug out a fat drumstick and took a large bite. He closed his eyes and moaned as he chewed.

"It really is finger-licking good," Eddie said. "Just don't get any grease on the seat."

For the next ten minutes there was no conversation between them, just the sound of smacking lips and gurgling beer. When they had their fill, Eddie took a handful of paper napkins, gave a couple to Lewis and they wiped their fingers, wrapped up the bones and tucked them into a bag. Eddie pushed a button on the tape player and the cartridge popped out. He grabbed a different one and shoved it in and turned up the volume. "That's Dusty Springfield. She can make you cry like a baby after a beer or two."

They listened to a few songs, then Eddie said, "You know what, let's turn the key off. I've been missing the quiet up here."

Lewis switched off the key and they rolled down their windows. A soft wind washed through the car. In the bright moonlight, they saw small waves rippling across the lake and breaking against the shore. Somewhere on the range, cattle bawled.

Lewis looked over at Eddie. He wanted to ask him why he went away like he did and let people think he was dead. That was so cruel. He knew his brother had a nasty temper that could make him do things he would later regret. Was that what happened? Had he made a hasty decision and was too stubborn to admit it?

Neither had said a word for the longest time, but Lewis had to know. "What happened, Eddie? Why did you take off like that, without telling anybody where you were going?"

Eddie took a sip of beer and sat back. "I was pretty screwed up back then. I just had to get away from here. Remember the guy I split shakes for? He told me his son was living in Valleyview, Alberta, with his grandmother. He was always going on and on about his son and how much money he was making in the oil fields. When I told him what happened and said that I wanted to go somewhere, anywhere, he told me that's where I should be. He even phoned and asked if I could stay with them, so that's what I did. When I got there, I got my first good-paying job at the Simonette gas plant. I made a dollar ninety-five an hour to start, then got a raise to two fifty."

Lewis was impressed. "No one around here makes that much. I think Alphonse said he got a buck an hour and he thought that was doing pretty good."

"Yeah, but that was a while ago. He'd get more than that now. Still, guys come from all over to work in the oil fields, the pay is so good. But it's never this quiet in that flat-ass place. We were so lucky growing up here. We could go anywhere we wanted to get away from people. Up there, all you can see are oil wells and gas plants everywhere you look. They have these tall steel chimney stacks where they burn off the hydrogen sulphide gas—poison gas, they call it. They say it's the second-deadliest gas after hydrogen cyanide, and that's what they used in the gas chambers. Five guys down in Fox Creek were killed the first week I was there. At night, when those flames shoot outta those stacks and bounce off the low clouds, it looks like they're touching the sky. And there's always the sound of the pipes hissing and whistling with the flames."

"Did you see many Indians up there?"

Eddie picked at his teeth and flicked something outside. "Sure. The Cree. Know what people up there call them? FBI. Fucking Big Indians. Maybe the white people thought I was a short-ass Italian, but I sure didn't bother to correct them. But the Cree knew who I was, and the very first time I started sniffing around one of their women, they beat the hell out of me. The only place I wasn't bruised were the bottoms of my feet. It took weeks before my ribs didn't hurt when I sneezed.

"I saw those guys around once in a while after that, but I made sure I stayed away from them. The prejudice is bad there.

It's like everybody has their own side to root for. The Indians don't like other Indians, the *summas* don't like Indians or the French. Sometimes I wondered if there was some kind of disease going around that made everybody act so hateful."

Lewis pulled a piece of chicken skin out of the bucket and popped it into his mouth. "So why did you stay if it was that bad?"

"Because the pay is so good. And they'll hire anybody, even Indians. If you know how to lean on a shovel, they'll give you a job. We worked six days a week, even seven, if you wanted, twelve-hour days, along with three hours a day just driving back and forth to the gas plant."

"Sounds like a stupid place to live, if you ask me, even if the money is good." Lewis went quiet for a moment. "Why did you tell Mom you're leaving tomorrow? You just got here."

Eddie drained his beer and burped. "I just wanted to piss her around a bit."

"But why tell her something like that?"

"Let's get outside so I can stretch my legs. I drove so long my ass fell asleep, and I can still feel the needles."

They stepped out of the car and went around to the front and leaned on the hood. Lewis waited for Eddie to answer, but he didn't say a word. So he asked again. "Why did you want to piss off Mom?"

Eddie lit a cigarette. "Lots of reasons. Remember when we were kids and she'd go to the beer parlour and leave us to look after ourselves? She always told us she'd be back on the bus later, but sometimes she wouldn't be there when we went to meet her. I still remember that. I wanted her to see how it feels when she doesn't know what will happen one day to the next." He blew out a smoke ring. "But me leaving wasn't really about Mom. Mostly I didn't want to be around where Eva lived. She was gone and I didn't like to be reminded." Eddie held up the cigarette to his mouth and let a gob of spit fall on the glowing end. It crackled. He dropped it to the ground.

"Why don't we talk about something else," he said. "What about you? What's going on with you?"

Lewis didn't know where to begin. "I dunno. Last year I was just going to school and it was kinda boring and nothing much happened, but this summer I stayed with Uncle Ned and Aunt Jean. Rosalyn is so smart, and little Cora is a live wire. And Marvin, now there's one tough kick-ass guy. They built a brand-new house and they got everything you can think of. I had so much fun. Then I met their neighbour, Loretta. She's a friend of Rosalyn's and after a while she was my girlfriend. We were together every day, almost, until she found out I was with another girl–a woman, I mean–and we broke up."

"Really? What did you do?"

"The two of us went to the Head of the Lake dance with Rosalyn and Marvin, and something happened. This woman, Lily Edwards, Alphonse calls her Tiger Lily. That's a perfect name for her because her red fingernails look like claws with blood on them. She gets real horny when she has a few drinks. Alphonse says she's worse than a man that way."

Eddie laughed.

"Every guy at the dance wanted her but she wanted me, so when I was in Alphonse's car, she . . . she . . ."

"What? She what?"

"She held me down, pulled off my pants and then she fucked me."

"Jesus. Really? She did that?"

"Damn right she did."

"What does she look like? Is she good-looking?"

"Oh man, she's more than that. She's pretty, deadly pretty. When she finished with me, she bit a piece of my ear off. Here, feel it." Lewis leaned over.

Eddie touched his earlobe. "She did too."

"The whole reserve was talking about it, and when Loretta found out, she told me to get lost."

"Did you like her?"

"No. But the sex was really something for my first time."

"Not Lily Pad, or whatever her name was, you horndog. Loretta, I mean."

"You bet I liked her. If we didn't go to the dance that night, we'd still be together."

Eddie looked Lewis in the eye and pointed a finger. "Okay, then. Tell me something and don't lie. If your girl never found out what you did that night and you could do it again, would you look up Lily?"

Lewis didn't answer for a long time. Finally, he said, "I don't know. I should have tried to fight her off, I guess, but I was never so scared of a woman. You should have seen the body on her. I haven't looked at *Playboy* since. She's like one of those Mexican women dancers I saw on TV. You just can't look away from her. I don't know if I would do it again. I miss Loretta a lot, though, so I hope not."

"Tough, isn't it?"

"You know what the funny part about the whole thing is?"

"No."

"Lily Edwards is Dad's girlfriend."

Eddie's mouth fell open and he looked at his little brother to make sure he heard right.

When Lewis nodded, smiling, Eddie slapped his leg and they burst out laughing and didn't stop for a long time.

CHAPTER 24

THE NEXT MORNING, Isabel hurried out of the bathroom dressed in her best town clothes, her hair backcombed and sprayed. She picked up her purse and was headed for the door when Grace whispered, so she wouldn't wake her sleeping boys, "Hey, where are you going all gussied up? You're not going without me, are you?"

Isabel whispered back. "I can go meet my brother by myself. Don't you want to spend some time with Eddie?"

"He's got his back up about something. Let him sleep and if he's got anything to say to me, we'll talk when I get back."

"Come on, then," Isabel said, and handed her the keys. "You can drive. The last time I went to town by myself, I almost ran over a jaywalker."

As they walked through the kitchen, Grace took a peek in the open bedroom door where Lewis and Eddie slept. Having her two boys together under her roof was something she had never expected to see again, and she felt good inside. Turning to go, she bumped into a chair and it banged against the table. Eddie jerked awake and looked around, sleepy-eyed and confused.

"Sorry, Eddie," Grace said. "Go back to sleep. We have to meet someone in town. Are you really leaving today?"

Eddie yawned and stretched. "No. I'm not going back for a couple of weeks."

Grace smiled at Isabel. "Okay, we'll see you before supper."

Eddie fluffed his pillow and turned over.

Grace pulled over beside Cenotaph Park and switched off the motor. This was where people from the reserve chose to park their vehicles in Vernon. It not only felt safer being around people they knew, but it gave them a place to sit and visit where they could keep an eye on their children while they played.

To the right was the Allison Hotel, where the side entrance for ladies and escorts led into the beer parlour. People going in and out were easy to spot. Across the street was the Greyhound bus depot, where a steady stream of travellers arriving in silver coaches disembarked, picked up their suitcases or boxes tied with twine and either walked to wherever they wanted to go or were whisked away in cabs. The depot café booths and counter seats could be filled one minute and empty the next.

Grace heard shouting and looked in the rear-view mirror. Three Indian children who looked too young to be left alone were jumping over the seats in the car behind them, back and forth, laughing and giggling in a game of tag. Then a little girl stopped, her eyes open wide and locked on something or someone. Grace followed her stare and saw a woman staggering toward the park. All three of the children squeezed into a corner as they watched her coming their way. She walked straight through a bed of flowers, crushing some plants. As she went to step over the drooping chain fence between the flower beds and the park, she tripped, tumbling heavily to the sidewalk. She rose on shaky legs and carried on toward her children. When she came alongside their car, she noticed Isabel watching her.

"What the hell you staring at?"

"Keep walking," Isabel said.

Watery eyes jerked in their sockets as she glared and swayed like a flag in a breeze. "Hah," she finally said, and then continued to her car. Her hand slipped as she pulled at the door handle, and she stumbled back onto the road. Regaining her balance, she opened the door and climbed behind the steering wheel.

"Holy cow, she's feeling no pain," Isabel said. "You ever see her before?"

"No. They must be travelling through."

The woman fumbled with her keys, started the car and drove away.

Grace said, "I hope those kids are going to be okay. I was never that bad, was I, Izzy?"

"We mighta got half-cut. But not like that, especially in broad daylight and with kids."

Grace pointed to a tall vagrant wearing a dirty suit jacket, sitting with his back against the memorial in the centre of the park. "There's that wino Alphonse told me about. He said he was crazy in the head." The man appeared to be sleeping, his shaggy hair poking out from under his cap. Then he jumped and jerked his head to swear at someone or something unseen. A mother walking by pulled her child close. They watched as the man scratched his nicotine-stained whiskers with dirty fingernails and bits of food or dried vomit fell to his jacket. Then, as if struck by a sudden fit, he dug his fingers into his ribs, scratching furiously at an itch. He looked like a man playing the washboard at a dance. Faster and faster he went and then, turning his head, he shouted, "Bastard."

A truck horn made the hobo sit up. After struggling to his feet, he wobbled to the street. As he disappeared down a narrow alley, Grace and Isabel couldn't help but laugh.

"There's always a drunk or crazy person here to put on a show," Grace said. "What time is your brother supposed to be here?"

"Around noon. In his letter, he didn't say what he wants to talk to me about, but it sounded important. Maybe it's something to do with Dad. When he died, he left both of us his place down at the lake. But I hope Theo gets here soon, so we can get something to eat. I'm starving." Isabel's eyes went to the bus depot. "Hey, do you want some french fries? I can nip over to the café there and get us some."

"I'll go. You stay here in case your brother shows up."

Grace stepped out of the car and crossed the road. When she opened the door to the bus depot café, the smell of coffee and meat sizzling on a grill hit her and her stomach growled. A man wearing dark glasses sat in a corner seat next to the tall windows, eating a slice of cake with a fork while sipping an orange drink from a sweaty glass. Grace noticed him staring at her and she turned away.

Two old men sat alone at the counter, blowing on their steaming spoons of soup, gumming bread. A heavy waitress in a white uniform dabbed at a stain on her stomach with a napkin while muttering under her breath. Shoving the napkin in her pocket, she wearily regarded Grace. "Yeah?"

"Two large french fries and two Cokes to go."

The waitress picked up a chrome scoop and filled two narrow brown paper bags with french fries kept warm on the grill. She squirted vinegar over the fries and the bag darkened with the liquid. Then she gave both a generous shake of salt and placed them and the two bottles of Coke on the counter. "Want them opened?"

"That's okay." Grace shoved a five-dollar bill across the counter and the lady opened the till and rattled around for change. Grace stuck the money into her jeans pocket, pinched the tops of the bags of fries together and grabbed the pop by the neck with her fingers. As she turned to leave, she came face-to-face with a man who was more than a little drunk. And before she could get past him, he grabbed her shoulder. "Where you going in such a hurry? How about having a drink with me?"

Grace jerked away from him. "Why would I want to have a drink with you? And keep your damn hands off me."

Face reddening, the man hissed, "Get your ass back here or I'll slap that look right off your face."

Grace glanced at the waitress, hoping she would say something, but she was busy wiping the counter. The hate in the man's eyes made Grace want to give him a quick punch, but her hands were full. She backed up and kicked him between the legs, and he collapsed to the floor with a groan, clutching his crotch, the stench of stale beer and his fetid body stink rankling her nose.

Before she elbowed the door open, she turned to the man still calmly eating his cake and yelled, "You Hollywood chickenshit."

Grace could feel her heart pounding as she crossed the street and handed the fries and pop to Isabel through the window. Sitting heavily in the driver's seat, she said, "Open one of them pops for me, would you?"

Isabel grabbed the bottle opener from the glove box and popped the cap, handing the bottle to Grace. "You're shaking. What happened in there?"

Grace drank, stopped to catch her breath and drank again. "Oh, that's better," she said, closing her eyes for a moment. She let out a long sigh. "There was a drunk in there looking for trouble. You could see he didn't like Indians and probably liked to smack women around for the hell of it. He came straight for me, but I surprised him. If his nuts were bells, you'd a heard them ringing."

"Oh, Grace! I wish I was there to help, but it sounds like you did pretty good by yourself. Now come on, you'll feel better after you get these fries down. They're so good with the salt and vinegar."

Grace took another long drink, felt her shoulders relax and began eating her fries. She looked over at the bus depot and spotted the cake-eating man at the crosswalk, tap-tapping his way across with a white cane. "Oh, look, Isabel. Jeez," she said, pointing. "There's the guy who just sat there while that drunk was grabbing at me. I called a blind man a chickenshit!"

Isabel began to laugh so hard she almost choked on her mouthful of fries. Then came a loud banging on the roof and Isabel's brother stuck his head in her window, kissing her on the cheek.

"Hello there, little sis. Sorry I'm late. What's so funny?"

Isabel calmed herself and lowered the door to the cubbyhole, where she set down her fries and pop. "You had to be there," she said.

Isabel's brother had moved away from the reserve years ago because he was always being picked on for preferring men as lovers. A group of boys once attacked him outside the day school because he didn't walk or talk the way they thought he should. They beat him so badly he ended up in hospital for weeks. When he came out, he had a new nickname: "Back-door Theodore."

He returned to the reserve a year ago with his boyfriend, Horace, a weightlifter whose huge biceps looked ready to explode. Now people stayed well away from Theodore, even when he was alone. Isabel stepped out of the car and hugged him while Grace came around the car to greet Horace, touching him on his massive arm. "Hello, Horace, what's new with you?"

He nodded at her.

Grace thought, *Not much of a talker, are you?*

"Hi, Grace," Theodore said and blew her a kiss. He looked sharp, dressed in a yellow short-sleeved shirt with a beige vest and matching slacks.

"So what's up?" Isabel asked. "And why did we have to meet in town? You know where I stay now."

"I'm too busy building my empire to go anywhere, but I got something for you." He reached into his vest pocket and pulled out an envelope. He handed it to Isabel.

"Feels heavy."

"Open it, silly."

Isabel pried the flap open and looked inside. "Jeez, Theo. Did you rob a bank or something? How much is this?"

"That, my little girl, is four hundred dollars from the beach lots I leased out to *summas*. There are so many of them looking for a place to build a summer cabin, I'm just getting started. That's your share."

"What do you mean 'my share'?"

"Dad knew the land would be signed over to me, but he wanted us both to have it. So whatever the lots lease for, you get half. Is that okay with you?"

Isabel's eyes filled with tears. "Damn right it's okay." She reached up to give her brother a big hug.

"Look, we have to pick up a few things, then me and my gorilla have to beat a trail outta here and get back home. I promise we'll come to you next time so we can have a nice long visit."

Isabel and Theo hugged again. Then she and Grace watched her brother and his boyfriend walk away, Horace looking back once to give a short wave.

Back in the car, Isabel said, "Damn, Grace, I wish he got here before we had the french fries. We coulda gone to the Top Hat Restaurant and had us a real meal. I heard their steaks are three inches thick, and for dessert, apple pie à la mode."

"That woulda been nice, but this is good," Grace said, popping her last fry into her mouth. "Izzy, that brother of yours is really something. Most men would have kept all that money for themselves."

Isabel rested her head against the seat. "He's always been like that. And we looked out for each other when we were little. People were so mean to him because he was different."

"Well, you got something to hide under your mattress now."

Isabel sat up. "I'm not going to do that. I'm going to pay the carpenter to put new siding on the old part of the house. And what's left over is just about enough to finish the whole job too, isn't it?"

"You shouldn't have to pay for work on my house."

Isabel looked surprised. "Well, I guess I thought I'd be staying there for good. So it feels like it's my home too. I like being away from Six-Mile and my nosy cousins keeping track of what I'm doing and saying things whenever a man drops by, like 'I wonder if he's poking her' or 'Gee, I hope she doesn't get knocked up.' I got no use for a man in my life now, and I don't want a kid either. Thirty-seven is too old to be wiping little asses and getting up in the middle of the night to feed the little bugger. I was lucky Ray was shooting blanks all those years. After Gregory died, I really missed him, and the thought of him still makes me want to cry. I don't want to go through that again. All I want to do is live in a place where nobody knows what I'm doing."

Grace said, "With you chipping in, Isabel, and with Eddie back, it seems like so many good things are happening all at once. I can't believe it."

They both turned at the sound of running feet to see Theo loping toward them. He leaned on the roof to catch his breath.

"Why are you running like that?" Isabel asked.

"Wait," he said, breathing deep. After a minute he stood and wiped his forehead with his hand and came around to Grace's window. "I almost forgot to tell you. Did you hear that something happened to your ex, Jimmy?"

"What do you mean?"

"He showed up at the dance on Friday night at Head of the Lake to pick up Lily. Then they were both at the Pastime Tavern on Saturday. Lily said he went out to his car for something and didn't come back. Then they found a big pool of blood in the parking lot and his car was gone. I thought you should know."

Grace didn't know what she should say. "I haven't seen him."

"Okay. Well, you both take it easy, and we'll get over to your place for a visit soon," Theo said, giving Grace a pat on the arm. He cut across the park and was gone.

"Jeez, Grace," Isabel said. "What the hell did Lazar do with Jimmy? He said he was going to drop him off at the hospital."

CHAPTER 25

"HOW IS THE OLD STUD?" Eddie asked as he and Lewis walked down the hill to visit their uncle.

"Same as always. He still goes to house parties down at Six-Mile. Sometimes he gets drunk and gets into a fight. And he looks at women, especially Isabel, with his tongue hanging out, and he doesn't care if she sees him. Abel says Alphonse is hornier than a two-peckered owl. He's never going to change."

Eddie laughed. "Sounds like him all right."

When the house came into view, Eddie stopped. "Jeez, it looks even smaller than I remember. I think I was at Grandma's house as much as at ours. Remember, Alphonse was still living down at Six-Mile most of the time, so she was on her own, and she was always glad to see me. We played a lot of rummy and solitaire. She couldn't read but she knew what the cards were. I can still picture her sitting at the kitchen table, tapping her fingers and looking up her road."

The faded white paint on the sunny side of the house had flaked and peeled, while on the north end everything looked as it always had. The wooden box nailed to the wall by the back door, Grandma's Indian fridge, was still there. The smudged windows, streaked by rain and smoke, looked like they hadn't been cleaned since she died.

On the roof ridge, the block chimney—darkened by years of creosote leaking down its sides like spilled black paint—sat crooked, with the stone aggregate showing. The trail to the outhouse and the river looked well used.

"I don't know how many times I went down that trail to get buckets of water at night," Eddie said. "On the way back from the river at night I always looked for the light from her coal oil lamp in the window, and when I saw her shadow moving around in there, I felt a little safer."

Rounding the corner of the house, they saw their uncle standing with Marvin in front of a rickety chicken pen. Poles leaned and the chicken wire sagged. Inside the cage, two enormous roosters with thick yellow legs pecked and scrabbled through blood-stained feathers that were scattered over the ground.

When Alphonse heard them coming, he turned. "Well, I'll be damned, lookit these two yahoos, Marvin. One just showed up out of his grave and the other one is still grinning like a cat because he nailed Lily Edwards in the back seat of my car. Now I don't let nobody sit back there."

"What about you, Alphonse?" Eddie asked sarcastically. "How's your sex life?"

"Oh, up and down, off and on."

The three boys laughed.

Alphonse walked up to Eddie, placed a hand on each shoulder and gave him a gentle shake. "Goddamn, I couldn't believe it when I heard you were here. I thought for sure you were dead. And now here you are, looking like a million bucks. How are you doing, kid?"

"I'm good," Eddie said. "I got a good-paying job in the oil field, so I can only stay for a couple weeks, then I have to get back."

"The oil fields. Jeez, sounds like you're getting high-toned."

Eddie reached around to his back pocket and pulled out a miniature oil derrick with a Valleyview, Alberta, label across the front and gave it to Alphonse.

Alphonse tested its weight. "Well, I'll be damned. So is this where you work, on one'a these?"

"Something like that." Eddie said.

"Isn't that something," Alphonse said. He looked up and pointed to Marvin. "This here is your cousin Marvin. He's all growed up now. They moved back here while you were gone, and now the valley don't feel so lonely."

Marvin and Eddie nodded a hello at each other.

"What are you doing here, Marvin?" Lewis asked.

"We got so much frozen hamburger, Mom sent some over to you so she could make room in the freezer for chickens. I gave Alphonse a couple packs and I was just about to bring some up to your house when I saw these roosters."

Eddie asked, "What happened here, anyway? Looks like there was a pillow fight to the death."

Bits of poultry meat, feathers and manure littered the pen and reeked ripe in the warm air. Drops of dry blood hung from the wire like red icicles. It was as if a chicken had exploded.

Lewis squeezed his nose. "Holy, those things shit a bucketful. Marvin's chicken house doesn't smell like this."

"I wanted to keep some chickens so I can fry one up whenever I want, and maybe eat eggs every day," Alphonse said. "I started with eight layers and then I had this idea I'd put in two roosters so I could get twice as many chickens."

Marvin smiled at his uncle. "Hens can only lay so many eggs no matter how many roosters you put in there. Funny they didn't kill each other."

"I know that now. My mom was the one knew all about chickens, and I guess I shoulda paid attention. Anyway, these two black bastards killed off every single one of my hens. Tomorrow, I'm going to sharpen the hatchet, cut their heads off and make a big pot of stew. I never seen birds mean as these. And look how big they are. They look like bull riders with those spurs on their legs. They'll scare the piss outta you when they come at you all puffed up, flapping their wings and squawking their death cry."

Lewis asked, "What did you do with the dead chickens?"

"They were cut up so bad, I dropped them off up on the range for the coyotes."

"Wow," Eddie said. "Are the roosters really that mean?"

Alphonse jumped at the fence, shouting, "Rawww!"

Both roosters charged, hitting the wire with ear-piercing screams.

"Jesus," Marvin said.

"These two is good for nothing," Alphonse said. "I thought maybe I should keep 'em a bit longer and sic 'em on the Indian agent. I seen the way he talked to your dad, Marvin."

"That's it!" Marvin shouted. "Lewis, these are exactly what we need."

Lewis gave Marvin a puzzled look. "For what?"

"Norris Husk. We sic them on old Norris."

Alphonse asked, "What are you talking about?"

"Marvin wants to get back at Husk because he's such an asshole," Lewis said. He asked his cousin, "But what about his dog, Max? She's as mean as these roosters, and we'd never get close without that dog hearing us."

Alphonse laughed. "He calls his female dog 'Max'? He really is a dumb bastard."

Marvin said, "I never thought of that, but there must be a way. And I think we have to hurry. Me and Dad were checking the fence by the river the other day and we saw him digging right where we found those arrowheads. He must have been there a while because he had a big patch of ground all dug up and we could see him scooping up dirt with his hands then holding up stuff and looking it over. Some pieces he just dropped to the ground, but he put the ones he liked into a metal bucket. What if he has a whole bunch of arrowheads hidden away someplace? We could set those birds on him and take them before he throws them in the river or buries them somewhere. He'll never know who did it."

"Hold on a minute," Alphonse said. "How do you know where he keeps them? I don't think they're in his house. He wouldn't want to be that close to Indians."

"I don't know for sure, but if they aren't in the house, they're probably in his granary. It's just a little away from the house. We sic these killers on him, and it'll give us enough time to go after the arrowheads. He might know about dogs, but I bet he doesn't have a clue what do when these things start in on him."

"All right, then," Alphonse said, "but we need to hatch us a plan. We gotta get that mutt away from there so she doesn't give us away. You know what, let's take a walk down the river so we can have a look at his place. I think I got a idea."

Marvin said, "Let me drop the hamburger off first."

The four came down through the trees and stood on the riverbank, looking across at Husk's farm. The grass was eaten down all around them and cow pies were scattered everywhere.

Alphonse, sweaty from the hike, unbuttoned his shirt and bent down to cool his armpits and face with water. And then he gave Marvin a brief history about Husk. "When your dad's cattle got into his place, Norris told Delbert at the store that he could have the Indian agent and Mounties there before the first cow shit hit the ground. Before your dad moved here, Husk's cattle grazed on your place for years for free. And up on the range too. I told the chief and council about Norris a long time ago but they didn't do nothing. He's got a 'lectric fence around his house and at night he just takes the holder off the post and lets his cows out. He uses Indian land whenever he can, even if it is just shoreline, because he's mad we took away his free feed."

"So what's the big idea, Alphonse? How are we gonna do this?" Lewis asked.

Eddie muttered, "There's a lot can go wrong here."

Alphonse turned to him. "This ain't the first time I done something like this, you Alberta puddle jumper." He looked around, making eye contact with each of his nephews. "You guys do what I tell you and wait for my signal. Then you turn all hell loose. We'll scare the shit outta old Norris so bad his hem'roids are gonna pop like Cracker Jacks."

At ten minutes to two in the morning, Lewis and Marvin stood with Alphonse on the riverbank, Marvin and Alphonse each holding a rooster in a sack. Even in the pale light of the thumbnail moon, they could see their surroundings. Alphonse pulled out his pocket watch and checked the time. "Ten minutes to go," he said. But just then they saw the lights of a car driving down the road in the direction of the store. The lights flicked off and on as the car stopped at the Husk driveway, a hundred yards away, and then backed up. Red tail lights showed a figure behind the car working quickly. Then the brake lights flashed, and the car revved again and again and honked its horn. Tires squealed, and it raced up the hill out of sight. Max barked.

Alphonse cussed. "Goddamn that little bugger. He's early. I hope he left enough dog food to keep that hound busy for a while. We better move our asses and get across there fast. Try not to bang them sacks now or them birds will start yowling."

Night bugs swirled around the flashlight as Lewis led the way across the river. Marvin, right behind him, carried the sack as gently as if it was a bag of dynamite. Alphonse, hanging on to the other sack with one hand and a walking stick with the other, jabbed into the riverbed for balance. Once they were all back on dry land, Alphonse whispered, "Look, he's got that big yard light on. After we get past the 'lectric fence and into the shadows, we should be okay. Let me go ahead and you guys follow."

Alphonse handed Lewis his sack. Crouching, he unhooked the electric fence holder and laid the wire on the ground. The three hurried to the back of the house. The bedroom window was wide open and there was no screen. "I don't believe it," Alphonse said. "Look how big that opening is, Marvin. When I let you know, you get to do the honours."

Marvin untied the knot on his sack while Lewis undid the other and hurried to the steer corral. Alphonse waited until both were in position and then snapped his finger twice. Marvin threw his bag through the bedroom window just as Lewis tossed his into the corral. Instantly, both roosters screamed their rage, attacking anything in sight. From inside the house came a man's frightened yell: "Aaaaaaaaah!"

A light went on for a split second, then went out, back on, then out again, like a strobe light, the rooster appearing to float as its wings flipped the light switch. The man screamed as if in a horror movie. The watchers wanted to give an ovation. Bawling steers smashed into the sides of the corral, trying to escape the monster rooster, rails splintering as they barged their way out.

The commotion alerted Max, who dashed back from the end of the driveway to the house. But there was so much going on, she could only bark at the confusion. Alphonse pointed to the granary. Lewis and Marvin ran to the door and ducked inside, searching by the beam of Lewis's flashlight.

It seemed to take forever but they found the pail, and they all hurried back toward the river. As Alphonse placed the holder back onto the electric fence, he looked back to the house to enjoy the show a little longer, not realizing he was illuminated by the bright yard light. When Husk appeared at the window, Alphonse knew he had made a big mistake. Husk stared across his yard at Alphonse, feathers and down floating like falling snow in circles around him and clinging to his blood-streaked face and hair. Then Ruth, untouched and in her nightdress, came into the bedroom and began to scream, a look of horror on her face.

The three ran for the river. When the dog barked, Alphonse looked back to see if she was coming for him, tripped and fell heavily into the water. Marvin and Lewis put their hands over their mouths to muffle their laughter as Alphonse sputtered swear words while stumbling to safety on the opposite shore.

Alphonse was up early the next morning to take down the chicken pen. He rolled up the wire and stashed it deep in the bush and then raked up all the feathers into a sack, added a big rock and tossed it into the river. As he came back, he saw a police car turn down the road to his house. Alphonse still smelled chicken manure, so he grabbed the shovel and threw scoops of wood chips and bark from the woodshed over the ground, returning the shovel to the shed just as the officer stepped out of the car, hat in hand.

"You Alphonse?" he asked.

"You bet."

The policeman approached, placing his hat on his head. "We got a call this morning that someone trespassed on a local property and turned two vicious animals loose on the owners—Mr. Norris Husk and his wife. Do you know them?"

"I know the sumbitch."

"So you do know him."

"Everybody does. Why are you asking me?"

"Because he said it was you who went onto his place."

As the officer stepped closer, Alphonse noticed a chicken head on the ground near the woodshed, sticking up as if the hen was buried up to its neck. "I'm tired of him putting the blame on Indians. I wish he was here right now. Know what I'd say to him? I'd say, go ahead and have a good look around. And if you see anything that proves it was me that let some vicious animals . . . What animals did he say?"

"Roosters."

"Roosters? What did they do, shit everywhere? I never heard roosters called vicious before, did you?"

The policeman shook his head. "Doesn't matter what I think. Mister Husk has deep cuts on his head and scratches all over his face, and there's blood on the bedroom walls. His wife was in the bathroom when it happened, so she wasn't hurt. He said he managed to grab a gun and kill the roosters. But not before one of them spooked his steers so bad they broke out of their corral. Now the steers're up in the mountains somewhere and his dog won't come out from under the porch. Husk says he saw three people running away, and he's positive one of them was you."

"I think you should arrest him for making bullshit up. Tell him to come over, like I said, and take a good look around. If he finds any proof it was me, he can punch me in the face as hard as he can, but if he doesn't, I get to punch him."

"Is that a threat?"

"No threat. It's just a deal. He doesn't have to do anything if he doesn't want to. But you should tell him to stop blaming Indians when he can't prove a thing. Isn't there a law against that?"

The policeman crossed his arms. "So you're saying it wasn't you?"

"What kind of person would do something like you said? You tell me."

The cop inhaled deeply, then breathed out. "Why do I smell chicken shit? I was raised on a farm in Saskatchewan, and I've known that smell since I was a boy."

"You prob'ly stepped in some of Norris's."

The officer strolled over to where the chicken pen had been. After having a good look around, he went back to his car. His hand on the door handle, he said, "You should know that Mrs. Husk told me she had a clear look at the person her husband saw, and she said it wasn't you."

"So what are you here for?"

"Look, my job is to deal with facts. I see feathers high up in that tree and in a corner of the woodshed. What do you say about that?"

Alphonse peered up. "Somebody's got pigeons across the river, and they roost here once in a while."

"Well, since Mrs. Husk said it definitely wasn't you and I have more important cases to investigate than people pulling a mean prank, I'll let it go."

Opening the car door, he removed his hat and placed it on the passenger seat. He got in, started the car and turned around. All he had to do was glance down at Alphonse's feet and he would have seen the evidence he needed.

CHAPTER 26

LEWIS CAREFULLY PLACED THE ARROWHEADS and odd-shaped fragments of stone on an upturned wooden box. He flipped them around, spacing them out and arranging them in neat rows. "Look at these," he said to Eddie, Marvin and Alphonse, who were all gathered around him at the front steps. His cousin's pieces and the collection he'd seen at the museum with Loretta had piqued his interest. Now he could feel in his fingers the importance of these artifacts left behind by a people he was beginning to learn more about.

Lewis envisioned a brown-skinned man, an ancestor perhaps, peering down the shaft of an arrow, smiling in approval at what he had created, and then sliding it into a deer-hide quiver. He hadn't been sure what Rosalyn meant that day at the swimming hole when she asked, "Where's our history?" Now he understood.

"Look at this," Alphonse said, picking one up. "See how small and sharp it is? This thing goes deep inside a deer or any animal if you hit the right spot." He laid it back down and picked up another one. "This is a lot heavier and rounded at the point. That's for killing rabbits and fool hens. You almost don't need an arrow to kill one of those. Just walk up and wring its neck. That's why spruce grouse are called fools."

"Norris Husk found all of these at the old fishing camp. Where are the ones for spearing salmon?" Lewis asked.

"They used different kinds. Some were arrows tied to a string or a harpoon. When we lived down at Six-Mile, we made our spears outta pitchforks that we heated up in a fire then shaped with a hammer. The really old ones were made outta bones or sticks, but they kinda looked the same."

Isabel and Grace came out of the house.

"Where did you guys get all those?" Grace asked.

For the longest time, no one said a word.

Finally, Alphonse said, "From a close friend."

"A close friend? What's that?"

"A friend that's . . . you know, close."

"You mean close to here?"

"Kinda. I know an old *summa* who collected these. He told me he always felt guilty keeping them for himself and he wanted me to have them because they belong to our people."

"You're so full of it, Alphonse. Since when do you have an old *summa* friend? I was just at the store and I heard all about how somebody threw some mean chickens into Husk's house. Is that your old friend?"

"Hmmm," Alphonse said.

She laughed. "You're such a bullshitter. Where are those two roosters of yours, anyway?"

"Up and flew away, the buggers."

The sound of crunching gravel made them look up to see a car coming down the road. But it wasn't the kind of dirty old car that usually showed up at their place, wobbling along the uneven road, springs squeaking and exhaust pipes rattling. This was a shiny new black car that seemed to glide over the bumps and hollows, the motor humming like a sewing machine.

As Lewis and Marvin gathered the arrowheads back into the box, Alphonse said, "Only one person I know can afford a brand-spanking-new Cadillac, and that's the chief."

Grace said, "Where does he get the money to buy a car like that?"

"Like I said, he's the chief."

"I didn't know he even knew how to get here."

"Maybe he's campaigning," Alphonse said.

"He won't find any votes around here, that's for damn sure."

The driver turned off the motor, opened the car door and climbed out. "Hello, Alphonse, Isabel, Grace," he called.

"Lawrence," Grace said. "Are you lost?"

"Nice to see you too, Grace. You should know, a couple weeks back your Jimmy came to see me at the band office." Lawrence cleared his throat, growing nervous under Grace's stare. "And he wants to move back here. Half of this land belongs to him now, and the other half is Alphonse's. Jimmy said he's not going to try to move in with you, Grace—he'll build his own house. Cookie from the Indian office told me to come out here to let you know. I think he's scared of you."

Grace took her time to answer, as Lawrence looked more and more uncomfortable. She said, "I heard you and Jimmy were scheming up something. And why wouldn't you, when he happens to be your first cousin and drinking buddy."

"We aren't scheming nothing. After your mom died, half the land went to Jimmy because he's a man and that's what they do."

"Who's they?"

"Indian Affairs."

Grace came down the porch steps and walked up to the chief. "I don't care who says what. This is my land. I was here long before Jimmy came around, so how could it be his?"

He took a step back. "I just told you. You think I made all this stuff up? I don't give a damn one way or the other."

"I heard they can't find him. Are you hiding him someplace?"

Lawrence bristled. "Nobody knows where he's at. I haven't seen Jim since he came into my office."

Grace poked his chest with her finger. "You really think I'm just gonna let him move back? If you do, then you're dumber'n I thought. Why don't you get back in that fancy car of yours and get outta here."

"You can't talk to me like that. I'm the chief," Lawrence said, as he walked back to his car.

"Hey," Alphonse yelled. "Why do you have all your windows rolled up? It's hot as hell out here."

"Air conditioner."

"One more thing, Lawrence," Grace said loudly. "I hear Norris Husk got a lot of money when the pipeline went through his place. Where's mine?"

Lawrence looked back at her as he opened his door. "It doesn't work that way and you know that."

Grace was angry now and went quickly toward the chief. "I hope you like riding in my car."

Slamming the door, he drove away, fine dust lifting from the road to settle on the car's polished paint.

Eddie spoke up. "Mom, do you really think Jimmy's got the balls to move back here when he knows what'll happen?"

They all looked at her, expecting her usual angry cursing at the unfair world, but Grace had her eyes to the ground, too deep in thought to answer.

CHAPTER 27

EDDIE TOOK A BACK STREET up a steep incline, turned onto Barnard Avenue and idled along until he stopped the car at what looked like a sheer drop-off. "They call this Suicide Hill," he said to Lewis, sitting on the passenger side. The tailpipes mumbled as the brothers looked down on the main street of Vernon stretched out below them. Traffic lights at the far end of town blinked red, amber and green. Off to the left, the hospital stood high on a hill overlooking Polson Park and the town. Eddie revved the engine. A horn honked behind them and Lewis looked back to see an impatient driver laughing as he revved his own car. The girl sitting next to him shifted nervously in her seat.

Eddie shoved the gearstick into first. "Well, Lewis, are you ready to die?"

He popped the clutch and gunned the engine, tires squealing as they flew down the steep hill. He speed-shifted into second and then into third as they came to what could have been a ski jump. Engine roaring, they lifted off and Lewis counted three seconds before the car slammed down onto the pavement with a bang, tires screeching. He looked back, expecting to see sparks showering the road behind them from a bottomed-out rear end, but there were none. Eddie fought hard to correct the car's swing to the right. When he regained control, he pulled over and stopped, laughing at the shocked look on Lewis's face.

"Did you see that oil slick at the bottom of the jump where somebody ripped out their oil pan?" he said. "I thought I was going to lose it there for a second. Whaddya think, wanna go back up and do it again?"

Lewis shook his head. "I'm good."

Eddie bounced in his seat. "Come on, let's do it just one more time."

"Once is enough. How did you hear about this place, anyway?"

"Camille, the guy I board with, spent his summers with his dad in Vernon after his parents broke up. He said it's just luck or a miracle nobody ended up dead on that hill yet. Now I know what he means. He also told me I should give Magnetic Hill a try. He said I'd freak. You ever heard of it?"

"No. What is it? It's not another jump like this one, is it?"

"Only one way to find out."

Eddie took a quick look around for police cars, did a U-turn and drove back up the street. On the outskirts of town, they came to where the pavement ended at a stop sign then turned onto a gravel road. They drove up and down, criss-crossing the back roads until Lewis was sure they were lost. In the middle of nowhere, they spotted a grey-haired man on the other side of the road, walking a small bulldog on a leash. Eddie stopped, rolled down his window and called to him, "Which way to Magnetic Hill?"

The man pointed to a road leading off to the right. Eddie drove on until the high beams lit up a road sign.

"There it is," Eddie said. "Dixon Dam Road."

When they crested a small rise and saw a pine tree with a Y-shaped top, a barbed-wire fence running alongside, they stopped. "This has to be the spot," Eddie said, and drove to the bottom of the hill. Shifting into neutral, he took his hands off the steering wheel and his foot off the brake. The car began rolling back up the hill.

"What the hell?"

"Jeez, look at that," Lewis said. "We're picking up speed."

Eddie braked at the top, drove back down and did it again.

"This is crazy, Eddie. How does it do that?"

"Maybe it's an optical illusion or something, because it sure doesn't make any sense." They went up and down until another car came along, and then they drove back toward town.

"I'm starving," Lewis said. "I'd love a hamburger right about now."

"How about we go where Mom and Alphonse used to take us? That's way better than any old burger joint."

Back in town, they drove down Main Street and turned left into Chinatown. Faded signs, in Chinese characters with English translations printed underneath, advertised boarding houses and a social club. During the day these buildings looked rundown, with their weathered siding, crooked doors and broken windows. But at night, under the street lights, they looked like the homes of ghosts and old secrets known only by the people who had lived and died there.

Cars and trucks lined the street near the Goon Hong, Lotus Gardens and Hong Kong Village restaurants. Because they served good Chinese food at cheap prices, all three eateries were seldom empty. Eddie turned into the parking lot of the Lotus Gardens, and they went inside.

After they slid into a booth and grabbed a menu, Eddie noticed a table of three Indian men watching them. "Look at those *skins* over there looking at us like they want to start something."

Lewis glanced over. "They're probably just wondering who we are."

One of the men turned in his chair and fixed a narrowed stare on Eddie, and it didn't sit well. Eddie went to get up, but Lewis reached over and grabbed him by the arm. "Are you trying to get us killed? There's three of them. Are you planning on fighting them all?"

Eddie jerked his arm away. "Does he think I'm scared of him?"

"What's wrong with you, Eddie? Since when did you start acting like this?"

Eddie couldn't let it go. "Where I live, you don't let people get away with looking at you like that. Next thing you know, they're laughing at you every time they see you. Then you get a name for yourself, and it never goes away."

Lewis couldn't believe this was his brother talking. "Jesus, what's it like up there, anyway? You know what I do when I see a drunk staring at me? I look away. If you want to get your ass kicked, do it when I'm not around."

A waitress came to take their order.

"Two chicken chow mein and green tea." Eddie closed his menu and slid it behind the condiments. "And sesame seeds."

Just then a big man came through the door, stopped and looked around the room. It was Hank. When he saw Eddie and Lewis, he walked over to the booth. He slid in and bumped Eddie with his shoulder. "Christ, I been hearing all kinda things about you. That you were missing or even dead. I bet your family was glad to see you."

"I guess. Good to see you, Hank," Eddie said.

Hank waved at the men in the corner, who were still eyeballing the brothers. The waitress set down a pot of Chinese tea, small cups and a saucer of sesame seeds. Hank grabbed a menu and quickly ordered. Eddie poured soy sauce into a saucer, dipped his fork into the black liquid, then pressed it down on the sesame seeds. He stuck the fork in his mouth. Lewis did the same, and soon the seeds were gone.

Eddie put down his fork. "Who are those Indians over there? The one guy is giving us dirty looks."

"Don't worry about them. They won't bother you unless you start something first."

Lewis said, "I think Eddie already did that."

"What happened?"

"That one drunk thinks he's so tough. When I got up to go see what his problem was, Lewis stopped me. Our dad used to look at me like that, but I was just a kid then. Now I don't let people get away with that shit."

Hank put down his cup, stood and went over to the table where the men sat eating. He talked with them for a few minutes and the table broke out in laughter. When he slid back into the booth, Eddie asked, "What did you say to those guys?"

"I told them you were a hothead just like they were when they were your age."

"What's so funny about that?"

Hank looked at Eddie. "I like you, Eddie, but you need to stop looking for trouble. Those guys are from Six-Mile. If I was you, I'd be making friends with your people instead of enemies. Because if you have a flat tire or your car breaks down there, you might not like who stops."

Lewis saw that Eddie still couldn't look away from the men. "It's like he's trying to scare me from way over there. If he wants a fight, why doesn't he just come and ask me?"

"C'mon, Eddie," Hank said. "Now they know you're friends of mine, they won't bother you anymore, so why don't we eat and forget about it."

The waitress came, balancing plates of food on her arms.

Lewis said, "Hank, you're like the Lone Ranger, always coming along to save the day."

Hank laughed. "Well, I'll soon be riding off into the sunset. I can hear the Kal calling."

When they were done, Hank wiped his mouth with his paper napkin. "Well, that was good as always, but I better get going."

"Did you bring your car?" Eddie asked.

"No, I wanted to stretch my legs."

Eddie reached for his wallet. "Let me pay for this and I'll drop you at the Kal. You can get me a case of beer, okay?"

"Sure, but when we stand to go out, I want you to wave to those guys and give them a little smile."

Eddie stood. He showed his palm and dipped his head toward the men, and they waved back.

Minutes later they pulled up behind the Kalamalka Hotel. Hank went inside and a few minutes later came out with the beer. "Here you go. You boys look out for each other, you hear? And don't go around picking fights. One more thing, when you open this case, you gotta drink all of it before it goes bad." He reached over and squeezed Eddie by the shoulder and went back inside the bar.

Eddie put the beer in the trunk and covered it with a blanket. Then he backed out of the parking lot and turned down the street, joining all the young drivers out doing mainers. There was only one reason for touring up and down the street, and that was to see and be seen. It wasn't hard to tell which cars belonged to the driver and which were borrowed from parents. A Studebaker with four girls cruised slowly past, staring at them, as "Crimson and Clover" blasted from their car radio.

"What are we doing?" Lewis asked.

"Trolling for women."

Lewis groaned. "Let's go home and have a beer on the range. I don't want anything to do with girls right now."

"Boy, that is something you'll never hear me say."

A green 1955 Chevy with glittering mag wheels approached from the west end of town. It sported yellow shackle extensions and a custom hood scoop. It stopped in the road and the driver stepped on the brakes then revved the motor, smoke billowing from the rear tires as the car crouched. When he released the brakes, the car raced down the street, tires squealing, muffler growling.

Girls on the sidewalk, walking in bunches, tried to appear uninterested while giving side-eye glances. Then a police car entered the line of traffic, red light flashing. All traffic slowed and pulled over until the cruiser turned down a side street. Engines roared again.

Eddie braked for two pretty Indian girls at a crosswalk. As they walked past, one of them did a double take when she noticed Lewis. It was Rosalyn, with Loretta beside her.

"Who is that cute thing looking at you?"

"That's our cousin Rosalyn."

"She's pretty sweet, but who's the Indian princess?"

Lewis didn't answer.

"Hey," Eddie said.

"That's Loretta."

"Your Loretta?"

"Yes."

"Now I know why you're so broken-hearted."

Rosalyn came around to the driver's window while Loretta continued on across the street, stopping to wait on the corner. She looked in every direction but at Lewis.

"Hello, guys," Rosalyn said. "Hi, Eddie. We haven't seen each other since we were little kids, but I'm Rosalyn. This sure is a nice car you got here. Marvin told us all about it. You out looking for a date?"

"I'm just showing my little brother the sights."

A horn honked. Rosalyn leaned over and said to Lewis, "I bet you're glad to see him again. Get him to talk to you about how to treat women. You could use a lesson or two." She touched Eddie's arm and hurried over to join Loretta.

As Eddie drove away, he asked, "What's her problem?"

"She's just sticking up for Loretta."

"Looks like everybody's heard about you screwing that woman. Well, it's too late to cry about it now. The only thing to do is get yourself another girl."

Lewis slid down on his seat. "I just want to go home."

"Let's do a couple of mainers. If nothing happens, then we'll go."

The brothers drove up the street and were coming back down when a car drove up behind them, revving its motor and flashing its lights. Then the black 1966 Chrysler pulled around and drove up beside them.

"Look at these car club greaseballs," Eddie said.

Three men, too old to be teenagers, sneered over at them. The lights from the stores and street lamps glistened off their oily hair. The driver, sporting Buddy Holly glasses, had his arm resting on the open window. The passenger in the middle leaned ahead and shouted, "Nice car, Cochise. Where'd you steal it?"

Lewis glanced at Eddie, unsure of what to say.

Eddie smiled. In a loud voice, he asked, "What is that, your mom's New Yorker?"

The driver looked over. "I could wipe your car off the face of the earth, man."

"That big old boat? By the time you get that car wound up, I'll be at the finish line waiting, Elvis."

The driver floored the gas, the car surging ahead, then braked heavily and sped up again, rocking his car up and down.

"That all you got?" Eddie yelled.

"Why don't you put your money where your mouth is," the driver yelled, and stomped on the pedal again. A siren wailed and the car pulled over to the sidewalk, the cop right behind him.

The brothers drove on, laughing. Eddie said, "I saw that cop car coming as soon as those guys started showing off."

Just as Eddie was about to turn off Main Street, he noticed two girls parked in a Volkswagen Beetle in front of Freddie's Records. He pulled up alongside. "Hey," he called. "What are you two doing? Looking for a party?"

A brunette and her blond friend looked over at the boys. "We're just having a smoke and thinking about going home," the blond girl answered.

"Jeez, why does everybody want to go home tonight? How about you park that Bug and join us? We'll supply the refreshments."

"You from the reserve?"

"You bet."

"Do you know Danny Hunt? He's from down in Six-Mile," the dark-haired girl asked.

Eddie shook his head. "Everybody's from Six-Mile. I heard the name, but I don't know him. We live on the other end of the reserve."

"He was going with my cousin for a while," she said. "I thought all you people knew each other."

"As soon as we get the new red pages from the phone company, I'll look him up."

"Ha ha. Very funny."

"Look, where we live, we don't have many neighbours. Do you want to join us or what?"

The girls talked to each other, then rolled up their windows and stepped out of their car.

"Just take a look at those fine ladies, Lewis. Do they look like teenyboppers to you? No way. They're at least a couple years older than us, so I bet they know their way around."

"Eddie, I don't want to do this."

"Maybe you don't feel like it now, but when the night is over, you'll be thanking me."

Eddie turned down a grassy road, switching off the lights and the engine. They coasted into the Pleasant Valley Cemetery and came to a stop.

"This is a graveyard," one of the girls said.

"Sure, but it's the quietest place in town. Nobody will bother us here. Why don't we have a beer and get to know each other. I'm Eddie and this is my brother, Lewis."

Eddie leaned over and turned on the sex lights.

"Ooh, those are nice," the dark-haired girl said. "I'm Caroline and this is Debbie. We pump gas for her dad at Spicer's Garage on Old Kamloops Road."

"Caroline. I love that name. 'Sweet Caroline' is my favourite song, how about that?"

The girls laughed. "This guy's a charmer, isn't he?" Caroline said.

"Debbie, how about you get in the front with Lewis while I get the sodas from the trunk. I'll hop in the back with Caroline. That okay with you?"

"Fine with me," she said with a smile. "So get hopping."

Eddie got out, opened the trunk and ripped open the case of beer. Lewis held the door open for Debbie, then joined his brother by the trunk. Grabbing his arm, he said, "Smooth move there, Ex-Lax. You're as bad as Marvin. Do those lines work on Alberta girls?"

"Watch and learn, little one. Watch and learn."

"I don't want anything to do with this. Just do whatever you're gonna do so we can get going. God, this reminds me of when we were small. You always had to have everything your way."

Eddie laughed. Lewis opened two beers, slid into the front seat and handed one to Debbie. It didn't take long before heavy breathing and sucking sounds came from the back. Then a snap popped and a zipper unzipped.

Lewis tapped Debbie on the arm and pointed out the window. They stepped out of the car. Lewis grabbed the blanket out of the trunk and they walked to where they couldn't hear what was going on. Lewis spread the blanket on the grass behind a headstone, and the blond girl sat down and leaned her back against the slab.

Lewis peered around at the inscription. "Holy cow, that's hilarious."

Debbie sat up straight. "What?"

"It says, 'Bend Over in 1960.'"

"Baloney, let me see."

Lewis pointed.

She said, "It says, 'B.D. Dover. Died 1960.'"

"Oh," Lewis said. "I guess it is a little dark."

"You're the one that's hilarious."

They both leaned against the headstone.

"So we're having a party in a cemetery, for Pete's sake?" Debbie said. "I feel so creeped out."

"Just take a look around at the freshly planted white people. You can tell which one was a big deal by how many plastic flowers are on their grave. This isn't scary at all. Everything is neat and tidy and boring here, but I dare you to stand in the graveyard on the reserve in the dark."

He leaned closer. "There's this story about a good-looking guy who showed up at a dance at Head of the Lake not that long ago. Nobody knew who he was or where he was from. He said his name was Samuel, and he was all dressed up in flashy clothes and smelled so good in his expensive cologne. And his teeth. Everybody said they never saw teeth so white. The women wouldn't leave him alone, so he danced all night with every one of them, except for one girl who wore a cross on a chain around her neck.

"When she realized she was the only one he was ignoring, she started toward him to ask why he didn't want to dance with her. When he saw her coming, he took off out the door. Her and some other people followed him and he ran into the graveyard. They couldn't believe what happened next. He gave that girl a little growl and then he turned sideways. *Pop.* He disappeared. My uncle calls him Sideways Sam. People see him once in a while, walking around the crosses and carved headstones in the graveyard like he's looking for something."

"You're stringing me along, right?" Debbie said. "Don't tell me a story like that. Now I'm going to be up all night."

Lewis looked over her shoulder, then his eyes bulged and his face twisted in terror.

"What?" Debbie spun around to look and Lewis brushed his hand lightly across her hair. She screamed and cowered against the headstone. When Lewis began laughing, she punched him on his arm. "You little shit!"

Lewis laughed and laughed. "Oh, you're so easy, Debbie. Did you pee yourself?"

"That's not funny, you moron."

Lewis wiped his eyes with his hand. "Look, I promise not to tease you anymore. Can we just sit here? Please. We don't have to do anything but finish our beer."

She made a face in disbelief. "Wow, first you scare me half to death and now you just want to wait around doing nothing? Do I turn you off or something? Am I not pretty enough for you?"

"Oh god, no, you're a good-looking girl. But I've been getting in trouble lately because of pretty girls. I always seem to screw things up."

Debbie took a long drink, sighed, then put her head on Lewis's shoulder. "I should be mad at you, but I can see something's wrong. What's her name?"

"What? Who?"

"The girl you can't stop thinking about."

"I'm not thinking about any girl."

"Any fool can tell you had your heart broken. I saw it all over your face when I got in the car. Tell me your troubles. I'm a good listener."

Lewis hesitated for a moment. "Okay, something did happen to me, but it felt like it was happening to somebody else, like I was outside my body, looking down. I took my girlfriend to a dance at the hall on the reserve and when I turned around she was gone. And the next time I saw her, she was hugging some other guy and kissing him on his cheek and . . ."

"Oh no. Oh my god, Lewis. Was it Sideways Sam?"

"What?"

Debbie laughed.

"You want to hear this or not?"

"I do. I'm sorry." She couldn't stop giggling.

Lewis looked up at the stars. "So at the dance I had sex with a woman, and my girlfriend found out and now she's not my girl anymore. I'll give you a million bucks if you can tell me how to fix this."

Debbie sat up. "I don't know what to say. Maybe you have to go to India and climb to the mountaintop and ask the swami."

"Or I could go to Chinatown and read a fortune cookie."

"Or you can stop fooling around on your girlfriend."

Lewis had no answer to that. He thought a while, then said, "I didn't mean to. It just happened."

Debbie turned his face toward hers to study him. "I never saw this kind of hurt on a boy before. It's obvious you still like this girl, but I don't know if she'll take you back. You could be the nicest person in the world, but you did something awful. Guys think they can have sex with another woman and then carry on like nothing happened. I don't think you're like that—heck, you won't even touch me. But there it is. You knew it was wrong and you feel bad now, but you still did what you did and I don't think she'll ever forget that. If you do get her back, she'll always wonder if she can trust you."

"You know, I really feel better now," Lewis said.

"Lewis, do you feel bad for what you did, or do you feel bad because you got caught? Ask yourself that, dummy. I think in the future you should do like the song says and love the one you're with."

Neither spoke.

"Hey, lover boy, let's go," Eddie called.

"Now that's what I call a quickie," Debbie said. "I don't think screwing in a cemetery is against the law, but I'm pretty sure it's a sin. Listen, Lewis, if you really want to win a girl over, don't bring her to a graveyard and tell her a ghost story. That's a bigger turnoff than getting stuck with an ugly gas jockey."

They stood. Debbie helped fold the blanket. As they turned to go to the car, she said, "Hold it." She gave Lewis a big hug and then kissed him on the lips. "You'll get over her," she said.

CHAPTER 28

ANY OTHER TIME, he and Marvin would be having fun together, talking and laughing, but tonight Lewis would have preferred to be alone. Debbie had him thinking again about what happened with Loretta. He felt guilty and he missed her, and it was making him miserable.

Marvin tuned the truck radio to a country music station, and the songs about love and loss sounded so corny that Lewis reached over and turned the dial. And when he found the song that he had been hoping to find, "Those Were the Days," he turned up the volume. There was something about the ukulele plucking away in the background and the female singer's sad crying voice that told exactly how it felt to lose your girl. He closed his eyes, leaned back against the seat and began to hum along.

"Oh, for Chrissake," Marvin said. He reached over and turned off the radio. "That's the third time we heard that song. Boy, that girl's really got your head spinning."

Lewis shrugged.

"Let's have another beer, eh? We came up to the range tonight to get drunk, and I'm already halfway there and you're just finishing your first bottle. So come on now, sit up straight and stop looking like you lost your dog. Look at Eddie: he goes through girls faster than you and me go through shorts. You wouldn't see him moping around like this. Fuck, fight and blow the light. That's his motto."

Lewis sat up. "What, is he your hero now?"

"I'm just saying you can have fun with a girl without falling in love with her. The next pretty girl you snag might have the best tits and ass you ever saw, but if you fall in love with her, she'll know it and then she'll move in for the kill. As soon as something goes wrong, she'll rip that heart right outta your chest and stomp on it."

"Is that all you think of when you see a girl, her tits and ass? You're just like Eddie and Alphonse, like women are there for us guys to use and we shouldn't care about them at all."

Marvin reached for the door. "You're boring the piss right outta me."

When he walked to the rear of the truck, Lewis heard a long, steady splashing on the dirt. Marvin came back and sat on the seat, wiping his fingers on his pants. "You know, Lewis, you're way too young to be this serious, and serious and beer just don't mix. God, I wish Eddie was here, he'd know what to say to you. Where is he, anyway?"

"He was in town all day. He said he had to see his roommate about something."

"Ah, we don't need him. We'll have us a little party by ourselves. Here you go, get this beer in your belly and you'll feel better." Marvin popped the cap and handed the bottle to Lewis, opened one for himself, upended it and drank the bottle dry.

"I don't know how you guys can drink the whole thing in one go like that. I did it once at the dance and look what happened. My girl left me."

Marvin laughed. "First of all, can we put away the violins?

And second, you're just a beginner. Come on, try to get it down without stopping."

Lewis lifted the bottle and began swallowing. Just as he was close to the bottom of the bottle, he choked, spewing beer over the dash of the pickup.

"Damn," Marvin said. "You just about did it."

Marvin had his empty bottle half in the case when he paused. "Hey, I got a good trick I need to show you. One time up in Lillooet a friend of Dad's came to the house after he had a few beers and showed it to us kids."

Lewis said, "You know, I never once saw your dad have a drink. He's such a good guy."

"Oh, he can go the other way if he gets mad enough. That's why he tries hard to stay calm when things get bad. Mom said when he came back from the war, he'd drink until he couldn't drink any more, and if anybody tried to pick a fight with him, he'd stretch the guy out. Then he just stopped drinking. I asked him about that once and he said it's because he drank a lakeful when he was younger and just didn't feel like it anymore.

"Okay, the thing about this trick is, the guy was pretty tipsy and it took him a few tries before he could do it. So booze doesn't help, but it sure makes it funny. We have to go outside to do this, and we need lights."

Marvin turned on the headlights and they stepped outside. Before they made it to the front of the truck, the lights began to dim.

"I think we had the radio on too long. You better make it quick before she dies," Lewis said.

"Don't you try and hurry me so I'll screw it up. Okay, I bet you a buck I can stand on this beer bottle with my right foot and touch my chin with my left."

Lewis rubbed his hands together. "It'll be worth a dollar just to see you fall on your ass."

Marvin set a beer bottle on the ground and placed his foot on top. Sticking the tip of his tongue out the side of his mouth, he positioned his heel against the bottle head, lifted his left foot off the ground and hopped up. Struggling to keep his balance, he stepped down. "All right," he said. "One more time." With arms out, he bounced and stepped up on the bottle, grabbed his left foot and pulled it up to his chin. When he stepped down, he bowed to an imaginary crowd. "Thank you, ladies and gents. Now, Lewis, either fork over a buck or you try. Double or nothing says you can't do it."

Lewis picked up the bottle, kicked stones and sticks out of the way, set the bottle down, and ground the bottom into the dirt so it stood straight and solid. Hiking up his pants, he put a foot on the bottle and swung his arms out from his side to steady himself. On the third bounce he lifted up his left foot just as the battery died and the lights went out. He fell, landing on his back. Marvin bent down to help, but he was a little drunk and fell on top of Lewis. The two rolled in the dirt laughing.

"You owe me two bucks," Marvin said when he caught his breath.

"For what?"

"You didn't touch your chin."

"I did too. You just didn't see it because the headlights went out."

"I knew you'd say something like that."

A loud noise made Lewis sit up. "Hey, I think there's somebody down below us." They ran to the edge of the hill and looked down to see a car spinning in a circle, the motor revving high, tailpipes giving a mighty roar. A manly spectacle. The headlights lit up the trees and brush as the car swung violently around, disappearing inside a cloud of dust, before rocking to a stop when the engine stalled. Laughter could be heard coming from inside, punctuated by a girl's high-pitched giggle. The driver started the car again and drove ahead, parked and switched off the motor.

"There's the kid himself. Only Eddie would do a power turn like that. Did you hear a girl laughing? Looks like he's gonna put the bone to her right about now," Marvin said.

"Boy, this guy," Lewis added. "It's all he ever thinks about."

They watched as the interior lit up in a red glow. "He just put his sex lights on. Looks like he's moving in for the kill. I bet he thinks he's got the whole place to himself. Why don't we get down there and scare the living Jesus out of him?" Marvin said.

"Oh, he'll be so mad, Marvin. Let's do it."

It was difficult navigating their way down the uneven ground in the dark. Lewis tripped over a stone and it rolled down the hill. He couldn't see which way it travelled but hoped it wouldn't hit the car. As they came closer to the bottom, Lewis slipped on cow manure and fell on his back. "Ow, dammit."

"Jeez, Lewis," Marvin hissed. "Be quiet."

Lewis stood and rubbed his foot on the grass to clean his shoe.

They managed to make it to the car unnoticed and stopped by the trunk to peek inside at two heads backlit by the sex lights. Murmuring voices could be heard over soft music from the radio. Marvin waved Lewis to the driver's door while he went to the passenger side. By the rosy glow of the sex lights, Lewis watched Marvin put up his hand and whisper the count. "One, two, three."

They yanked the doors open and the interior light came on just as Marvin and Lewis began rocking the car, yelling and howling. The girl jumped and screamed as Eddie threw his hands up as if fending off the devil himself. When Lewis saw the look on his brother's face, he wished he had a Polaroid camera. It would have been so good to have something over Eddie.

The girl recognized Marvin and stopped screaming. She turned toward the driver's side. When she spotted Lewis, her hands went to her mouth. Lewis couldn't believe his eyes, and blinked as if to wash the image away, but she was still there. It was Loretta.

And she was with his brother, whose main goal in life was to fuck a girl and take her panties. This wasn't what a person who cared about his brother would do, but someone who kept count of all the women and girls he bedded. Hurt and stunned, Lewis wanted to run away.

"Hey, Lewis, it's not how it looks," Eddie said.

Lewis didn't believe him. Smoke from two cigarettes smouldering in the ashtray floated out the driver's door. Loretta didn't smoke and had always said it was a filthy habit, but Eddie must have charmed her into giving it a try. Then he noticed that an open box of Big Elephant popcorn had spilled on the floor by Loretta, and the memories of the times they had shared the pink treats, in their short-lived time in the tent or sitting by the river or parked on the range, came rushing back.

He hit Eddie twice before he could defend himself and then grabbed him by the hair, dragging him out of the car.

"Lewis, stop," Eddie yelled. He managed to work himself free from Lewis's grip, and hit him on the jaw so hard, bright bursts of light filled the night sky like fireworks. Another punch landed on his ear, sounding like a bomb had exploded. Another glanced off his cheekbone.

Lewis grabbed Eddie by the arms and swung him around, and their legs became tangled and they fell to the ground.

Marvin ran around the front of the car and jumped into the driver's seat. He started the car, spun it around, the battlers caught in the headlights' dusty beams. They rolled one way and then the other, Eddie kicking and trying to pull his arms free. Then he head-butted Lewis on the nose and Lewis let go, reeling back to grab at his face, blood leaking through his fingers. He heard Loretta say, "Marvin, you have to stop them."

"No," Marvin said. "They're going to settle this here and now or they'll hate each other."

Loretta went to open her door, but Marvin clamped a hand onto her wrist. She bent down and bit a finger, and he yelled, "Aaah, Jesus."

She hurried out the door. Searching in the headlights for a good stick, she spotted one at the side of the clearing.

The brothers scrambled to their feet and squared off, bringing up their fists. Eddie charged but Lewis was ready, and he grabbed his brother, tossing him to the side. Eddie landed on his back, with Lewis straddling him. Lewis threw punches, striking his brother over and over. Then the blows were coming down on them.

Loretta shouted, "Stop it, you two. Stop it."

She beat them with the stick, but they wouldn't stop. Looking around, she saw a fresh pile of cow manure and shoved the stick into it, rolling until there was a healthy-sized lump on the end, a dung lollipop. She went back and smeared their faces.

"What the hell are you doing, you fucking idiot?" Eddie shouted as he struggled to his feet, pawing at his ears and neck, retreating from the manure spreader.

"Don't you talk to her like that," Lewis said, breathing hard.

"For god's sake, you two, what are you trying to do, kill each other?" Loretta screamed.

Eddie rubbed his eyes and looked over at his car. Marvin hadn't turned the motor off and the smell of exhaust in the air made him cough. He touched a cut on his ear and looked from Lewis to Loretta to Marvin, then he walked to his car and climbed in. Slamming the door, he floored the gas pedal. Rocks flew out from under the rear tires, pinging and banging off the metal. The three had to turn and cover their heads with their hands as sticks, dirt and cow shit sprayed over them.

The car vibrated over the cattle guard and sped up Range Road toward the highway. Eddie was going too fast, and Lewis held his breath as the car fishtailed and came close to crashing into the trees. The car straightened and went out of sight.

Lewis couldn't face Loretta. "Marvin, can you take her home?" he said. "I'll ask Alphonse to pick up the truck tomorrow."

CHAPTER 29

GRACE WAS ANGRY. "Take a good look in the mirror. You look like a raccoon with those black eyes. I know what happened, Lewis, so don't bullshit me. Marvin told his mom all about it, and she told me. Jean said you and that damn girl were together all summer until you got caught with your pants down at the dance. The only thing I don't know is who was the slut you were rolling around with in the back of Alphonse's car. Nobody'll tell me her name, but I'll find out. Why the hell didn't I have girls instead of boys? And where is your brother?"

Lewis left the house in such a hurry, he forgot to bring his jacket. He went downriver by the big tree and sat cross-legged on the ground, glad to be outside, alone.

Tossing a pebble into the water just to hear the sound it made, Lewis watched the rise and fall of the current, and was soon absorbed by its constant motion. A storm upstream had stirred up mud and silt, turning the usually clear water a murky grey.

When a cool gust of wind blew over him, he shivered and wrapped his arms tightly around himself. The temperature had dropped the night before, bringing with it an early touch of frost. The salmon run would be under way in a matter of weeks, the water red with hundreds of sockeye. Everything it seemed, even the weather, had changed overnight. School was a week away and Lewis couldn't wait to get back.

He debated going back to the house to see if there was any news about Eddie. Lewis hoped he was just sleeping in his car somewhere and that nothing bad happened to him. He pulled out a handful of dry grass and tossed it in the air. A single thread landed on the water and he watched as it drifted away.

His thoughts turned again to Loretta. He imagined her walking through the rooms of her house, helping her mother sweep and wash the floors, and then dashing outside to pet old Duke. She told him that at night she liked to lie on her bed and read until she fell asleep and, in the morning, find that the book had slid to the floor without waking her.

And here he was, without Loretta, and without Eddie.

Touching his sore, swollen face, he felt the betrayal of catching them alone together all over again. That's when he decided he needed to find his brother and have it out in the cold light of day.

As he stood, Alphonse came out of the trail, brushing spiderwebs and leaves off his shirt. "That musta been one helluva scrap you and your brother got into," he said. "You look like you came out the wringer of your old clothes washer. This is like a Zane Grey Western—a girl gets between two brothers and they fight over her. Wonder how this one ends. What are you doing down here? Hiding out?"

"Staying away from Mom. I can't stand to hear her going on and on about everything."

"I just came from your place. Your sweetheart is up there right now with Isabel. Looks like she's on her way to see you for round two."

Lewis said, "She can't point her finger at me anymore and bring up Lily. Not after I found her with Eddie in his car, getting ready to—"

Alphonse rapped his knuckle on his nephew's head. "Wake up. Don't you see, the foot is on the other shoe now."

"What?"

Even though his uncle could mess up the simplest saying, Lewis knew he was right. "So what am I supposed to do? What do I say to her?"

Alphonse shook his head. "Christ, this sounds more like a Harleykin romance than a Western. I can hear the fiddles already. Do you want this girl to slide her shoes under your bed or not?"

Lewis didn't answer.

"Course you do. So tell her it was all her fault, or some of it was. Spin it around on her."

Lewis scratched his head. "If I want her back, I'm supposed to blame her? I don't know what you're talking about. She won't believe a word I say. I don't know much about women, but Lily Edwards? She'll never let that go."

"When are you going to learn? Stop being so honest. It's not like you sweet-talked Lily into it. She's the one who wanted to crawl all over your young body. You just didn't fight back, that's all. Jeez, who would? I'd lay there like a log with her ass a-gyrating on me.

"I better get going before your girl gets here. Just think about what I said. I never seen you so sad, boy. You're all alone in the middle of a deep lake and it's a long way to shore, so either you start dog-paddling or you're gonna drown. I'll see you later."

Alphonse turned and hurried downriver.

Lewis dreaded seeing Loretta again, but it wasn't long before a shadow floated over him where he sat. He looked up, shielding his eyes from the light.

"Hello," she said.

As she walked around him to the shore, the expression on her face reminded him of Lily. A beautiful anger. When he caught the faint smell of her shampoo, he felt an ache inside. He jumped to his feet, ready to face whatever she had to say, but she calmly held out his jacket. "Isabel told me where you might be and said to give you this because you might need it. Boy, you got some good shiners there. You look like a raccoon."

"So I heard." Lewis put on the jacket, feeling her eyes on his face.

"I can see why your mom is mad at me," Loretta said, "but I'm not the one that caused all the trouble. I just wanted to come over here to say a few things, so you know the facts. I was going over to visit Rosalyn when Eddie came down their road. He stopped and asked where you were. When I said I don't keep track of you anymore, he asked me to get in. I didn't want to go with him because of his reputation, so I said, 'No, thanks.' But he promised he just wanted to talk to me about you.

"I didn't know if I could trust him, but I got in his car because he was so insistent, even though when I go to bed at night and close my eyes, I can still see you at the dance staring at that woman with that goofy look on your face and it makes me sick. You know what? Forget it. This was a stupid idea." Loretta turned and began to walk away.

Lewis yelled after her, "Hold on a minute. You're not going to hear me out? That's bullshit and you know it is."

Loretta stopped. She looked as if she was having a hard time deciding whether she should keep walking or stay. She turned and came back.

Lewis didn't know where to begin.

"Cat got your tongue?" she said.

From the way she held her chin up and shifted her weight from one leg to the other, Lewis realized that despite her tough words, she was close to tears. He wanted to hold her in his arms to try to make her feel better, but he knew she wouldn't let him. And he had too many questions that needed answers.

"What about the cigarettes?" he asked.

"What?"

"The two cigarettes burning in the ashtray. One was for him and one for you. Eddie got you to start smoking, didn't he?"

Loretta made a face. "What do cigarettes have to do with anything? He asked me to try one, so I took a puff and almost choked. I just left it in the ashtray."

"I would never have asked you to do something like that. You wanted him, that's why you tried one."

Loretta stepped closer. "Nothing happened that night. Well, except for me and your brother in the back seat of his car fucking. Oh, wait a minute, that was you and her. Oops."

"Damn, I'm glad we're breaking up because I wouldn't want to be married to you."

"Married? You got high hopes."

The tears at the edge of her eyes were gone, her face pinched with anger.

He said, "The first time I make a tiny mistake over some little thing, you'll be in my face barking like a dog."

Loretta gave a steady glare. "Lily Edwards was no little thing."

Lewis wanted to defend himself, but she was right. The time for lies was over. He looked away. When he faced her again, he lifted a hand to say something, but the words wouldn't come. They stared at each other. "You're right," he said.

He started walking down the trail to home.

Loretta called after him. "Now who's walking away? Did you really think Eddie and I were going to do something?"

Lewis looked back at her. He wanted to keep going, but he couldn't after seeing how she stood her ground, arms folded.

"When you opened Eddie's car door and saw me sitting there, did you even hear what your brother said to you? He said that it wasn't how it looked. He was going to explain but you didn't want to hear him. You just dragged him out of the car and started to punch him."

Lewis tried to keep his voice calm. "What was I supposed to think? We watched while you guys did power turns and I heard you laughing. I could tell he was putting the moves on you."

"I did have a good laugh. Him doing donuts with his car was his way of cheering me up. And he didn't put the moves on me. He told me I should give you another chance. That got me to thinking that maybe I should, but then you came charging in and spoiled everything. So *you* did all this. You were wrong, dammit. You're just so . . . so dense."

Lewis didn't want to continue going back and forth but there was one thing he had to know. "Who was that guy you were with at the dance? You were looking in his eyes like you were in love with him. And then you gave him a big kiss."

Loretta laughed. "You're right. I love him and I did give him a kiss, on his cheek, you jackass. That was Vincent, my brother. He drove up from Wenatchee for a funeral in town and then he came out to the dance. It was just a fluke we saw each other. So all this time you thought I picked up a guy, and you were jealous." A smile began tugging at a corner of her mouth.

"All I saw was you giving him a big hug and going all ga-ga over him. I didn't know he was your brother."

"So? That's why you screwed that woman—to get back at me?"

"No."

"Why, then? Look, Lewis, you got nothing to lose, so go on, spit it out."

Lewis wondered if there was a way he could tell her about Lily so he wouldn't look bad. But he knew it was impossible, so he might as well tell her the truth. The Alphonse way. "Me and Alphonse were at the door when I saw Lily and . . . well, I couldn't help but stare at her. You saw her yourself. Alphonse said every man at the dance wanted to take her to bed but nobody trusted her because she did things that hurt guys."

Loretta listened, a stiff soldier.

"So after you walked away, he took me to his car to have a beer. I guess he felt sorry for me because I embarrassed myself in front of the whole dance hall. He went back into the dance, but I didn't want to. I had a few more beers and fell asleep. You know I'm not much of a drinker. Anyway, when I woke up, I got out of the car to look for you and she showed up. One minute I was minding my own business and the next thing she shoved me in the back seat of that car like I was a little kid. I banged my head on the door. Everything went fuzzy after that, and I couldn't think straight. Before I knew it, she was gone."

"Did you scream for help? Did you try to buck her off?"

"I couldn't. She held me down."

"So she was on top of you. Did you put your hands on her?"

"No."

"So you didn't kiss her?"

"No. Not really."

"Not really? What's that supposed to mean?"

"She kissed me."

Loretta paced in a circle. When she came back around, she stopped and jabbed her finger in his face. "I was there, remember? I saw she got you so hard you couldn't even blink, so don't tell me you didn't kiss her or touch her."

Lewis raised his hands. "I didn't."

"You had this gorgeous woman on top of you, and you wanted her so bad and you didn't touch her? I don't believe you."

"She wouldn't let me."

"So you wanted to, but she wouldn't let you?"

"Will you slow down for a second? Stop jumping on everything I say. What I mean is, she told me to shut up and lay there and not move."

Loretta thought for a moment. "Did you blow your load?"

Lewis looked down to the ground, up to the sky, then back. "I didn't know what was happening. The next thing I remember was Marvin was on his knees, sniffing down there to see if the air freshener covered the smell. But like I said, I bumped my head and couldn't think straight. I was going to tell you all about it, but then I saw how mad you were. It's not like I picked her up and sweet-talked her. I don't know how to do stuff like that. I'm not like Eddie and Marvin. When it comes to girls, I get all tongue-tied and kinda stupid. You know that."

"You were pretty smooth to me at the ball diamond that day. Remember? When you saw I had a Coke, you asked if I needed rum."

"I never would have thought that up by myself. Marvin told me what to say."

Loretta had another question. "So how come you tried to beat the shit out of your brother, but you let that woman push you around?"

Lewis's head began to ache. "I told you. I was drunk and woozy and she caught me by surprise. Don't tell anybody this. I was scared of her and what she'd do to me if I didn't listen. The way Alphonse talked about her, she might have had a knife. I don't know. Look what she did when I wouldn't do what she wanted."

Lewis pointed to the bottom of his ear. "See that? She bit the end right off."

Loretta walked up closer for a look "Oh for Pete's sake, you probably caught it on her earring when you were sucking her neck. But maybe what you say is true."

"What, that there wasn't anything I could do?"

"No. That you're stupid."

Lewis grabbed her by the shoulders. "I only said that to make you feel better."

"And I only agreed with you. You know, if you had a red nose with those black eyes, you'd look like a rodeo clown."

Lewis couldn't think fast enough to keep up with her. "You never run out of words, do you? You just can't help yourself."

"Stupid clown."

"Shut up."

"Or what? You gonna beat me up?"

"Want me to?"

"Go ahead, clown."

"Stop that, Loretta."

"Bozo."

Lewis pulled her against him and planted a hard kiss on her lips.

Loretta pulled away so fast she almost fell. "What do you think you're doing?"

"Shut up."

He pulled her against him again. This, time she put her arms around his neck and kissed him back.

CHAPTER 30

AS LEWIS AND LORETTA walked back up the trail, he reached for her hand, but she pulled away.

"I'm not ready for that yet," she said. "I still think you're a brat."

Coming around the corner of the house, Lewis noticed a strange car parked out front. A man came out of the house, followed by Isabel.

"Bye-bye, honey," he said. "Sorry I'm too busy to stay for a visit. I just didn't know if you heard the news or not."

After a brief hug, he ran lightly down the steps, waving at Lewis and Loretta, got into his car and drove away. Isabel waved as the man turned up the road and honked his horn.

"Who's that?" Lewis asked.

Isabel turned and smiled when she saw Loretta standing beside him. "That was my brother, Theo. It's too bad you weren't here to meet him. Hello again, Loretta."

"Hi, Isabel."

"I'm glad to see you two patched things up, but Lewis better run you home now. Grace was in the bath when you were here earlier. I didn't tell her you stopped by. Let's keep it that way for a while. I'm not telling you anything you don't know, but you're not very popular with this boy's mother. Why don't both of you get in the car and stay outta sight while I get the keys."

Lewis said, "Mom better not say a word to her about anything."

"Look, it's none of my business what you two get up to, but you need to get Loretta out of here. Theo just told us that Eddie is in a lot of trouble. Get her home before Grace sees her, and then you get right back here."

While they waited in the car, Loretta said, "She looked scared. I wonder what happened?"

Isabel appeared at the window and handed Lewis the keys. "Now get a move on."

When Lewis returned, he found Isabel and his mother at the kitchen table, Grace staring into a mug of hot tea. She looked up. "Want some?" He shook his head.

"I seen you and that girl sneaking outta here. I don't know how a little thing like that can make two brothers try and beat each other to death. I bet she could charm a rattler, that one. Just because she's pretty—"

Lewis cut her off. "Never mind about Loretta, Mom, just tell me what happened to Eddie. Isabel said he was in trouble."

Grace put down her cup. "I don't want that girl around here. Hear me? You keep her away. Theo said him and Horace were sitting outside at the Dairy Queen last night."

"Horse?"

"Horace. Theo said they were sitting at a table, having an ice cream, when two cars went flying past, drag racing. One of the cars rear-ended a delivery truck that turned onto the street. Theo said when the cops showed up, they were out of their car like they caught a murderer. The driver was laughing and howling like a dog when the cops put the cuffs on him. Then a paddy wagon showed up, the Black Mariah, and took him away. Theo didn't know who the driver was until he ran into Hank this morning and he told him it was Eddie."

Grace rubbed her face. "That's all we know. Eddie will go to court and hear what the charges are. How could he do something so stupid like racing on the street? He's lucky he didn't kill anybody. You two are turning out to be just like your dad."

Lewis shook his head. "You act like we're the biggest disappointment in the world."

"How do you think it looks with both of you riding around town in Eddie's fancy car, fighting over a girl and drinking all the time? Now he gets picked up for drunk driving and I don't know what else."

A loud knock made them all jump. Alphonse stuck his head around the door. "Is it safe to come in?"

"Grab a cup and sit down," Grace said.

Alphonse went to the counter and filled a mug with tea, then joined them around the table.

"It's Eddie," Grace said. She told Alphonse everything.

Isabel said, "We should go in and see him, Grace. He could be hurt."

"I don't want to look at him on the other side of those bars. But I hope they keep him in there so he'll see what it's like to have to ask the jailer to be let out of his cell so he can take a shit. That'll soften up his attitude."

"Okay–I think you're better off staying here," Isabel said. "He don't need to hear stuff like that, because he's probably feeling bad enough. We'll take him some clean clothes and cigarettes. He's gonna be dying for a smoke by now. And a couple of pocket books to help pass the time."

"Put 'em all in a cloth sack," Alphonse added. "After he has a shower, he can throw his dirty pants and shirt in there and use it for a pillow. He'll need both blankets they give you, cuz them steel beds can cool down beer. And take him some paper matches. I'll stay back and keep Grace company."

As Isabel and Grace rounded up what Eddie would need, Lewis grew impatient and went out to wait in the car. Alphonse followed him and stood looking down at his nephew. "You never set foot in a jail before, right?"

Lewis's gaze shifted to his uncle. "You know I haven't."

"I woulda never thought one of you would end up there. I guess Abel knew what he was talking about when he said that every Indian has to spend time in jail at least once. It's like losing your baby teeth or getting your tonsils out. Still, I always thought you both were smart enough to stay out of that kind of trouble. I don't like to think of Eddie cooling his beehind on a iron bed. I was in there a couple times. Once I was laying there staring up at the bottom of the bunk above and I seen where somebody scratched the paint off and wrote, 'In for murder. I killed a bottle,' and put his name under it. I even knew the guy."

Lewis looked away. "You and Mom don't think much of us, do you?"

"I'm just telling you this so you know, so listen. If Eddie's lucky and lands in cell eleven, tell him he can slide that small bulletproof glass window back a hair and look outside. Not much out there to see except cop cars, but you can just see the sky.

"And tell him he's gotta be on his toes all the time cuz just doing the smallest thing wrong in there can get you a good asswhipping. If you turn over in bed and it goes bong, somebody bigger and meaner than you will tell you to quit rolling around and keep still. If you're walking in circles in your cell, you wanna go slow and make sure you don't drag your heels or somebody will swear at you to pick up your feet. If he don't look anybody in the eye and or ask questions, he should be okay."

Alphonse wasn't done. "I hope the judge doesn't send him to Oakalla Prison or even worse the BC Pen. That's where the young ones go and get corn-holed by a three-hundred-pound murderer that's got nothing to live for."

A policeman ushered Lewis and Isabel into a visiting room that wasn't much bigger than a telephone booth. They sat on the narrow bench, waiting. There was a small chrome grill in the glass partition for them to talk through. It seemed a long time before the door swung open and Eddie stepped inside. Flecks of blood dotted his rumpled shirt, and his top lip was swollen.

"What happened to your lip?" Lewis asked.

Eddie ran a finger over it. "I banged my mouth on the steering wheel when I ran into that truck. You don't look so hot yourself."

"Are you gonna be okay?" Isabel asked. "How are you feeling?"

Eddie looked away from his visitors and grunted. "Peachy."

"Don't get smart with me. I didn't put you here."

Eddie looked at Isabel, surprised. "I'm sorry, Isabel. I'm a little on edge. Where's Mom?"

"She couldn't stand to see you in here, but she got some stuff together for you. We don't know how long you'll be stuck in here, so there's two pairs of pants, shirts, shorts and socks, a few books and two packs of cigarettes."

"Jeez, I haven't had a smoke since I got in here. But they don't let you have matches. You have to ask the guard for everything, and he doesn't come every time you call him."

Lewis took the book of matches out of his pocket. He tore them off, one by one, and passed them through the grill, with Eddie tucking each one into his shirt pocket. After the book was empty, Lewis ripped off the paper striker and passed it through.

"Thanks, Lewis. These are like gold in here."

"I wish you weren't in jail. You've been gone for two years, and I act like a jealous little kid."

"Don't worry about it. If that was all the trouble we had, we'd be doing pretty good. What is today, anyway?"

"Sunday," Isabel said.

"Jeez, it feels like I been locked up longer than a day. After court tomorrow, I hope I can come home. Sitting here, I think I figured out what I'm going to do. What about you and Loretta, Lewis? Do you think you and her can ever get back together?"

"We already did, but Mom's not happy about it."

"Pfff. Never mind what she thinks. She never did like me talking about girls."

"She doesn't like sharing her boys," Isabel said. "Eddie, we can't stay long and we need to get back to Grace. She'll want to know if you're okay."

"Are you coming to court tomorrow?"

"Yes, and I'll bring your mom if I have to drag her. Don't expect Alphonse, though. He won't come because he's scared the cops will keep him."

Eddie stood. "I'm dying to get back in there to have a smoke, so I'm gonna go."

"I'm really sorry about all this, Eddie. I was so stupid," Lewis said.

Eddie chuckled. "I'll see you tomorrow."

Eddie knocked on the door and a guard opened it wide. As he was about to leave, he looked back. "Tell Mom thanks for sending everything."

Isabel beamed.

———

The next day in court, Lewis sat between Isabel and his mother. As a line of prisoners were led in through the door, he remembered what Alphonse said about Indians and jail. Only two of the eight prisoners were white. Eddie usually stood out in any crowd because of the way he dressed and looked after his hair, but he looked as worried and guilty as the others.

A guard pointed to a row of seats behind a low railing at the front of the courtroom. As he took a chair, Eddie glanced back and gave them a weak smile. Lewis noticed that his lip didn't look as bad. A lady came through a door at the back of the room, followed by the judge, his long black robe flowing behind.

"All rise," the lady ordered.

They stood. After being helped to their feet, a few elderly people held the arm of the person beside them to keep their balance. Lewis felt sorry for an old woman who remained seated, clutching a wad of Kleenex in her bony hand, dabbing at her damp eyes.

The lady read from a paper, formally announcing the judge's name and the date, then bowed to the judge. "Be seated," she said.

The morning dragged on as Eddie's cellmates learned their fate. Some received a small fine. Others were sent to prison, over their lawyers' loud protests that the sentence was too harsh. After each case the judge banged his gavel and a sullen detainee was led by the arm out through a separate door.

When the court clerk finally announced Eddie's name, he stood and walked to the table, where he faced the judge, accompanied by a tall, skinny man carrying a briefcase.

After the charges were read and Eddie pled guilty, the judge spoke to the lawyer. "Do you have anything you'd like to say on behalf of your client?"

"Thank you, your honour. I would ask that you consider that this is the first time my client has been in trouble with the law. I don't need to tell you that he has a tough road ahead to pay the repair costs of the vehicle he damaged as well as his own car's, and cover the fine. But he has a good-paying job in Alberta, where he has been employed for two years. If he can get back up there sooner rather than later, he can start to straighten all this out."

The judge stared at Eddie. "Mister Toma, I'm not going to waste time lecturing you, but I have to ask, what's a decent-looking chap like yourself doing here in the first place? If you come before me again, I will not be amused. I'm fining you six hundred dollars and suspending your driver's licence for a year." *Bang.* "You may go."

CHAPTER 31

LEWIS STABBED THE SAUSAGE on his plate with his fork and cut off a chunk. He shoved it in his mouth and sat back in his chair, chewing slowly. He was still surprised by how much the place had changed. The new windows in the addition made the house so bright. He remembered a time before they even had electricity when he begged his mother to let him light the coal-oil lamp in the evening. He loved standing on a chair to touch a match to the wick, setting the globe back on the lamp and then watching how it lit up the dreary room.

The water pails and basin stand that had been a part of their everyday life were nowhere to be seen. Instead, the kitchen and bathroom hot and cold taps stood ready to be used at any time. No more walks down to the river in the dark to fill the buckets. Sometimes, as a kid, he'd hear a sound that was scary enough it gave him all the power he needed to run uphill with two full pails. By the time he set the buckets on the stand, they were only half-full.

A large roll of linoleum sat against a wall, close to where the door that used to lead outside now opened into the new addition. Grace said, "I kept the old door so we could close it to keep the noise from the TV out of the bedrooms. They're coming out tomorrow to finish off the floor. I can hardly wait."

Isabel and Grace had even convinced Alphonse to move the wreck out of the yard, and the place looked so much better. When school started again, Lewis thought that he wouldn't mind his classmates seeing for themselves how he lived.

Eddie sat quietly, studying the linoleum roll in the corner of the new addition.

"What are you thinking about, Eddie?" Grace asked.

He said, "I was thinking that you and Isabel did this, Mom, nobody else. Last night I had the best sleep and it's because the house feels so different. That, and my bed didn't make any noise when I rolled over."

Eddie placed his fork on his empty plate, blew the steam off his cup of coffee and took a noisy slurp. "I almost forgot what good food tastes like. Camille's grandma died a year after I got up there, and then it was just him and me in the house, and neither of us can cook worth a damn. We're lucky he has an aunt who takes pity on us and drops stuff off once in a while."

"Where's his mother?" Grace asked.

"Took off somewhere. Nobody knows."

"You guys just have to get yourself a cook," Isabel said. "Look for a good chunky girl with burn marks on her arms from loading wood into a hot stove and taking a turkey out of the oven. And little scars on her fingers where she cut herself with a sharp knife. That's how you know you got yourself a good one."

Eddie said, "I think we'll be eating more frozen dinners, thank you. I got enough troubles."

"When are you going back?" Grace asked.

"I'm going with Camille, so it's up to him, but I think three or four days from now. I wish I could go back in my car, but I have to kiss it goodbye. Since I won't be allowed to drive for a year anyway, I sold it to the guy at the repair shop. But before I go,

I want to take Lewis up to the high country above the range. I thought a lot about that in jail. What do you think, Lewis?"

"When can we go?"

"As soon as we get packed up. I'll ask Alphonse if he'll drop us off at the old Smith place and pick us up early Friday morning. I want to be up there as long as I can."

After putting their bags with food and camping gear in the back of the pickup, Eddie and Lewis climbed in beside Alphonse, who started the truck and pulled away from the house.

Lewis noticed that his uncle seemed anxious to say something. "What are you smiling about, Alphonse?"

Alphonse banged the steering wheel with his palm. "You're never gonna guess what I gotta tell you boys."

They looked at him, waiting. Then Eddie asked, "Do we really have to guess, or are you gonna tell us?"

"Did you guys hear a siren about a hour ago?"

Lewis said, "I did. I figured it was a policeman after a speeding driver."

"No, it was an ambulance, and it was headed for Norris Husk's place. I was walking to the store when I seen old Abraham Jenkie coming up the road in the other direction. I was just thinking I shoulda gone by his house and asked if he wanted me to get him something, when he brought up his shotgun and let go both barrels. Jeez, that boom rolled around them hills for a long time. Sounded like a jet. When Norris heard it, he jumped in his truck and drove down to the end of his driveway to see what the hell was going on. That bugger gave me some dirty looks, let me tell you."

"I heard that big gun go off," Lewis said, "and I didn't think anything of it. We hear the odd gunshot from hunters all the time."

"So what happened?" Eddie was getting impatient.

"You know how Abraham's been looking for that wolf all these years? I guess Norris's dog turned even meaner after them roosters got done with her, because she came after the old man, growling and snarling. Abraham shot that mutt right in the head. Maybe finding that wolf was all he was living for, because his poor old heart gave out on him and he died right there. When they were sliding him in the ambulance, it sure looked like he had a smile on his face."

Lewis glanced at Eddie. "Wait'll Marvin hears that. He'll have a good laugh when he finds out who killed that dog. Instead of one of us Indians, it was a weak old *summa* who happened to be on the road at the right time."

Alphonse dropped the brothers and their gear off and drove away, leaving them at the bottom of a mountain. "Is that where we're going?" Lewis said. "Up there?"

Eddie nodded. "You bet."

"It looks straight up."

Eddie clapped Lewis on the shoulder. "I bet I can get up there before you. I'll even give you a head start."

Lewis settled the full rucksack on his back and then stared past Eddie as if he had noticed something far away. He pointed. "Is that a bear?"

When Eddie turned to look, shading his eyes with his palm, Lewis took off up the mountain, scrambling on all fours.

"You dirty swine," Eddie yelled, and he hit the hill running, reaching ahead of him for anything to grab onto. Lewis was fifteen feet above him, kicking dirt down, gaining even more ground, but then he stumbled and fell to his stomach. Eddie caught up to him, then grabbed Lewis by the leg to pull himself higher. Lewis scrambled to his hands and knees as Eddie passed, and they raced up the hill like spiders going up a wall until both were so out of breath they needed to stop.

"Only a couple hundred more feet to go," Eddie said.

"Let's just rest," Lewis said, panting.

After a few minutes lying on their backs, they continued climbing at a much slower pace. When they finally reached the plateau, both collapsed on the ground underneath an old pine tree.

"Holy Jesus," Eddie said. "I thought I was gonna die back there."

Lewis pressed both hands to his heaving chest. "Have a cigarette, why don'tcha."

Minutes went by before they were able to stand and go through their supplies. Lewis pulled out an old wine jug Isabel used to water her pansies, even though they never stood a chance growing in the hot ground in front of the house where the cat buried its poop. He tipped up the jug, humming as he drank. After passing the bottle to Eddie, he sat back down and leaned against the pine tree.

Across the valley, he heard a train's horn, the sound echoing off the hills. When he spotted it on the tracks above the highway, he pointed. "Look how far away it is, and you can hear it so clear."

Eddie sat beside him, looking toward the chain of railcars inching its way along. "Just listen to that, Lewis. Do you know what that sound is?"

"I don't hear anything but the train."

Eddie closed his eyes. "Besides that. The sound is . . . no people. That's what that is. Just listen."

A soft wind washed through the pine needles and across their faces. In the cloudless sky an eagle wheeled upward, screamed, then levelled to glide toward the water. Hawks and crows scrambled to get out of the way. The eagle carried on, indifferent.

"You been up here before?"

"I came close to here when I was little," Eddie said. "Mom and Alphonse took me with them when they went hunting. There was hardly any deer close to home, so that's why we had to walk so far. I remember Alphonse yelling at me to hurry up when I fell behind. Then he told Mom it was my fault the deer stayed away because he'd had to holler at me. Do you remember what a prick he was back then? He couldn't stand us little kids. Mom finally told him to shut up and leave me alone."

"Where was I?"

"Home with Grandma."

"Did you sleep up here?"

"No, we had to walk all the way home. I remember they hardly talked because we had to be quiet for the deer. They never saw even one. I slept like I was dead when we got back."

Lewis looked around the plateau. "Where are we gonna sleep? Right here on this cliff edge?"

"Yep, right here. Just make sure you don't roll over in the middle of the night—it's a long way down. Why don't we set up camp before we do anything else. It doesn't look like it's going to rain, so we can sleep out in the open. And the wind is blowing away from us, so we can hang our asses out over that way to do our business," Eddie said, pointing. "After we gather some wood for a fire and put these old blankets on the grass, we can take it easy."

After the wood was collected and readied for the fire, the brothers lay on top of their bedding and stared up at the sky.

Thinking how good it felt to be up here, Lewis propped himself up on his elbows and looked over at his brother. Eddie hadn't spoken for a long while, but he was smiling.

Lewis asked, "What's going on over there?"

"What?"

"You're not talking. Why are you so quiet?"

"I was daydreaming, I guess, about that last day I had with Eva. I can remember what I did, what I ate, what I felt. I can even remember what I was wearing."

"Why are you thinking about her now?"

Eddie pulled a cigarette from the pack and offered it to Lewis.

"No, thanks, I just can't get the hang of those things."

Eddie lit a match, took a long drag and exhaled through his nose. "Because this is where I came after I found out she was dead.

"Remember Grandma's funeral? I took off under the bridge to get away from all the people at the house. That was only a couple of days after the big fight I had at school, and I was pretty beat-up-looking. Eva found me there. When she saw me and touched my face, oh, her hands felt so soft and cool. A couple of weeks earlier, she got mad at me when I stole a kiss, but now she invited me to have lunch at her place. When we got to her house, she kissed me.

"I couldn't believe it. Lewis, I felt like I was floating off the floor. Then her mom and dad came back from church, and they let me know in so many words that I didn't belong at the table because I was an Indian. Her uncle and cousin were there too for Sunday lunch. The uncle said his son was off to a military school back east and was already feeling homesick. Then he told him he just needed to find himself a squaw for the night and he'd soon feel better. I was so mad I had to get away from there.

"Eva caught up to me on her brother's horse and I jumped on behind her. She whipped the horse and we came around the corner flying. We were going to go through the gate, but I forgot I closed it before I went to the bridge. She was pulling those reins hard to get the horse to stop, but it kept running and tried to jump across the cattle guard. Its front feet went down between the rails and we both landed on the road. That's all I remember until I woke up in hospital.

"I asked everybody how Eva was, but nobody would tell me anything. Then after I came home, Alphonse told me she died. He must have told you that much, Lewis. About the horse, I mean, and what happened?"

"Sure, he told me and Mom what he saw."

"When I heard Eva was dead, I was going to take my gun and crawl inside my old tree and end it all where nobody would find me. But once I was in the tree, I cried myself to sleep. When I woke up, everything changed."

CHAPTER 32

A HAWK CIRCLING IN THE SKY, searching for small game below, saw what appeared to be a lifeless form curled up fetal-like where no human should be. But a slight movement showed that the person was only sleeping.

Tears had pooled in Eddie's eyes. When he looked up, he felt like he was underwater, so he turned his head to the side and a line of liquid ran across his cheek and down his neck. A scratching sound drew his attention and he saw a mouse speeding up the inside of the hollow tree trunk. Just as the mouse reached the top and paused to look around, clawed feet snatched it up and it was gone.

Bits of wood landed on Eddie's face. When he shook his head, the ache in his skull began all over again. Then he felt the strange weight of the gun lying across his chest, and he remembered where he was and why he was there. It was like waking from a terrible nightmare. He sat up and jerked back the bolt, and the bullet landed on the ground beside him. He picked it up and pushed it into his pants pocket. Shoving the rifle ahead of him through the stump opening, he squirmed and twisted to free himself, more wood raining down. The more he struggled to get out, the more chips fell—the old tree was ready to go at any time. With a final push, he dragged himself free and stood, brushing off his clothes and hair.

The world outside felt changed somehow. The river was loud in his ears and the air was sharp in his nose. A squirrel chittered, a crow squawked and other birds and creatures cheeped and shrilled as though mocking him for his foolishness. The wind, washing through the forest, moaned like a ghostly choir.

Eddie found it hard to believe he had planned on hurting himself, and he grabbed the yellow kerchief from his pocket, his last reminder of Eva, and tossed it inside the tree opening. Holding on to a souvenir of her seemed useless. She was dead and gone, and nothing could bring her back. Suddenly furious, he stepped back and ran at the tree, hitting it hard with his shoulder. It shook and a large chunk split off to land beside him. He hit the tree again and more debris fell. With a last effort, he gritted his teeth, ran at the stump and jumped, slamming into it hard with both feet. It collapsed in on itself as he rolled out of the way. The smell of wood rot hung in the air. Old, decaying, dead, still.

He walked over to a log by the river, sat down and put his head in his hands. The pain hammered inside him with a new strength; he could feel the throbbing with his fingers. He squeezed his head hard and rocked back and forth until the pain began to ease. Resting his elbows on his knees, he cradled his jaw, trying to think of what to do next. The one thing he knew for sure was that he needed to get as far away from home as he could, because he couldn't live here anymore, not one more day. The only question was where to go and how.

He watched the birches and poplars on the far shore, their leafless branches trembling in the wind. The grey sky was showing blue just behind the mountains to the north, and he could see their broken reflection in the moving water.

Eddie had a feeling he was being watched. He checked the trail behind him. Then something below him caught his eye. Sitting at the water's edge was a fat, bug-eyed frog, bobbing up and down as if doing push-ups while staring at him. Eddie thought frogs always looked old and grumpy, the way their mouths hung down at the corners and their throat bulged when they breathed. It wasn't the first time a frog had sat close to him unafraid, like it wanted to spend time with him. But he had no patience for that now, so he kicked at the frog and it leapt, plopping into the water to swim gracefully downstream like a scuba diver.

Eddie stood and stared up the path to his house. He had no idea how long he had been holed up in the tree or if anyone was out looking for him. He took a last look around, picked his gun off the ground and started up the trail, breaking into a run. There were no vehicles parked near the house. He leaned the gun against the porch then threw open the door so hard it banged against the wall. As he searched for something he could use to carry clothes and food, he remembered the flour sacks Isabel had washed and smoothed with a stove iron. Why she had wanted to save them, he didn't know. He found them stacked in a corner of the pantry with the towels and pulled out two.

He went to the big dresser in the corner of the bedroom he shared with his little brother and took out pairs of pants, socks, shirts, underwear and his jacket. After stuffing them into one of the bags, he rearranged the rest of the clothes so it would seem as if nothing was missing.

Back in the kitchen, he opened the top door of the hutch. When he was little, the shelf was mainly empty except for dust and mouse turds, but now it was lined with cans of pork and beans, creamed corn, shrimp and sardines and other treats that his mother could never have afforded. After Ray and Isabel had moved in with them, they kept it well-stocked, giving Eddie the feeling that the family wouldn't go hungry again. He was careful to take only one can of each, but there were so many he doubted anyone would notice a few were missing. The bread box was half filled with Isabel's tasty buns, so he stuffed four into the food bag. He would really miss Isabel's cooking. She could make something delicious out of anything.

He took down a box of matches from the top of the pantry and placed it with his clothes. Then he noticed a rusty pocketknife alongside the canvas water bag Ray tied to his car grill to cool as he drove. Eddie pocketed the knife and grabbed the water bag and shook it to see if it still held any water, dust floating to the floor. He filled the bag from the water pail and hung it around his neck by the strap. It felt cool on his skin when he lifted it against his face.

As he took one last look around to make sure nothing looked out of place, he spotted the box of tea bags. Tea would be the only drink he needed when he sat by himself at the fire, so he grabbed a big handful and slid it to the back of the shelf. Then he realized he needed something to boil water in, so he hurried to the garbage pit near the outhouse and spotted a yellow lard pail. He remembered his mother washing the little pails for his school lunch bucket when he was a kid and wondered for a moment how many had ended up floating downriver after he tossed them from the bridge.

He picked up the pail and looked it over to make sure it was usable before he stuffed it into a bag. Then he tied the bags together with a rope. Satisfied, he threw the sacks over his shoulder and grabbed the rifle. With the clothes sack in front and the food bag on his back, he hurried toward Range Road.

"Shells, dammit," he muttered. "I'll never get out of here."

He would need more than one bullet where he was going, and the only place he would find ammunition was down at his Uncle Alphonse's. He also knew exactly where the shells were, because his uncle had often sent him to fetch them when he needed more. He stashed the bags and the .22 in the bushes and crept toward the house, watching for any sign of his uncle. He was about to go down when the door slammed, shaking the glass in the window. His uncle came around the corner of the house with a bucket in his hand and headed down to the river.

Once he was out of sight, Eddie ran to the house. Slipping inside, he went to the small bedroom and over to where his uncle's favourite picture hung on the wall. Cut out of a magazine, it showed a mounted cowboy aiming his rifle at the bear that had spooked his horse. Eddie lifted the picture off the nail and reached into the hole in the wall behind it, where three boxes of .22 shells sat on a two-by-four ledge. He grabbed a box and put the picture back. His uncle would know who took the bullets, but Eddie hoped he wouldn't be sure when they were taken. After adjusting the picture, he turned to go. That's when he saw his uncle's thick blanket on the small couch. He quickly rolled it up. Then, through the window, he saw the top of his uncle's head pop into view, coming up the river trail.

He went out, closing the door quietly, and ran for the trees, where he stopped and stood in the shadows to watch the house. The window rattled again as the door banged shut. He saw his uncle put the water bucket on the stand in the kitchen, then sit at the table with his back to Eddie to roll a cigarette.

Eddie stuffed the blanket into his clothes sack then slung the bags over his shoulder and ran. Then he stopped and crouched down to see if a tracker could spot his footprints. It was late enough in the day that the grass was dry, and he saw no trace of his passing on the matted trail. Satisfied, he took off up the path to Range Road, loping along the grass verge to avoid leaving tracks in the dust. At the trail up to the range, he stepped carefully across the cattle guard and slowed to a walk.

He passed a thicket of hawthorns and skirted around ponderosa pine that grew taller the higher he went. At the bottom of a steep hill, he stopped to study the sheer face. It was almost vertical. He dreaded the climb, but he knew it would save time.

At the top, legs burning, Eddie stood with his hands on his hips while he caught his breath, his head throbbing.

He wasn't high enough yet to see the lakes below the range, but he felt good about his progress. He had a half mile to go before he came to the old Smith place, a homestead built by a white squatter family that had been deserted many years ago, and then another half mile straight up to the high country where he wanted to set up camp.

The ground was riddled with gopher holes, so he kept his head down to make sure where he stepped. Many wild horses had snapped an ankle here and died a slow death. Once, he and Lewis had come across the body of a bay mare lying bloated under a tree, its mouth and nose covered in crawling flies. Running back and forth beside the dead horse, eyes white with terror, was a young colt. Its whinnying sounded like screaming. He wondered whatever happened to the beautiful little horse.

Finally, he reached the cow trail that led to the old Smith place, which made for easier walking. When he reached the homestead, he took a bun out of the food bag and sat on the doorless threshold, looking across the valley to the far hills. Here, the land changed completely from rolling prairie to high mountains, ramparts guarding a secret from the rest of the world. The wind shifted direction to the north, lifting his hair, as the nearby pines announced the change. Weighty boughs creaked and cracked like old man's bones as they stirred from their torpor.

Deciding to rest here a little longer, Eddie walked around behind the house, where he sat on the ground under a big tree, leaned back against the trunk and closed his eyes. He felt the long roots flexing under him and the sound of the wind in the boughs was like a soft voice humming him to sleep. He hadn't intended to doze and he still had more ground to cover, but in his mind-weary state he couldn't keep his eyes open. As he dozed, he felt he wasn't alone. He was walking in bright sunshine with someone, and he was happy, something he hadn't felt in a long time. Then he saw who was beside him. It was Eva, his beautiful Eva, watching him with eyes so striking and alive that he reached out a hand to touch her. But then she was gone. Shouting her name, he was awakened by his own voice to find himself truly alone.

He jumped to his feet. Throwing the sacks over his shoulder, he walked into the wind toward the high ground. Something bothered his eyes and he swiped at them with his hand and then dried his wet fingers on his pants.

A half mile later, Eddie was at the bottom of a high mountain. Pulling the plug out of the water bag, he took a long drink and studied his second steep climb. This would be even more difficult than the first, but at the top he would be completely alone, just like he wanted. He took a deep breath and set off. Using the .22 as a walking stick, he pulled himself forward, grabbing brush and mulleins that he hoped wouldn't come out of the ground in his hand.

Just as he made it to the top, his legs gave out. Winded, Eddie lay on the ground for the longest time. When he could breathe normally again, he rose to his hands and knees and crawled to the edge of the drop-off to look out at the range below him. A cooler wind carried clouds his way. He rushed to make a crude shelter out of boughs and branches, and hung his food and clothes bag up a tree, as high off the ground as he could manage. When he was done, he leaned against the tree.

It was dark when the rains came, gently at first, then harder. Thunder rolled across the sky and he sat in the downpour and let the rain wash over him.

CHAPTER 33

"WEREN'T YOU SCARED, being up here all by yourself? I know I would be."

"No," Eddie said. "Back then, I would sooner have trusted a skunk than another person. But moving to Alberta wasn't easy. At first, I couldn't even imagine going to a place where I didn't know anybody, but then I knew it was my only chance to get out of here.

"'Valleyview, Alberta. Long, long ways,' my old boss Frenchie would say. 'Drive twelve hours. Only stop for gas and a piss.' So after a while I packed up here and hitchhiked to town and went to see the Frenchman. He even lent me money to get me started. That old white guy really helped me out. That same day I was on the Greyhound headed for Valleyview. Before I left, I made Frenchie promise not to tell anybody where I was, no matter who asked."

Lewis doubted he would have the courage to leave home like that.

"Camille's grandma really looked after us. It felt good to come home after working all day and eat good food and sleep in a clean bed by myself. Sometimes in the morning when I didn't feel like getting up, I reminded myself about the money I kept in my dresser drawer, and I'd throw off my blankets and get going. Camille told me to put it in the bank, but I said no, what good is it going to do me where I can't even see it? Some nights before I went to bed, I'd hold the money in my hand, so happy it was all mine. I worked hard for it and I didn't need to suck-hole to an Indian agent for help. With money, I was better than all the *summas*."

Lewis rolled onto his side to face Eddie. "It must have felt nice to pick up that money and let it fall out of your hands. I saw that in a movie once and always wanted to do that. But, Eddie, we all thought you were dead. Why didn't you at least let me know you were alive and okay?"

Eddie sat up and took a drink of water, then turned to face Lewis. "If I told you, you would have told Mom, and I didn't want her to know.

"My whole life she was always telling me what to do. She picked out my clothes and shoes and everything until I was fourteen, when I said that's enough. It wasn't just her, though. It was the white kids that called me names, teachers who didn't think I had a brain, the Cluffs thinking I didn't deserve Eva. When we were kids, Mom would rather sit in the beer parlour instead of staying home to look after us.

"She could have helped us out by buying an old bike so we could at least ride over to the store and get a can of beans to eat when she was gone. I even saw a girl's bike at a rummage sale once and showed her, but she just turned up her nose and walked away. It felt like I was always mad at her."

Lewis interrupted his brother. "I still don't understand why you'd leave without letting me know."

Eddie shook his head. "Like I said, I wasn't thinking straight. I knew you were going to be okay–you always had somebody to look after you. First it was me, and when I left, you had Mom and Isabel. But nobody looked after me here and nobody looked after me in Alberta. I did think of you, and I wanted to tell you I was okay, but I couldn't. That's the only thing I would go back and change."

Lewis lay back and put his hands behind his head. "If coulds were woulds, we'd all be lumberjacks," he said. "I don't know. Maybe that's why you were so mad all the time. Mom drove you crazy. Me and Isabel were talking once about all the fights you had at school."

Eddie said, "I can count on one hand how many you've ever had. Half a dozen, I bet, not counting the one you had with me."

Lewis sat up again. "Half a dozen? You don't know what you're talking about."

"Okay, let's say a dozen. Hell, I could do that at recess. Do you want to know why? I'm the *skin* and you're the *summa*."

An old feeling from childhood of being provoked by his big brother came over Lewis. "Don't you call me that. I'm no *summa*."

"I'm just saying they left you alone because of your skin. Now don't get mad at me, but you do look like a white boy."

"Come on, Eddie. People know I'm Indian and you're my brother."

Eddie said, "When you started school, I kept an eye on you in case guys started picking on you. Most of the time they'd leave you alone, but the trouble I had off the reserve could be the same trouble you're going to have on the reserve. Indians will fight other Indians, especially if you're not from where they are or you're different. You stick out because you look like a *summa* to them. It's wrong to fight your own people, because it doesn't change anything. At least, I think that way until an Indian pisses me off. But we're all in the same boat. It's like that up in Valleyview. White people hate us and they hate the French. It doesn't make sense." He sighed.

"And talk about stupid fights—look what we did. For two years you thought I was dead, but that didn't stop you from trying to kick my ass, all because of a girl."

"That was stupid for sure. I guess you know a lot more about those things than me. But then, everybody does." Lewis stood up. "Anyway, let's do something. If we had a gun, we could go shoot gophers or do some target practice. Whatever happened to your old .22?"

"My gun. I forgot all about my old gun. Hah. I stashed it. And some other stuff too."

"Where?"

Eddie pointed uphill. "See that big rock that looks like a nose, sticking out on the face of the mountain? That's where."

Eddie took off running. Lewis knew another race had been called and ran after his brother. When Eddie stumbled, Lewis was able to catch up, both scrabbling for higher ground until they were neck and neck again. They slapped a hand on the big nose at the same time.

Eddie crouched beside a broken log that he had lodged in a hole behind the rock. He pulled at it, but the wood wouldn't budge. Looking around, he saw a large branch, jammed it below a gap at one end and they both put their weight on it and pried. At last the piece came loose and they pushed it out of the way. Eddie felt around inside the hole until he touched what he was looking for. Pulling out a long object wrapped in a fusty blanket, he set it down on the ground. Reaching in again, he came out with a sack. He unwrapped the rifle and handed it to his brother.

"There you go, Lewis. It's yours now. There's still half a box of shells too. Boy, I can remember the day I got this. It's the only thing Dad ever gave me. So you look after it. With this thing in your hand, you can walk anywhere, even at midnight, and no boogeyman is going to get you. Keep it loaded, but make sure you have the safety on."

"Oh man," Lewis stared down at the rifle. He tested the weight in his hands then ducked his head through the strap, letting the gun rest on his back.

They walked back to the fire with what they found. Then Eddie said, "I'm hungry and I bet you are too. But first we better get some water. I know a place pretty close."

Lewis grabbed the jug and the water bag while Eddie took the old kettle from home, and they set out for the little spring. With Eddie leading, they crossed a draw then made their way up an old horse trail until they came to a stand of birch trees that hid the watering hole. Squatting on his heels, Lewis filled the water bag and wine jug while Eddie scrubbed out the kettle with gravel. After it was cleaned, he filled it with water and clapped on the lid.

Back at camp Lewis built up the fire again while Eddie drove a green stick into the ground so they could hang the kettle over the flames. They opened two cans of Chef Boyardee spaghetti and set them on the coals. When they looked through their gear for spoons, they couldn't find any, so Eddie grabbed a large, dry stick and whittled out something resembling spoons. Once the cans were hot enough, they each grabbed one and scooped out their supper. The plan was to ration the buns to make them last longer, but the boys ate them all.

It was dark when Eddie brought out two cups and dropped a tea bag into the kettle. He let the tea simmer then took out the bag and placed it on a flat rock. "You know, Lewis, we were so poor that I saw Mom use the same bag at least three times. She saved every one and, when she was out of fresh ones, threw them all into a boiling pot and drank it. I never touched the stuff because it smelled like piss."

They sat leaning against the tree like they were in the front row at a theatre and sipped their tea. Under a waning moon, they watched the headlights of cars and trucks on the highway a mile away reflecting off the water of Madeline Lake. Wild horses crested the hill above the lake and walked across the range in single file, their heads bobbing up and down like merry-go-round ponies. Lewis followed the shadows of birds swimming across the uneven terrain, but when he looked up, he couldn't find them. Invisible night birds seemed normal in this place.

At the west corner of the range, headlights bounced as a vehicle crawled up a steep hill before levelling out on flat ground, its high beams clouded by the dust of running horses. As the vehicle came closer, they could hear a voice shouting as if cursing. It was their mother's truck.

"Only person I know pissed off enough to chase horses all the way out here is Alphonse. He must have left the gate open at the bottom cattle guard, and they probably shit all over his yard," Eddie said.

Alphonse stopped the truck, honked the feeble horn and banged the door with his hand. They saw him look up the hill to try to spot them, but they were too far away. He waved anyway.

"That guy is something else. He can be a mean old bugger one minute and tell funny stories the next," Eddie said. "You see how he was swearing at those horses? I bet right now he's probably whistling a tune."

"Yep, he's a big talker," Lewis said.

"He's a bullshitter is what he is," Eddie added. "All right, little brother, I'm tired. I think it's time to hit the sack."

"Fine with me," Lewis said.

They piled wood on the fire to keep it going through the night and crawled into their blankets. In the quiet, Lewis heard the rustling of little feet on the dry grass and the hiss of wind. Looking up, he watched stars falling like sparks across the night sky until he fell asleep.

The next morning Lewis rubbed crusts of sleep out of his eyes, surprised to see that Eddie was already up and had a fire going and he hadn't heard a thing. The burning wood popped and snapped, and steam rose from the kettle. His brother sat with his back to the pine tree at the edge of the cliff, his legs dangling, sipping from a cup with the rifle resting on his lap. Lewis pulled back his blanket, stood and stretched. Then he poured himself a cup of tea and joined Eddie. "Is this all reserve?" Lewis asked.

"It is on this side of the highway for a ways, but it goes back and forth. On this side of Range Road, the reserve runs south from the river as far you can see. Do you know the names of the five lakes around here?"

"Not all of them."

"There's Cluff Lake, named after Eva's great-grandfather, who *summas* say discovered the place even though Indians been using it for years. Madeline Lake is the shallow one by the highway. Little Madeline, the one closest to Range Road. Heart Lake is the one below our house. And Round Lake, the lake with no bottom, is off to the left."

Across the valley, Blue Grouse Mountain rose steeply before them, its sharp face flattened by landslides. The railway right-of-way was cut into the mountain just above the highway, meandering past Moffat Creek to the north and Mann Creek to the south, then on toward Vernon and Okanagan Lake in the distance.

Lewis said, "I wish we had Uncle's Ned binoculars. I didn't know the reserve was so big."

A grouse landed on a branch ten feet away and, without hesitation, Eddie raised the gun. A single shot to the head and the grouse fell at their feet. "Oh shit," Eddie said. "I should have let you do that."

Lewis laughed. "You're like an old Indian hunter from way back when. I can see you climbing a tree with a knife blade between your teeth."

After plucking the feathers and pulling out the guts, Eddie took the grouse and washed it in the spring. They cooked the bird in boiling salted water, taking turns poking at it for over an hour. By the time the grouse was cooked and cool enough to eat, they were really hungry. They sat cross-legged on the ground and began to pull the meat away from the bones, popping pieces into their mouths.

"Know what?" Eddie said, swallowing his mouthful. "This doesn't taste as good as I thought it would. What do you think?'

Lewis held a piece up to his nose and sniffed. "I think I'd sooner have a cold can of pork and beans."

Eddie tossed the meat into the bush. "Good idea."

After they were finished the beans, Eddie ran a finger around the inside of the can and licked his finger. 'We're going hafta do a lot better than this at supper, but the beans should keep us going for a little while. Let's head 'er. There's a lot to see on this mountain.'"

Lewis pulled the unburned wood away from the fire as Eddie emptied the canvas water bag onto the hot coals. Then they shook out their bedding and spread it over bushes to air out. Eddie grabbed the water bag and Lewis shouldered the gun, and they set off.

Their first stop was at the spring to fill the water bag and wash their faces. Then they headed toward the eastern side of the mountain. When they came across a tree blackened by a lightning strike, they noticed claw marks high up the trunk. On the ground were deep holes made by a hungry animal searching for mice, voles or other underground dwellers.

"Just take a look at those gashes," Eddie said. "They're six feet off the ground. That's a black bear marking its territory. And see how he ripped that rotten log to pieces."

At the bottom of a shale slide, Eddie pointed to an opening near the top edge of the steep-faced cliff. They made their way uphill on solid ground before carefully stepping across the shifting plates to the opening. Poking their heads inside, they were hit by the strong odour of bear. It looked like someone had taken a broom and swept away everything except for paw prints on the dirt floor.

Lewis took the gun off his shoulder, but his brother said, "That .22 won't do anything to a bear but make him mad, unless you're close enough to stick the barrel in his eye and maybe the shell will go into his brain. We'll just have to keep a lookout for him and hope we see him before he takes a run at us."

The sun felt hot on their faces as they came out into the open at the crest of Rose Swanson Mountain. They stood looking down on the little community of Armstrong sprawled below them. Eddie pointed. "See the rodeo grounds right across the road from that creek? Those are the barns and corrals. Do you remember us sitting in the grandstand with Mom and Alphonse watching the whole show? It was dark by the time it was over."

Lewis said, "I remember that. I had the best hamburger and hot dog with lots of fried onions and ketchup and mustard. They were so greasy it ran down my face. I can almost taste them right now."

"Is that all you remember about the rodeo? The food?"

"Yeah. I was hungry. What do you remember?"

"The barrel racers. Jeez, there's just something about the way a barrel racer walks around in her tight Wrangler jeans and she doesn't care what guys think because she knows she can make a horse do things they can't. I think it's the saddle that makes their ass so perfect."

"So I'm hungry and you're horny. What a surprise," Lewis said.

They watched a train pull away from a tall grain elevator and roll down the tracks that sliced through the middle of town. On the main street, businesses with false fronts looked like they were out of a Western movie. Houses built after the First World War lined the residential avenues, while an old brick school stood on a tree-lined road.

"Let's take a break," Lewis said. He laid the gun down, then stretched out on the grass and crossed his arms over his eyes. Eddie sat beside him, plucking a grass stalk to chew on. Lewis dozed in the warm sun until crows roosting in the treetops suddenly began squawking and cawing at something crashing in the trees below them. It made such a racket running through thick brush and breaking limbs, Lewis sat up. "What's that?"

"I don't know, but I sure don't want to come across whatever it is. C'mon, sleepyhead, let's get back to camp. You can snooze there."

It was dark by the time they made it back. They were both so hungry they downed a tin each of pork and beans and another of spaghetti. After they ate, the brothers sat by the fire, drinking tea and watching the stars while little eyes watched the brothers from the darkness of the bushes. Soon the night grew chilly, and they fed the fire and crawled into their bedding.

"You know, Lewis, two years ago this was the best place for me to hide out. I could just sit in the quiet and think of Eva. After a while even the memories that made me sad eased up a bit. But now I'm here with you and it's not a sad place at all anymore."

When Lewis didn't respond, Eddie glanced over to find him already asleep. Then Lewis let out a rolling fart and Eddie had to smile. It was just like they were kids again.

CHAPTER 34

EDDIE WAS UP and had gathered an armful of firewood, which he tossed onto the ashes, poking at the embers until flames shot up with a *whump*. After the fire settled into an even heat, he tucked two potatoes into the coals and placed the kettle on the tripod.

Lewis stood, shook out his blanket and spread it on a bush. He kneeled by the fire and watched as Eddie opened a can of creamed corn and pushed it near the potatoes. Then he twisted open a can of Spam with the key and cut it into slices that he skewered onto a stick and propped near the heat. Soon the corn broke soft bubbles as sizzling fat dripped from the rectangles of meat, making little flare-ups in the flames. When the potatoes felt soft, Eddie rolled them away from the heat to cool.

Neither brother spoke until they finished their breakfast, then Eddie stood and arched his back. "Sleeping on that ground is like my bunk in jail." He sniffed at the air then at himself. "And I'm starting to smell pretty ripe. I bet you are too. How about we go for a dip in Round Lake? Be nice to be clean again."

"Yeah, sure." Lewis was staring into the far distance, at the knoll overlooking Heart Lake where he and Loretta had parked.

It brought back the image of the tear-streaked face of the frightened young soldier. "Did I tell you that one night when me and Loretta were parked above Heart Lake, we found a lost cadet wandering all over the place in the dark? He got separated from his group and he was scared to death because they found some human bones that day and he thought a ghost was following him. He said it was close to a big rock with a wide quartz vein running through it. Do you know where that is?"

Eddie paused to think. "Alphonse talked about a rock he found somewhere that he was sure had gold in it, but I thought it was another one of his bullshit stories."

"That's probably the one. It's supposed to be by a landslide. You know what, that was the second dead guy that was found this summer. At the end of June, they dug up the bones of an old Indian on the hill just above the road near our bottom gate. They think it was a chief. He was wrapped in birchbark, and they figured he was hundreds of years old."

Eddie thought for a minute. "There's only one slide around here that I know of and that's above where the army does target practice. A birchbark coffin, eh. I didn't know that. I wonder if only chiefs were buried like that or if they did that with everybody. Jeez, we don't know a thing about how they did things, do we?"

"Why don't we go up there and see what we can find? There might be other graves up there, or even gold. And then we'll go for that swim at Round Lake." Lewis swung the gun over his shoulder.

"Well, as Alphonse says, let's give 'er snoose," Eddie said, picking up a walking stick. "The only thing I don't like about going down the hill again is coming back up."

They stood at the edge of the cliff and looked down. Eddie shook his head. "Boy, that's steep. I just hope one of us doesn't trip on the way down."

Lewis patted his brother on the back. "Aah, you Albertans get scared of a molehill." He jumped and began leaping down the hill.

After taking two steps back, Eddie charged. A high-pitched scream made Lewis look back over his shoulder to see his brother thrashing on the ground, hanging on to his foot.

He climbed back up to him. "Jesus, what happened, Eddie? What should I do?"

Eddie looked up, his face twisted in pain. "You can . . . you can . . . you can kiss my ass, sucker." He pushed Lewis to the ground, jumped to his feet and took off down the hill. Lewis chased after him, but Eddie beat him to the bottom.

"You might as well just give up, little brother. I win every time. Maybe when we get back, you can have a foot race with Mom and Isabel."

"Very funny. At least they don't cheat."

With the warm sun overhead, a light wind at their backs and the bunchgrass crunching under their feet, they set off at a fast pace, two brothers walking together through a land they felt they alone had discovered long ago. They passed enormous dead pine trees, dry and twisted into shapes of snakes and dragons, patches of their scaly skin blown away by the unrelenting wind. Others stood where they had died like monuments. Vibrating in the wind, the hardy shrubs held fast.

When they came to the army rifle range, they turned uphill and continued to climb. Halfway up the face of the precipice, they stopped to rest. Breathing hard, Eddie pointed to a depression on the side of the mountain. "That's where we're going."

They climbed past a tumble of boulders where an old landslide had brought down a large part of the mountain. When they came across a well-used trail—the smell of horse was strong and the turds on the path looked fresh—Lewis looked up to see how much farther they had to go.

Finally, the land levelled off and they stood in a large clearing, one side bordered by trees, the earth on the other side ripped away. Just ahead was the large boulder with the white streak running through its centre.

"Jeez, I thought we'd never get here," Lewis said. "It's like we climbed Mount Everest."

The ground around the boulder had been disturbed by many feet. Lewis said, "Maybe the bones were taken away and buried in a different place. That's what they did with the chief."

They spent half an hour searching under fallen branches and trees, finding no sign of bones or gold.

Eddie said, "All they left are piss holes in the dirt."

Lewis looked into a ravine where anything that had rolled down from where they stood would have ended up. Rocks, pine needles and cones, horse droppings, dry leaves and weeds that had been picked up by the wind, all deposited at the bottom of that stony wall. "I'm going to look in that stuff against the rocks. Maybe I'll find something."

Lewis slid down to where the debris was stacked. With his foot, he cleared away withered mulleins and burdocks but found nothing. Then he picked up a stick and started digging under a half-rotten tree trunk. He pushed loose rocks away and pulled out pieces of branches and was about to give up when his stick hit something that gave a metallic sound. He went to his knees and dug around, then stood, holding up a round piece of rusty metal.

"Hey, look at this!"

Eddie scrambled down the hill. Lewis handed him the object and Eddie brushed dirt away with his fingers. "This is an old belt buckle. Jeez, it looks like it was pretty nice at one time. There's a raised star in the middle and it looks like engraving at the top. You're gonna need to scrub this thing with a brush and soap and water to get some of this shit off. Good luck with that."

He handed it back and Lewis stuffed it in his pocket.

"Come on," Eddie said. "So much for finding a graveyard or gold. This was a waste of time. Let's go have that swim. We're even smellier than we were this morning. Alphonse told me Round Lake is fed by an underground spring and it's always cold as a witch's tit, but I don't care. I gotta get this stink off me."

It was afternoon when they finally made it to the lake's shore. They were covered in sweat, and flies landed on their hair and crawled on their necks as they stood staring at the clean water.

"Well, there's nobody here to see us, so let's get naked," Eddie said.

They peeled off their clothes and dove into the water. When they surfaced, moaning and gasping, they immediately made for shore. "Jesus, that's cold," Lewis said, wading out on dry land.

Eddie pointed. "It sure is. Look at your little pecker all shrivelled up."

"Me? Look at you. Yours is so small you need to shake some pepper on it and when it comes up to sneeze, grab it with tweezers." Their laughter echoed around the lake.

They put on their clothes as fast as they could and then sat on the ground, tying their runners. Lewis was still shivering.

"I think we should start back," Eddie said. "We don't want to be caught out here in the dark. The horses and cows aren't the only ones that water here. You'll warm up on the way."

Lewis picked up the gun as Eddie grabbed his walking stick, and they turned to go. The ponderosa pine that grew close to the water had dropped so many needles the ground was red and felt slippery underfoot. "Why are they doing that already?" Lewis asked.

"Every few years, the older ones lose a lot of needles. I don't know why."

Eddie stopped and bent down to examine something in the mud. "Come and look at this."

Lewis went to his knee. "What is it?"

"That's a cougar track. See how deep it is? It's got to be a big male. And the track is fresh–you can see how soft the mud is here at the edge. Have a feel."

Lewis crouched and felt the ridge where mud had been forced up between furred toes. He wondered how his brother had become such a well of knowledge. "I never ever seen a cougar before," he said. "How come you know so much about stuff like tracking?"

"Alphonse taught me. Remember, when I was about twelve, he started to take me with him when he went hunting? But I had to be so quiet. If I sneezed, I got a kick. Grandma showed me some stuff too, whenever we went for a walk. She was always trying to teach me things you never learn at school. Speaking of school, what grades are you getting?"

"Mostly B's. I got an A in social studies."

"See, right there, that's where you and me are different. I did okay in arithmetic and spelling, and I liked drawing and poetry, but compared to me, you're an egghead. This here, outside by a lake or river, that's my school. If I brought my old teachers up here and left them on top of the range and told them they had to stay for a week, they'd be scared shitless.

"Up in Alberta I met this Indian at work. A Cree, of course. He was only a year older than me, but he was like an old man, he knew so much. I'd go with him fishing or we'd hunt partridge in the bush. He said his grandpa took him out when he was little and taught him all about tracking and showed him how to make a shelter so you could stay dry when it rained. It took a while before I found something I could do better than him, and whenever it sounded like he was talking down to me, you know what I'd do?"

"Name a girl's body parts?"

"Shut up. I'd kick his ass playing pool. He couldn't play worth a damn. I always remember that no matter how smart you think you are, there's always somebody better than you. I always keep trying to be the one people try to beat."

"You mean like how I kicked your ass in the pretty girl department? Don't forget Tiger Lily and Loretta."

Eddie grabbed Lewis and rubbed his knuckles hard across the top of his head. "You're a turd." Still holding his brother in the crook of his arm, Eddie pointed across the lake. "Look, look. See over there?"

Lewis pulled free and looked across the water, past coots swimming in a circle, and saw a lone owl perched on top of a dead tree. "I see it. Jeez, I never saw an owl so light-coloured before. He looks like a Christmas tree angel sitting up there, doesn't he?"

"I'm not talking about the owl. Look on the ground, close to that poplar with no top."

Lewis narrowed his eyes to search along the shore and spotted movement. As it stepped out into the sunlight, a cougar stopped in its tracks and fixed its stare on the brothers.

"Wow. He's looking right at us."

Eddie laughed. "He's a little too close for me. Just a little run around the lake and he'd be on us in a minute. I think now would be a good time to get outta here. You make sure that gun is ready to go. Aim for his head."

Lewis pulled back the bolt and slid it forward, loading a bullet into the chamber. He pulled the bolt into safety. "You think he'll come for us?"

"You never know. I'm just glad we can see him, because that way we can keep an eye on him. When you can't see him, that's when it gets scary. They don't make a sound when they walk and they like to work their way around behind you. You never hear them coming. Then, when he makes his move, all you'll feel is a little pinch on the back of your neck and then the lights go out."

"How do you know that? Who told you? Was it that Cree Indian again?"

"No."

"Who, then?"

"Walt Disney. Let's go."

That evening back at camp they each ate a large can of beef stew and drank hot tea. After the camp was tidied and the fire stoked, they stretched out on their blankets and looked up at the starry sky.

Eddie said, "I guess we go home tomorrow, because I have to leave the day after that. But why don't we sleep in and take our time getting back. I sure don't want this to end. Up in Valleyview in winter, you can see the northern lights, and sometimes when they really get going, people say you can hear them. I never did, and I'd rather have this any day. I dreamed about you and me up here, camping out. How about you? I bet you can't wait to get back so Mommy can give you a glass of milk and tuck you into bed."

Lewis laughed. "I don't want to go home, because it means you'll be going away and I don't know when I'll see you again. But I could use a good shower about now. It'd be great if the work on the house is finally done by the time we get there and the shower is finished."

"Me too. We're so dirty, even after a shower there's gonna be a ring around that tub."

"I know. I'm so itchy it's driving me crazy." Lewis reached into his pocket to scratch himself and paused when he felt the contents. "Hey, I almost forgot. I found this down by the river and I been meaning to show it to you." He pulled out a yellow cloth.

Eddie recognized the kerchief instantly. "Where did you get that?"

"Under that big hollow tree of yours next to the river."

Eddie didn't speak. He could only stare.

Lewis said, "Do you know what it is? You were the only person who used that place."

Eddie reached over and took it out of Lewis's hand. "This was Eva's." His voice broke. "I took it from her closet."

CHAPTER 35

BUBBLING WATER RAN DOWN the ballooning legs of the wet blue jeans as Grace fed them through the washing machine ringer. They made a squishing sound as they came out the other side, damp and flat. The jeans were the last of the laundry, so she unplugged the cord from the wall and stuck the machine's drain hose into the black pipe that went down through a hole in the floor and ran outside to empty in the bushes. Then she went out to hang the clothes.

Birds perched on the clothesline flew away when she held the pants by the waist and gave them a hard snap. She draped them over the line and held them down with clothespins. After the basket was empty, she went up the steps to go inside just as Isabel came out with the mop and pail.

"Floor's still wet. You're going to have wait until it dries." She walked to the edge of the porch and tossed the dirty water into the weeds.

Grace sat down on the bench and leaned against the wall. Isabel came to sit next to her. "Wouldn't it be nice, Izzy, to have one of them new spin washing machines right about now, and a dryer? Those clothes wouldn't take no time at all."

"I wish we could have everything all at once too, but I think we're doing pretty good, don't you? Remember, at the beginning of the summer, Lewis still had to get water down at the river. Now all we have to do is turn a tap. And the kitchen looks even bigger with that old wood stove gone. That electric range is like cooking on a dream."

"The only thing I don't like is giving money to Bennett's Hardware every month to pay for the damn thing," Grace muttered.

"But if it's something you need, then that's what you gotta do. You pay a little every month until you're clear. That's the way you do things now. Seems like everything is changing and we hafta keep up. But it sure is nice getting used to all this new stuff, isn't it? I think all them years of you bitching to the Indian agent was worth it."

"Hah. If we didn't work our asses off packing apples, we'd have the bathroom built but nothing in it."

Isabel pulled at her blouse to let in cooler air. "The new part of the house is going to look empty for a while yet, but we'll get there. And never mind that, how did it feel taking a hot bath in your own house for the first time yesterday?"

Grace closed her eyes. "I never seen water so dirty. But lying in that warm, soapy bath, I didn't want to get out. Eddie and Lewis are gonna be surprised to see the shower is all ready to go. And aren't they supposed to be home by now? It's gonna be supper soon. I hope nothing happened up there."

"They're probably just taking their time. Lewis really missed Eddie. He came to me after school was out, asking all kinds of questions about him."

"I wonder why he asked you and not me."

"Because you're just like your mom, that's why. Do you remember what she was like when we were teenagers? We'd ask her about boys and she'd say, 'How the hell do I know?' Remember?"

"I'm not like that, am I?"

Bluebirds landed on the top wire of the clothesline. "Oh, look at that. Funny how they like that clothesline," Isabel said. The birds chirped, their little heads searching about. Then they flew away. Isabel turned back to Grace. "You *are* like that. How about when Alphonse came to see you that time he was half cut and almost in tears, and he said to you, 'I think I'm in love, Grace,' and you said, 'What are you telling me for? You don't like talking about stuff like that and everybody knows it.'"

Grace said, "Damn, I wish I could be like you and not get mad and clam up every time. I'd ask Eddie why he hates me so much."

"He doesn't hate you, Grace. He's mad at the whole world. But you need to talk to him. How are you gonna know anything if you don't ask. He's leaving soon and who knows when you're going to see him again. You don't want another two years to go by."

"I know. It's just that I'm feeling good right now and I don't want anybody to spoil it. Remember when we were out on the front porch of our little house in Oroville feeling like we had no troubles in the world?"

"And then Mabel came along," Isabel said, "and told us all about Jimmy. I remember."

Grace shook her head. "Every time we start feeling good about things, another damn car drives in with bad news. We were doing so good, and then Jimmy's bullshit spoils everything. I should feel guilty he's gone missing, but I don't. And it was so nice taking that money out of his wallet. It was probably the biggest help he ever gave me."

Isabel said, "Just remember, Lazar's the one should be on the lookout for the cops. Not us."

"What if he did drop Jimmy at the hospital and that girlfriend of his didn't know it? What if he gets better and shows up here? What do we do then? That Lazar, you seen how he is. He's crazy and he's stupid. If he gets caught, what if he tells the cops what happened?"

Isabel swatted at a fly buzzing around her face. "Grace, we got no reason to worry. Lazar's the one who hurt Jimmy, and he won't talk anyway. Him and all the other jailbirds hate stool pigeons."

Grace stared at the clothesline, hoping the bluebirds would return. "If Jimmy's still alive, then he and anybody else who thinks they can move onto my land will find me sitting here waiting for them. I'll put a bullet into the first person that steps on my ground."

They heard a shout and looked up to see Lewis and Eddie waving from the back of the truck as Alphonse drove down the lane.

CHAPTER 36

LEWIS WAS THE FIRST into the shower. Lathering himself with a bar of Irish Spring soap and stepping under the warm spray of water, he could feel the dirt and smell of the last few days roll off his body and disappear down the drain. After drying himself, he stepped in front of the mirror, parted his hair in the middle and shook his head, fluffing out his hair. "Oh yeah, the dry look."

He dressed and glanced one more time in the mirror, then opened the door to find Eddie leaning against the wall, waiting, reeking of sweat and smoke, his hair standing up in brittle spikes as if he had brought home half the dirt of the range on his head.

"What were you doing in there so long, pulling your wire?" he whispered. "I hope you left me some hot water."

He undressed and dropped his dirty clothes on the floor, pushed Lewis out of the way and went into the bathroom, naked, a foul odour following behind. He shut the door with a bang.

"Boy, look at you, all shined up," Isabel said as Lewis came into the kitchen. "You're just in time to help me with the dirty clothes. Looks like I'll have to add extra soap to get them clean. What did you two do up there? Roll around in cow manure? Round up your stuff and bring it all to me."

Lewis shoved the clothes into the washer as Isabel added powdered soap, paused, then added more.

Lewis sat in the chair. "Hey, the washing machine is indoors. I just noticed that. Nice."

"You bet. We shoulda put in that drain a long time ago. You should have seen your mom crawl under the house like a gopher to hook up the hose."

She put on the lid then turned on the machine. "So how was it up there? What did you two talk about?"

"I don't remember what we talked about, we just had fun. It reminded me of the time when we were little and a dump truck brought out a load of lumber ends from the sawmill. We couldn't believe we had all these building blocks and we played for hours making tunnels and corners. Up there it felt like we were kids again. We had races and went swimming and hiked to the other side of the mountain and looked down on Armstrong. We ate out of cans and drank water out of your old wine jug. And we saw a cougar." He was silent for a minute, then said, "I didn't want it to end. If Eddie wasn't leaving, we'd still be up there."

Isabel peeked into the washing machine. "Holy cow, look how dark the water is already. This thing can really beat the hell out of those clothes. Sounds like a cement mixer, it's so noisy." She placed the cover back on. "Did he say anything about your mom?"

"I dunno. Like what?"

"Grace thinks he hates her."

"He doesn't hate her."

"I think she wants to have a talk with him, but he's probably too tired right now. After breakfast tomorrow, let's you and me leave them by themselves for a while."

Eddie and Lewis were both so tired they ate the supper that was put in front of them and then crawled into bed.

In the morning Lewis walked into the kitchen and found Eddie already seated at the table. "Look, Lewis, it's like the breakfast at the Woolworths lunch counter in town."

Grace said, "Hey, ours is better than theirs any day."

Bacon and eggs and fried potatoes sat waiting on a plate as Isabel spooned whole tomatoes from an open can into a bowl. Golden-brown buns fresh from the oven sat cooling on a round pan. "I hope you guys are hungry," Isabel said as she dabbed the tops of the buns with a piece of wax paper dripping with butter. "Sit down and dig in before it gets cold." Isabel poured coffee into mugs while Lewis pulled his chair closer to the table and filled his plate.

Lewis looked up from his food long enough to notice that the old wood cooker was gone and in its place in front of the chimney was a new electric range. "When did that thing get here?"

"A truck from Bennett's came out while you guys were on the range. You both must have been pretty tired last night, because you walked right by it and never noticed," Grace said. "They hooked up the new one and dragged that poor old wood stove out to the porch, and Alphonse and Abel took it away."

"Abel?" Lewis said. "I thought he was living with his woman."

Isabel shook her head. "Not anymore. But this one lasted longer than the last one."

"This isn't the same house," Eddie said, looking around. "I never thought I'd see stuff like this in here. Hey, Lewis, if you could pick only one thing to keep, the running water or the toilet, which would it be?"

Lewis answered without hesitation. "The toilet."

"What about water? Wouldn't you have to start hauling those heavy buckets up from the river again?"

Lewis shook his head. "No. I'd just dip water out of the toilet." Everyone laughed.

When his plate was empty, Eddie broke a bun in half.

"Do you want some peanut butter on that? We got the crunchy stuff," Grace said.

"Oh no. I wouldn't spoil these." He wiped his plate clean with the bun and popped it into his mouth and sat back. "I don't think the canned spaghetti and beans we had up at the range were as good as we thought they were."

Lewis reached for his coffee. Eddie added two spoons of sugar and canned milk to his mug as Isabel took his plate away. Grace poured herself another cup, then sat down at the table across from Eddie.

"Lewis," Isabel said. "If you're finished, can you come outside and give me a hand? I need to get those clothes in."

Lewis took a quick drink of his coffee and pushed back his chair. When he stood, he remembered the buckle in his pocket.

"Hey, Mom, look at this. I was up on the range in the old truck one night in the summer and came across a lost cadet who told me him and some others found human bones up at this old slide. Me and Eddie went there yesterday. We didn't find any bones, but we found this." He pulled the buckle out and set it on the table.

There was a single knock on the door. Alphonse swung the door open and stepped inside. "Damn," he said. "Looks like I missed breakfast." He reached into the cupboard and brought out a mug, filled it with coffee and sat down at the table. Spotting the dirty object on the table, he asked, "What you got there, Grace?" He blew on his coffee.

"I don't know," she said. "Lewis was the one found it."

CHAPTER 37

GRACE PICKED UP THE BUCKLE. She turned it over, then reached over to the sink for the dishcloth and rubbed at the caked-on dirt. Eyes narrowed, she looked closer, then she dropped the buckle on the table as if it was hot.

"What's the matter?" Alphonse asked.

"Look at that thing. It's Dad's. Don't you remember? He wore it everywhere, showing it off and telling everybody how he won it at a rodeo. Where did you say you found it, Lewis?"

"Above the target range, close to a huge rock at the old slide."

Grace reached for it again. "Jesus, I forgot all about this. This buckle was his pride and joy, and he wore it every day." She went into the bathroom and came out with a tube of toothpaste. She squeezed some onto the cloth and rubbed at the tarnished metal. "See? It says right here: 'Winner, Pendleton, Oregon.' I can't read the rest. He loved rodeos and sometimes he'd be gone for months."

Lewis and Isabel leaned over Grace to see for themselves. "So what was it doing up in that place?" Lewis asked.

"You said there were human bones?"

"Yeah, the cadet said they were spread all around by animals, probably coyotes. But the chief and council must have moved them, just like they did with the birchbark Indian."

Lewis looked at Eddie. "Remember how Grandma would get mad if you asked her anything about Grandpa?"

"I sure do."

Grace rubbed her chin for a moment, then she said, "I was twelve when we rode up here on horses for the big salmon run. We stayed for days, catching salmon, smoking them and salting them. One day, Mom and Dad saddled up and headed for the range. Mom said they were going to look for medicine plants and they told me to stay off my horse because she had a stone bruise and needed to rest. But I didn't want to stay in camp by myself, so as soon they were out of sight, I jumped on my horse and went after them. I didn't think her bruise was that bad. Mom just didn't want me to go with them."

Lewis interrupted her. "You sound like you knew a lot about horses."

"We raised a few, just like other people on the reserve. To get around, you know?

"I remember it rained a little the night before and I found their tracks and followed them. I stayed back so they wouldn't see me. It got foggy higher up and my horse was a little old and couldn't keep climbing, so I tied her to a tree and kept going on foot. I came out of the fog and it was so pretty up there, all dusted with a little snow, and I forgot all about them. Then I heard a shotgun blast below me. It sounded like Mom's gun. She was scared of bears after what happened to me and Jean."

Eddie held up his hands. "Hold it. What do you mean? What happened to you two?"

"We got a little close to a bear once. That's all. But it put a scare into her and she took her shotgun whenever she was out riding or walking up in the hills.

"I ran back in the direction of the shot, which took me a while. Right about where you said you found this buckle, I came across scuff marks and . . . blood. I tracked the marks up to this big windfall of trees and I saw somebody had dragged something heavy inside, so I crawled in. That's when I found my dad. I knew right away he was dead. His eyes were half open and he was looking right at me."

Everyone in the kitchen watched Grace, waiting. Finally, she continued. "I screamed and got outta there fast. When I got back to camp, Mom saw me leading my horse and grabbed me. She wanted to know exactly where I was riding. I told her I went up to Moffat Creek for berries. She gave me a licking because I took my horse and now she could hardly walk. She told me she didn't know where Dad went, and we never said a word about it ever again. But it took years before the dreams went away."

Alphonse stared at his sister. "Jesus, you knew this when you and me used to talk about him and wonder where he was? Why the hell didn't you tell me about this before?"

"I was scared. I was just a kid, and maybe I thought Mom would kill us both if I told you."

Grace looked around at the people seated at the table. She could see their minds spinning, just as hers had been all those years ago. Such secrets were best kept tucked away, never to be shared.

Eddie spoke up. "Grandma really did that?"

Grace reached for the buckle. "She sure did."

Alphonse sat considering the dregs at the bottom of his cup.

"So why were you on the trip with them by yourself? Where were Aunt Jean and Uncle Alphonse?" Lewis asked.

"They stayed home with their grandma and went to day school."

Eddie took the buckle from his mother and examined it, then

slid it to his brother. "Boy, women are hard on men up here, aren't they, Lewis."

"I never would have thought our grandma could do something like that," Lewis said.

Everyone stared down at the buckle until Isabel nudged Lewis and said, "Let's get out there. We need to get them clothes in so we can get Eddie packed up."

She looked at Alphonse and jerked her head toward the door. Alphonse stood and took his mug to the counter. "I guess I'll join you."

The three went out and closed the door.

Grace asked her son, "What time is your ride going to be here?"

"Around ten."

"So soon? We never had time to visit for more than a few minutes. You were always on the go."

"It's not up to me. It's Camille's car and he wants to be on the road early because it's twelve hours of driving and we both have to work next week. When we get back up there, he wants a day or two to take it easy."

"I just wish we had more time." Grace stared at her cup, turning it around with her thumb and finger.

"Time for what? To visit, you mean?"

"Yeah."

"What do you want to talk about?"

Grace drummed the table with her fingers, staring at the cup as if she couldn't bring herself to say the words she wanted to say.

"Isn't that something about Grandma?" Eddie said. "How could you live with her after she did that? If I knew you killed my dad, I'd never turn my back on you."

Grace looked up, unsure what to make of his remark. "You think I could do what she did?"

"What, murder somebody? Damn right, Mom. You were like a grizzly bear if anybody hurt me or Lewis. You're one scary chick."

Grace said, "So I'm a chick now, am I?"

Eddie smiled at her. "Something like that. You know, I'm glad I came back, and I'd like to stick around a little longer, but I have to work so I can pay my fine and the lawyer, and I only have three months to do that. The judge said I'm not supposed to drive, but I'll get a cheap junker to bomb around in for a while. But you should know, I got my eye on something big."

"What is that?"

He leaned his chair back on two legs. "You'll find out soon enough. I can't wait to see all your faces when I pull in here."

Grace said, "Things sure change, don't they? One minute you're falling out of a tree with no shoes or socks on, and the next thing you show up with a new car and money in your pockets. Here I was thinking you needed to stay in school so you could get ahead. Who'd a thought?"

"Getting kicked out of school after that big fight I had was the kick in the ass I needed. That and other things."

Grace knew he was thinking of Eva. She leaned toward him. "Listen, we got bigger things to worry about now. Bad things. Did anyone tell you your dad was planning on moving back here? He's gonna build down by the river and make a living stripping stolen cars."

Eddie tipped forward in his chair, the legs hitting the floor with a bang. "What? How do you know that?"

"Do you remember Mabel?"

"A bit."

"She's the one who told me. And then the chief showed up and said my part of the land is Jimmy's now and he can do whatever he wants with it. Two guys were here looking the place over, but Alphonse ran them outta there and shot up their truck."

Eddie looked puzzled. "I thought this all belonged to you and Alphonse after Grandma passed. How could it be Jimmy's?"

"All the reserve land from this side of the Salmon River Bridge down to the small bridge by the store belonged to your grandpa. When he disappeared, we all figured it passed on to your grandma. We moved up here so you two boys could go to school in Falkland. When your grandma died, we never thought anything about it. But now the chief and the Indian agent say it's split between your dad and Alphonse."

Grace saw the anger in her son's face.

"Jesus, maybe I should stay so me and Lewis can take of care of Jimmy when he shows up. Does Lewis know?"

"Yes. I thought he woulda told you."

"He never said anything. Maybe he didn't want to spoil the good time we were having." Eddie scraped his chair away from the table, moving restlessly. "I don't want to leave you guys all alone. After what he did to us, I wouldn't trust him as far as I could throw him. I'll get a job down here and we'll be all right. The worst thing Jimmy could do is to come poking his nose around here." Eddie banged his fist on the table.

Grace said, "But there's no jobs, Eddie. Not for Indians, anyway. Pete Thomas from down at White Man's Creek was looking for a job and his sister Doreen told him to try the new plywood mill in Armstrong, where that huge parking lot is always full. She told him to go in on Monday morning first thing, because somebody's bound to get drunk on the weekend and not show up for work. He went every Monday for a couple of months, but no luck. He wanted to just forget about it, but Doreen told him to keep going back for a little longer if he had to. She said they'd get sick of him showing up at the office and hire him to make him stop. So he did, but they still wouldn't even look at him. Finally, he gave up. You might have seen him walking on the side of the road collecting beer bottles.

"Eddie, if you stay, you'll probably end up doing something like that, right after you get out of jail for not paying your fine. Do you know how lucky you are to have a good job in the first place? You're crazy to think about staying."

A car horn honked and Grace jumped. They slid back their chairs and went to the window. "It's Marvin in his dad's car."

As she went to open the door, Eddie grabbed her arm. She turned and saw he was smiling at her. The softness in his eyes was there again, and she swallowed hard.

"Okay, Mom, now it's my turn to tell you something. Jesus, this day is full of surprises, and you're not going to believe this one. Do you know who that woman was bareback riding Lewis in the back of Alphonse's car at the dance?"

"Oh Jesus, Eddie, why do you have to bring up something like that?"

"Just listen. The whole reserve is talking about how Lewis banged Lily Edwards, Jimmy's girlfriend."

Grace stared wide-eyed at Eddie. Then she put her hands to her face and walked over and leaned against the kitchen counter and stared at the wall. Then she turned, her eyes on his. She went to him and grabbed him by the shoulders. He did the same, the closest thing to an embrace they'd had in years. Together they began laughing.

Isabel came back inside and placed the basket of folded clothes on the table. She put her hand on her chest, watching.

"I hate to break this up, but you both should get out here. I'll pack your clothes in your suitcase, Eddie, while you go out. Marvin wants to say his goodbyes."

As they went outside, both were wearing huge smiles and wiping their eyes.

Marvin was chatting with Lewis and Alphonse, holding a small box. He walked toward Eddie. "There's some food in here for the road, and a present from Cora."

He handed over the box. Eddie shook it and something rolled around inside. He pulled back the flaps and saw sandwiches, cookies and plums.

"Mom doesn't want you to get hungry on the way back. Those plums in there might be a little green."

Isabel came out the door. "If you can't eat them, just put them on a windowsill for a few days," she said.

Alphonse reached inside the box, grabbed a plum and took a bite. "Tastes pretty good to me."

Eddie moved the box away from his uncle. "Thanks. What are these?" He pointed at the comics tucked alongside the sandwiches.

"Cora and Mom were at a rummage sale and she told Mom she had to get these for you."

Eddie flipped through the pages. "Now how did she know I liked comics?"

Marvin reached into the box. "This is the one I couldn't put down. It's about two Indians in a prehistoric valley and they fight dinosaurs and bears and cavemen. *Turok, Son of Stone*. It sounds like it might be a little young, but I think you'll like it. It reminded me of you and Lewis camping in the mountains."

Eddie looked at his cousin. "How did you know we went camping?"

Marvin grinned. "Alphonse."

The sound of a rock spinning out from under a tire made them all look up to see a police car turn the corner. The car came slowly down the lane, the light on the roof a watching cherry eye.

"I wonder which one of us outlaws he's looking for this time?" Alphonse said.

When the car came to a stop, the policeman stepped out of his car, settling his hat on his head. "I'm Officer McKinney. I'm looking for Grace Toma?"

"That's me," Grace said. "What's going on?" Grace felt her hair prickle when he opened his notepad.

"Do you know James Allan Toma?"

"Yes."

"Is he your husband?"

"Not anymore, he's not."

"When was the last time you saw him?"

There was something in the way the policeman spoke to her that didn't feel right, as if he already knew the answer before he asked.

"About two years ago. Did he send you here to kick us off this land?"

Marvin interrupted them. "I'm going to get outta here. Have a good trip back to Alberta, Eddie. We'll see you again sometime." Marvin hurried to his car, started the motor and drove away.

Grace was becoming impatient. "Can we get this over with?"

"I still need to ask you a few questions. Do you keep in touch with him?"

"No. Why the hell would I do that? If I saw him, I'd—"

"Grace," Isabel said.

302

Grace placed her hands on her hips. "I came to you guys for help with that man before, and you didn't do a damn thing, so either you tell me what he's up to or you can piss off outta here."

The officer folded his pad. "I have some news about Mister Toma. Do you know where Nahun is located?"

Grace turned away. "Oh, for Chrissakes." She turned back. "Sure I do. Everybody does. It's halfway to Kelowna on the Reserve Road."

"So you know how treacherous that part of the road can be, and only one car at a time can make that hairpin corner? It looks like Mister Toma's car went off the road there and rolled into Okanagan Lake. Fisherman spotted the car hung up on rocks in the water and notified us. A barge pulled it out yesterday morning. If that car had made it any farther into the lake, we never would have found it."

Isabel spoke up. "What? He's dead?"

"Well, that's what I wanted to tell you. The vehicle was empty. There's a layer of mud and silt on the bottom of the lake that could swallow up a tanker truck, so he could be under there somewhere, so we're going to keep looking. All we found inside the car were empty beer bottles and a wallet with his birth certificate inside. Do you have any questions?"

Grace shook her head.

"No? You call the station if you think of anything. Have a good day." He pocketed the notebook and went to his car, got in and drove away.

"I'll be goddamned," Alphonse said.

Isabel placed her hand on Grace's arm. "I don't know what to say, Grace. I don't know whether I should feel bad or jump in the air and kick my heels together."

"Oh, don't do that. Let's just leave it and see what happens."

Lewis asked, "What are you gonna do, Mom?"

"If we knew he was dead for sure, I could have some peace and think about something else besides him. You don't know what it was like this summer, hearing about what he was up to. I was always on the lookout for him, worrying that he could show up any minute. And it's not going to be over until I shovel dirt on his grave."

Grace took a deep breath and looked at her boys. "And don't you two feel sorry for that man. He was mean to all of us and he was going to kick us off this land, and it was all done according to the law. Wherever he is, I hope his asshole's sucking slough water and the fish are eating his eyes."

Alphonse laughed.

"But what's going to happen now?" Lewis asked. "This is just . . . I don't know."

"We'll have to wait and see. But I'm not going to take back what I just said, even if it makes you both mad at me."

Eddie said, "C'mon, Mom, I know you think Lewis and me are still kids, but we know what an asshole he was to you, right, Lewis?"

"Yeah, we remember. And we'll go to war if anybody tries to take our home."

Just then another car turned down their road.

"There's Camille," Eddie said. "I better grab my stuff."

Eddie walked into the house as the car pulled up and stopped. The driver stepped out, gave them all a little wave and went around to the back to open the trunk.

Eddie came down the steps and placed his suitcase in the trunk and the box of food in the back seat. "Everybody, this is Camille. The worst cook in Alberta."

Camille smiled. "Hello, everybody," he said, giving handshakes.

"This is my mom, Grace, this is my other mom, Isabel, this is Uncle Alphonse, and my little brother, Lewis."

Camille gripped Lewis's outstretched hand and squeezed hard. "So you're the one he always talks about. It's nice to finally meet you."

Lewis flexed his fingers when Camille let go.

When Eddie got into the car, he looked as if he didn't want to leave, but he stuck his head out the window as Camille drove them away and gave a smiling salute as everyone waved. They all stood there watching until the car was out of sight, in case there was a chance Eddie might come back.

Lewis said, "I'm gonna take the truck and go to the store. You wanna come, Alphonse?"

"I know you're off to see your sweetheart. But I got nothing better to do, so I'll tag along and you can drop me at Ned and Jean's."

Lewis started the truck. Alphonse stepped into the cab, complaining, "My bum back's been bothering me for a week. Just trying to set down on that toilet hole is a pain in the ass." He pulled the door shut but it wouldn't close. "Jesus, this damn thing," he said, slamming the door hard until it stayed shut.

After the truck turned down Range Road, Isabel and Grace sat down on the porch steps side by side. Isabel said, "It was sure nice to see you and Eddie laughing it up in the house, just the two of you. Everything has worked out for the best. Just look at Eddie—if anybody can get back on his feet again, it's him. And Lewis isn't moping around anymore. So we're doing pretty good. And the land will go to the boys in the end, and you'll never have to think about that man again."

Grace let out a heavy sigh. "The longer I sit here, the more I wonder about Lazar Alexander. Why would he take the car to Nahun?"

"Well, he did say he was going to dump it somewhere. Maybe he went down and pushed it in the lake."

"Maybe."

Isabel said, "Who knows what that squirrely ex-con was thinking or where he was going."

"Yeah, he could be thinking of coming here to be with you."

"Don't say that, Grace."

"I wish I could be like you, Isabel. You say everything is gonna be good and that it's all worked out for the best, like it was tied together with a pretty blue ribbon. But I don't think like that. Everything isn't that easy."

Isabel said, "You know what, why don't I make us a pot of tea. It'll calm us both down. It's gonna be okay, Grace. You'll see. Be right back." The screen door banged behind her.

Grace rubbed her eyes. Maybe the anxious thoughts in her head would go away and she'd be able to see the world differently once she had a cup of tea. Her mother believed tea was the cure for all that ailed.

On the ground in front of her, Grace saw two ants, a red one and a black one, twisting and rolling in the powdery dirt in a life-and-death rumble. She brought down her foot and squashed them both, dust lifting to drift away. And then she heard someone whisper her name. "Grace."

She looked up, but there was no one there. Senses crackling, she noticed an odd vehicle parked up the road, strange in the way it glittered and flickered like a road mirage. *Will-o-the-wisp.* The interior was so dark even the bright light of the sun couldn't penetrate the glass. Then it began wending its way slowly down her lane. Sunlight shimmering off the unsoiled paint, sparkling glass and mirror-like trim gave the car an appearance unlike anything she had ever seen before.

She waited. A train blasted its horn up at the Moffat Creek crossing, and the steel wheels shrieked and squealed on the rails as the car came on, soundless.

ACKNOWLEDGEMENTS

Thank you to the Canada Council for the Arts.

Thank you to my agent, Denise Bukowski, for believing in me, and to my editor, Anne Collins, from whom I have learned so much.

Thank you to Susan Mayse, for opening that first door and showing me the way and a special hug to Taryn Boyd for trusting her instinct and publishing my first book. Without her, none of this would have been possible.

A big thank you to my brothers, who inspired me: Don, Tim and Steve.

To my son Brodie and his wife, Karen, and their children Sienna, Rebel and Huxley: thanks for being such a big part of our lives.

Thank you to SʔímʼlaʔxʷMichelle Johnson, PhD, of the Sylix Language House. A note on a few words in the novel. *Mow'-itsh* is Chinook for "deer meat." I've spelled this *mowitch* for ease of pronunciation. *Spalq* is n̓syilxčn̓ for "penis." *Sámaʔ* is n̓syilxčn̓ for a non-Indigenous Caucasian person, which I've spelled *summa* for ease of pronunciation.

BRIAN THOMAS ISAAC was born in 1950 on the Okanagan Indian Reserve, near Vernon, British Columbia. After completing grade eight, he found work in the Alberta oil fields and in construction, eventually retiring as a bricklayer. He came to writing late in life. In 2022, his bestselling debut, *All the Quiet Places*, won an Indigenous Voices Award, was a finalist for the Governor General's Literary Award for Fiction and the Amazon Canada First Novel Award, and was longlisted for the Scotiabank Giller Prize and CBC's Canada Reads. He lives with his wife in West Kelowna, BC.